Nicole Locke discovered her first romance novels in her grandmother's closet, where they were secretly hidden. Convinced that books that were hidden must be better than those that weren't, Nicole greedily read them. It was only natural for her to start writing them—but now not so secretly!

THE KNIGHT'S
RUNAWAY MAIDEN

Nicole Locke

MILLS & BOON

First Published in Great Britain 2021
by Mills & Boon, an imprint of HarperCollins*Publishers*
1 London Bridge Street, London, SE1 9GF

© 2021 Nicole Locke

ISBN: 978-0-263-28395-2

MIX
Paper from
responsible sources
FSC™ C007454

This book is produced from independently certified FSC™ paper
to ensure responsible forest management.
For more information visit www.harpercollins.co.uk/green.

Printed and bound in Spain
by CPI, Barcelona

To my family, extended and close.

To my aunts and uncles, cousins, nephews and nieces,
who kept me company during the many days of
writing and who fed, watered and sheltered me,
and took me out on walks.

Thank you for sharing yourselves, your homes,
and just—well, being there like family.

Love you all very much.

Chapter One

France, 1297

'I must confess, Séverine, your living here like this was…unexpected.'

Séverine of Warstone, once Séverine de Marteldois, the name she secretly still called herself, slowly stood from her hunched position stacking kindling and hoped the shadows in the woodcutter's hut hid her reaction. It wasn't the use of her true name that alerted her to a threat. Nor the fact that she had been identified despite her poor gown, the ash brushed through her tightly bound hair, and the vigilantly patted sheep dung around her ankles.

No, her imminent endangerment came through the carefully cultivated construction of that sentence. Just a few words purposefully measured in a cadence to exploit fear.

Ian of Warstone only used that tone of voice when he was about to strike. The tenor was different, but the control of it was the same, as was her reaction. That cold Warstone voice had always crystallised dread like hoarfrost along her spine.

Only now it was terror that stopped her. Because of what she had done to him and his family. Because of the punishment that would be enacted, the torture, the public rebukes. The certain lifetime confinement.

Because she had fled and disappeared from Ian of Warstone, her husband, and he would leave her with no merciful choices. Not that she expected any. After all, she'd stolen coin, priceless artefacts…his two only sons.

Running and hiding, actions she had effectively done for almost six weary years, were futile with him this close. Ian of Warstone, the eldest child of one of the few families feared by monarchs, kingdoms and emperors, had found her. He'd seize her before she took one step away.

Her life was forfeit, now she had to protect her sons. *His* sons. As long as no harm came to them, she would do whatever was necessary. In truth, she'd hidden from him far longer than she'd expected to. Long enough to avoid her sons from becoming the monster their father was. If fortune favoured her at all, it would always be so. For now, she would face the consequences. If only...

But the slight uneven scrape of his boot against the ill-swept floor indicated that the figure behind her was not a figment of her nightmares. However, his presence was curious.

Warstones weren't known for being quite so impulsive. Ian would have secured her by now. Never would he have announced himself first when there were two doors to the outside and one was near her.

There was also something about his step that was odd. Every one of his family was uncommonly graceful. Her husband's lone faltering step was almost alarming...but heartening. Was running possible? Perhaps he was injured and too slow to catch her. But...her children. She knew where they *should* be, but there was no certainty, and there was no risking them. Not ever, no matter what would happen to her.

Thus, Séverine, with a bundle of sticks cradled in her arms, turned to face a fate that was never meant to be hers. Only to be mired in more obscurity than her thoughts.

She was correct that the shadows hid

expressions—it certainly hid her husband's. The light from the opened door behind him outlined the man he'd become in the years since she'd seen him.

He had always been broad, but there was something more substantial about his shoulders; something entirely different in the way he held himself. More raw than elegant.

'Ian,' she said.

He inhaled sharply, as if she'd said something surprising or painful. He took another step inside the building. The light behind him receded, allowing her to discern almost familiar cheekbones and long lashes framing eyes below a lowered brow. The light didn't allow for his distinct colouring, other than to see his hair's natural waves edging along his nape, and that it was still as dark as midnight.

Warstones were always dark.

She remembered the first time she had seen that family at her eldest sister's lavish betrothal announcement. Séverine had never cared for spectacle, but she did like to observe and listen. And many a jest had been made that day that there were four Warstone brothers for four Marteldois sisters. When she'd first overheard it, Séverine had had to cover up her snort with a quick cough. Though her sisters were expected to make advantageous marriages, as any royal member would, Séverine had had no such desire for herself.

Her father, ever indulgent, had agreed. After all, she was far younger than her sisters, and not the prettiest. She was also…different. Her penchant for snorting, scoffing and giving any sort of reaction at all was one of them.

Further, she had eschewed any knowledge of household management and fripperies. Instead, she'd enjoyed hiding in private chambers with her needlepoint, or meandering in abbeys to steal glimpses at books. While her sisters had conducted their lessons as if they were insignificant social gatherings, Séverine had badgered her tutors until they had begged her to stop her questions.

She was fortunate. Her family were great patrons of the arts and music, and her enthusiasm had been encouraged. No, a husband was not for her. The life in the abbey was the one she wanted.

And one she was denied by her husband, Ian, who had originally been meant for her sister, Beatrice, but who had demanded her hand instead. A man who was not the one in front of her.

She clutched the kindling in her arm. 'Who...?'

'Not Guy,' he said with malicious amusement.

No, not Guy. She heard he'd met a violent death a few years before by some men he had crossed. Such a demise had always been a plausible end to the second eldest Warstone brother.

Not Ian, or Guy. He certainly wasn't the father or Reynold, the third brother, who had always been singular. He was far too strategic a warrior to limit his sword range by entering a small woodshed. That left the youngest Warstone brother...

'Balthus,' she said.

The man stepped forward, and shadows scattered.

It was indeed the youngest Warstone, though he had greatly changed since she'd last properly seen him the day of the betrothal announcement. That one tentative moment when she had turned her head and caught him staring at her. That odd singular time when she had, because she'd been either perplexed or bemused...or perhaps embarrassed or equally arrested, returned his stare. That moment before an icy hand had manacled her wrist and wrenched her away from a life she'd thought she would be living to something else entirely.

Balthus was truly here in front of her. Over the years she had imagined that moment that had stretched before them until something had warmed her chest, and she had felt herself leaning towards him. Until his mouth had curved at the corner, and her heart had hammered, waiting for his smile. Snatched away too soon, she'd waited forever.

She'd thought she'd exaggerated that moment, but he was here, and she felt the hitch in her chest all over again.

He was beautiful, like all the Warstone brothers were beautiful. Dark hair, grey eyes, chiselled cheekbones and a cut jawline, features softened by ridiculously long lashes and lips that were upturned just at the corners as if he was internally amused. He had the assurance of wealth, power and the intimate knowledge that with either precise kindness or cruel malice he could have anything he wanted.

This boy turned man was indeed of that loathsome family, but there had always been something different about him, and she was again slammed with that realisation. She greatly resented it.

* * *

Almost six years since she'd disappeared from his brother's life, many more years since she'd disappeared from his...if it was possible to say she had ever been part of his. Yet two memories of Séverine struck Balthus.

Her smile was his earliest memory of her. All encompassing, lighting up the darkest spaces in a young man's soul. He'd never seen a woman smile with joy like she did, and for an entire day at his brother's betrothal celebration, while people had knowingly alluded that the youngest sister was for him, he couldn't stop staring at her, and when she'd turned...when she'd looked back at him...he'd imagined his life illuminated by such bright happiness.

Until his brother had strode across the great hall and announced it wasn't Beatrice he desired, but the youngest sister, Séverine. So with swift change of mind, and change of fate, the young maid who'd carried joy had become his brother's unintended wife.

Many years had passed since then, but now he had two memories that would torture his dreams...when he dared have them. That smile, and his last memory of her, the way she, at this very moment, said his name.

'Do you need help with the kindling?' he asked, indicating with his chin.

Jumping back from him, some of the sticks in her arms fell to the floor. A step or two more, and he bent to pick them up, but her quick step back warned him, and he straightened immediately.

'Clever,' he said, feeling familiar yet unwanted suspicion slither down his chest as he registered her attempt to trick him. 'Let the man pick up the kindling while you take the other exit and escape.'

'I wasn't—'

'I don't remember you being a liar.'

He didn't care that she flinched at the word he'd used, and it didn't matter if she lied or not. He certainly wasn't here for any truth from her. He was here for a piece of parchment that she'd stolen from his brother. Given her history of running from his brother and taking Ian's sons, him being lost in forfeited memories had no place here.

'I don't want to remember you at… What's wrong with your arm?' she said.

'It is—' He released his grip on his wrist and tucked both limbs under his cloak.

She'd noticed, even in the dim light of the wood hut, which he'd thought would hide his

disfigurement from her. This day was both for-
tuitous and not. One, he'd finally found her,
but now she knew his weakness. He hated it
that he'd almost told her the truth, that his arm
was agonising…it *was* agony. The pain made
everything he did clumsy and ineffectual. At
times, like now, simply walking jarred his
entire body and caused him to stumble. The
pain was meaningless compared to the veri-
table truth that his left hand had been severed
a few months earlier.

Since then anything he did in any sense was
ugly. He couldn't tie the laces of his own boots.
He didn't have an impairment, *he* was impaired. And this woman, who had haunted the
last remnants of his young adulthood, whom
he compared to all other woman simply from
the way she *smiled*, knew.

If he could rage away that pain of shame,
he would. All his achievements had been re-
duced to this woman, and how he'd glimpsed
what happiness looked like. His brother, his
impairment, ensured she could never be his.

He didn't want to be here. His hand…or
lack thereof…ached. It always made him lose
his bearings. It was the reason Henry, a servant, was on the other side of the door behind
Séverine to guard it in case she escaped. There

was no mistaking Henry for any mercenary or trained guard, but he was built like a boulder. If she ran, Henry would catch her.

A pinched look marred her forehead as she eyed his movements. 'Where are my children?'

'Wherever you left them.'

Eyes flashing to his, hands clenching the sticks, she demanded, 'Tell me!'

All too simple finding her, all too easy if he simply blurted the truth. He'd come to Séverine's family's estate expecting to find clues to her whereabouts, not the maiden herself. Did she think her disguise sufficient? Though she stank and did well to smear some sort of dirt through her red tresses, no matter what, nothing could hide the green of her eyes or the bump on the bridge of her nose.

'Does your family know you are here? Are they poor of coin and need you to be a servant?'

She clenched her lips. 'You have no right to know my family.'

'Given that you wed my brother, I'd say I was family,' he said.

'You're not my family. I want nothing to do with any of you, and I made that clear by my leaving.'

'Yes, but I'm here now, and—'

'Tell me what you want and be done with whatever else you need.'

'What are you expecting, Séverine? Of course we'd want to find you. You have the Warstone grandchildren, after all.'

'Don't pretend you care. As if your family has any concept of children, and what it means to be a parent. You and yours only want abominations without conscience. Killers without morals, controllers without care. Why are you here?'

'I suppose the logical answer would be I'm here to capture you and the boys, and—' Her stricken eyes! He couldn't finish that sentence. 'I should be hurt by such an expression. Currently, your boys are as safe as you have made them without the protection of my brother.'

'Typical cryptic response. Can your family ever speak plainly?' she scoffed. 'I assume that you already have them secured and you're baiting me. Stop your games, Warstone, and tell me what is expected. What is it you want?'

That was a question he would answer only when he obtained the parchment she'd taken when she'd fled from her husband. As far as he could see, this hut contained nothing but piles of wood, spiders and debris. Dressed as she was, there was also the possibility she'd sold the decorated parchment for coin in the years since she'd fled.

'I am not here in jest, but in earnest, and as to what I am doing here?' he said. 'That seems like an odd question, given the circumstances. It's been terribly long since we've conversed as family, and I have yet to be introduced to your youngest.'

'We've never sat down for conversation.' Her eyes shifted. 'You think I want you to speak to my boys when I have done everything I can to keep them away from you?'

Oddly, he did want to meet them. She might have covered her own tresses to darken them, but the boys had unmistakable red shining through their Warstone black strands. It had been easy to spot them with two village men, out in the fields, as if they'd no royal blood in them at all. Here, Séverine was dressed in rough brown wool, and fetching kindling.

He hadn't expected to find her on her family's estate. Not this close to Provence, and certainly not pretending she was a mere servant. It was believed she wasn't in her own country, let alone France, since she'd evaded his brother's efforts to find her all these years. Instead, she had been unexpectedly close. Clever Séverine. Which meant he had to be clever, as well.

Telling her that her boys were unharmed, unaware of his presence, and out of his reach meant the likelihood of her using that door behind her.

'I want to converse with you as well. So much has occurred since we last saw each other. Let's call a truce, shall we?' he said. 'It's cold here. Certainly, no matter your dress and obvious labour, your family isn't letting their grandsons catch frostbite. I could use a warmed wine, couldn't you?'

Hurling two sticks at him, she shrieked, and ran out the other door.

'Séverine!' Balthus reeled in the agony she'd inflicted on his arm and staggered to a wall to brace himself against falling. She couldn't get away, he had to chase after her, he had to—

A cry, sharp and quick. Forcing his body to move, Balthus rushed outside. Henry lay crumpled on the ground, and Séverine and the boys in the field were gone.

Chapter Two

***

Two weeks later

'I don't want to play hide-and-seek again,' Clovis said.

Séverine bit back her impatience at her eldest child. Clovis was only eight, and this journey, which had taken over a fortnight if she counted the days they'd hidden in the tunnel under the fields, had been especially arduous.

The last few days reminded her of when she had first run, always looking over her shoulder, sleeping in short bursts, waiting for the shadows to reveal an enraged husband. She'd been that way for the first two years, while she'd implemented her plan to stay hidden from Ian and his entire family as long as possible.

Which was difficult when everyone wanted to be noticed by such a respected family. The

Warstones had the ear of not one king but England and France. They'd gained so much wealth that both kingdoms taxed them heavily, but it was a well-known secret they hid their coin. It was also known, and hardly a secret, that both kings wouldn't press too hard for anything more.

What wouldn't a family do to gain their notice, let alone marry into one? No father with any daughter would deny it, yet she wished with all her being that her father had.

Perhaps the marriage would have been different with her sister Beatrice, but on that betrothal day Ian had announced *her* as his chosen bride. To save her family from embarrassment and certain ruin, she'd agreed.

She'd thought the insult to her sister and her sister's hatred towards her was the worst of it, but she'd been wrong. In public, the Warstones showed a united front. Never a curt or unkind word to each other, and they displayed a camaraderie that appeared like familial love and respect.

However, she had been allowed behind those doors into their private world. After all her studies and imaginings of Hell, she'd never come close to the horror, to the cruelty, the family evoked when they thought no one was

looking. She'd thought she'd be sealed forever
in the tomb of her marriage until that fateful
day when Ian had taken her and the two boys
to the aptly named keep, Forgotten. A place
she'd never heard of, and hardly a keep at that,
but a crumbling tower under repair surrounded
by splintered wood that once was walls. She
could ask no questions of him, though, for he
left them that very day. She'd waited one, two
weeks for messages or his return, all the while
formulating a way out of it all for her sons'
very souls.

She'd had to. After years of attempting to
understand her husband and failing, she had
concluded he wasn't understandable. He had
been gone more than at home, and even when
he'd been there, he'd sequestered himself in
his private chambers. When he had conversed
with her, it had been with odd sentences and
expressions that had seemed open but would
quickly turn bitter…she'd had no guidance
when it came to him! There had been rare
times when they'd shared a bed, even rarer yet
if he'd fallen asleep. Then in the dark of night
Ian would mutter and sometimes he would talk
favourably of her and the boys. But it wasn't
enough.

Ian *frightened* her, and all the more when

he'd prepared that caravan and woken her and the boys in the early morning and rushed them away.

When he left them at Forgotten Keep, she'd made a vow she'd rip out her own heart rather than have her children follow in their father's footsteps. She'd waited for him to return or send a message, and when he hadn't, she'd approached two servants who'd helped her sequester as much of his coin, jewellery, enamelled boxes and any other trinket or book she could find. When they'd procured several more servants loyal to her to help, she'd left that home in the middle of the night. That had been six years ago.

Over the years, those stolen artefacts and the servants were left behind in various villages. For extra measure, she commissioned traps beside or near their homes if anyone got too close. The servants assured her that Pepin and Clovis would have some place safe, hidden, and secure for their future.

In all those years of travel, the children had been easy to carry and care for. They'd never questioned anything because that was all they knew.

When no word from her husband reached her, and no mercenary aimed a knife at her throat, she'd eased her restrictions. They stayed longer in the many villages in France, made connections, friends, they began to place roots, which she now realised had been a mistake. She should never have stopped looking over her shoulder.

Every day since Balthus had taken her by surprise, she'd thought of him. Not only of him but she now searched her surroundings more, but also…

How guarded his gaze had been when he'd greeted her. He'd had all the control and power when he'd surprised her in that hut, and yet… instead of caustic words or threats he'd offered to help her with the kindling.

She'd married and lived with Warstones, and they were never helpful, yet something about his mannerisms was different. Did he pose more of a danger to her and her children? She couldn't take the chance either way.

Though it was earlier than she wanted in her planning for their future, and though she wasn't certain it would be enough to stop any Warstone, they now travelled to her former servants at one of her hidden locations. One with a trap…just in case.

'One more day of our game, and we'll arrive to our new home and you can play with the other children,' she said. 'But today it's hide-and-seek.'

'It's not fun, no one ever finds us,' Clovis replied.

That was the point, but already Balthus of Warstone had found them, and she'd curse his name if she hadn't already voiced a thousand curses on the entire family. How soon would it be before Balthus notified Ian of her whereabouts? Now that they had a point of reference for her location, the parameters of where she and her children were had been narrowed. A few Warstones and their mercenaries could circle the countryside and catch them all too neatly.

She shouldn't have been weak, shouldn't have given in to her to longing for her parents. She prayed her family, who'd harboured them, wouldn't now be the subject of any Warstone wrath.

She'd known better. In all the years of running she'd never returned to her home once she'd disappeared. During that time, she'd sent three letters via messengers. The first to let them know what she had done, the others to let them know she still lived. She'd never given her location and had moved the moment she'd sent them. She'd taken every precaution...

except she wanted her parents to know her children. So she'd come to them as a servant, they treated her like a servant, and the children never knew. Except now they had been discovered by the very people she'd sworn to protect her family from. She couldn't let it happen again.

'They never find us because you're so good at it.' She rubbed Clovis's head, loving the way his hair stuck out. When he quickly ran his hands over to smooth it, she smiled. She often teased him that he'd straightened his baby gowns every time he'd crawled, and yet she worried over that trait of his. It was so endearingly him, but would he ever allow himself to make mistakes?

'No one can find us in tunnels and hay carts, can they, Mama?' Pepin skipped in a circle, kicking up the dirt around him, making his clothes, if at all possible, dirtier than they'd been moments before.

'Quieter, you,' she said, though she had no hope that he would be and neither would she demand it. He was silent when it counted the most. After she'd struck that man, she'd run to the fields and grabbed her two boys, a few more steps and they'd dropped into a hidden hatch to a tunnel below. A field worker had stood on top so no one else would accidentally find it. Pepin, nearly seven years old, had stayed quiet as muffled voices above them had indicated how easily they could be found.

A day later, and supplies had been dropped to them, however, they'd waited a week more though it was reported that Balthus and the other man had left after two days.

When they did finally emerge from that damp cavern supported by thick but cold beams, it was night, and they were quickly assisted into a hay cart to be whisked away for three more days. Now they walked the rest of the way to their destination. It was cold and the sun was quickly disappearing. They'd need to find shelter soon.

'Do you like hide-and-seek, Mama, because you don't like to hurt them?' Clovis said.

Séverine stopped while Pepin skipped ahead unawares, and her heart dropped a few steps behind them.

'Clovis, what are you saying?' she choked out.

'That man found us,' Clovis said. 'Then you hit him, and we hid.'

Pepin spun around and shoved his brother. 'Mama doesn't hit anyone.'

Staring at his chest where his brother had

marred his tunic, Clovis brushed the fabric straight before he slugged his brother, who skidded to the frozen ground. Séverine knelt to cradle her younger son. She brushed his face with the hems of her sleeves. There was a little blood leaking from his nose, his grey eyes wide, stunned. When the pain hit him, the all-too-familiar mutinous look mottled his expression, and he tried to shove her away... so he could then shove his brother in the dirt. She'd been here too many times before, and they didn't have time for it.

Holding him tighter, she said, 'None of that.' She looked up and pinned her elder son with a warning glare. 'From both of you. Agreed?'

Once they acknowledged her, she released her younger son. Clovis held out his hand to help her up, which did more to ease her frustration at both of them than anything. Her elder child made the courtly gestures every so often. More so now. Placing her hand in his, she pretended that he pulled her up, and she brushed her own skirts.

'Mama doesn't hit,' Pepin repeated.

'She didn't hit, she was punishing. You know...like when she gets cross at the foxes?'

Séverine's knees gave out, and if she hadn't locked them, she would have fallen over.

Pepin turned to her. 'That man was trying to steal hens?'

Clovis huffed. 'For breaking the rules of hide-and-seek, isn't that true, Mama? You weren't happy about that because we had to start all over again.'

She couldn't breathe. She couldn't. How could her children have guessed this already? She was meant to protect them from the games of the Warstones and try to escape them.

Pepin shoved his brother again. 'Now you've upset Mama.'

'Did not! You did!'

How had she come to this? Her children. Her sons, physically similar, but their personalities different. No sooner did she learn one way of talking with Clovis than she had to learn another with Pepin.

Travelling with them had been easier when Pepin was an infant, and they didn't argue amongst themselves. Now they fought all too often. Now they had eyes and thoughts separate from her own.

Which she loved, but Clovis's domineering ways and Pepin's keen observations weren't like those of other children, or were they? She didn't know if all boys were like this and, worse, there was a terrible deep part of her that constantly questioned.

Was this how a boy behaved, or did Pepin shove because he had cruel tendencies like his father? Did Clovis observe because he was curious, or did he watch for weaknesses like his uncle Reynold? Was Clovis kind to help his mother up, or did he do it to control her emotions to escape punishment?

Were they Warstones or *her* children? Was she fighting a battle she could win, or against Fate? These thoughts meant nothing unless she got them to safety.

'I'm not upset, and no shoving or hitting. I can't mend you in the middle of a forest.'

Clovis kicked the snow under his feet, a reminder that they were leaving a trail. Taking Pepin's hand, she dragged them deeper into the woods so their footprints would be partially obscured by the underbrush.

'It's cold, walking,' Pepin said, his body leaning outward so he almost dangled by her hand. 'I liked the hay cart.'

'Can't they find us like this?' Clovis said.

'I can't find foxes.' Pepin twisted around to look behind them.

'Paul said the point of hide-and-seek is to

make someone "it",' Clovis said. 'Why is your game different?'

'Mama's game is the true game,' Pepin said. 'Paul lies!'

Paul was correct, but Séverine couldn't have him thinking she was wrong. Then… Oh! She needed to stop. Clovis was older, and she'd known this day would come. Their time with hide-and-seek was coming to an end.

'Paul's twelve. The other boys said it was so.' Clovis's eyes shifted to her, and Séverine had a horrible thought: Could he know they were hiding from his father? She'd left when he'd been very young, but since then he'd experienced families with homes. He must wonder about his own and yet he'd only asked once when he was much younger. The answer then had been easier. She'd said he had a father, and they'd see him soon. When she'd said that, she'd believed it. She'd thought she'd be caught. Pepin didn't remember his father and never asked.

But was Clovis wondering now?

Pepin tried to walk backwards in front of them before he stumbled, and she caught him. Giggling, he straightened and skipped forward with every word. 'We've been playing this game for years and years and years, and no one is ever "it". It's only hide. Like Mama plays.'

'Paul says there's a seek,' Clovis stated, his tone challenging. 'That man found us, and Mama—'

'Clovis!' Séverine said, putting as much warning as she could in her tone. He went quiet. 'There is a seek. I find you.'

'You're the one who hides us, which makes it no fun. I want to be caught by someone else.'

'You mustn't get caught for then you'll lose,' she pointed out, aware that she was in a negotiation with her children, but the boys liked games, and the hiding had always been exciting for them. Best of all, they grasped what they were to do: to stay unseen and quiet. What were they to do now?

'I want to lose! I'm tired of dark places and logs, and that last place we went to, I almost got stuck.'

Clovis's thin body barely kept up with his sudden height. He was eight, but a full head taller than he was last year. If he was like any of the Warstone brothers, her hiding them in small spaces wouldn't be possible much longer. The game that had worked for years wouldn't work anymore. She needed to find another way to travel. In the meantime, she had to get them to safety.

Clovis was tired, but she also wondered if there was another reason for his complaints. For a few precious weeks he had been surrounded by her family. Not that either of her sons knew that, but she was recognised immediately by her parents. For a time, and in small ways, the boys had had some attention from those who loved them. It made it all the harder to leave, which was exactly what she'd feared.

Now she had to begin her other plan. The one she'd been quietly setting up from village to village for years and on which she'd spent almost all the coin she'd taken from her husband. She had over ten locations. Surely ten hideouts and traps would be enough? Enough shelters to hide them until they were young men. They could make decisions on their own then; would know what was right and wrong and not turn out to be monsters. They needed empathy, not cruelty. Compassion and understanding, not control. The world was full of people, not games.

She'd never returned to those previous villages where her friends and loyal servants lived, where the secrets places were. Instead, she'd travelled as a widow with children. Her fine gowns had been replaced with poorly spun wool dresses, her hair bound tight, linen covered and ashes through it. When she'd felt it necessary, she'd smeared dung around her ankles every morning to keep men from looking too closely.

Clovis and Pepin had no cares. All they wanted was a place to rest and play, and when she was fortunate they wanted her. In every place she went, she ensured they had some education. She taught them reading, arithmetic, good manners. In each new village they learned skills. In their small way they could trap and fish, and no matter where they went, the boys picked up sticks for sword fighting or wrestled. It wasn't proper training but then, she'd seen how the senior Warstone trained his men. She wouldn't want that for any child.

She'd also learned tasks she never would have if she'd remained sequestered in wealth and privilege. Skills she was proud of— cooking, tilling fields, cleaning, serving, and one year she'd travelled with a healer and learned to set broken bones and assist women to birth babies. So much had happened over the years it wasn't inconceivable that she wouldn't immediately recognise Balthus, and even so he was different after so many years.

The way his gaze had taken her in. The hut had been dark, but his eyes had roved over her as if he couldn't believe he'd found her. Not surprised, not predatory, but pleased. The emotion displayed hadn't been haughty or cold but…uncommon. Unexpected.

The way he'd moved…something wasn't right with his arm, and he'd hidden it before she could look at it more closely. It'd pained him. She wished she could— Séverine shook her head. He was a Warstone! If he'd injured his arm, he'd have a thousand healers taking care of him.

Most likely, it wasn't injured at all because Warstones had others do their will, to be harmed or killed in their place. How many times had Ian and his brothers left her in the care of his parents?

Ian's mother was the dagger she had never seen coming. Moments after Ian had announced at the betrothal celebration that he would marry her—moments when she should have run or laughed or played his words like a jest—she'd felt the iron grip around her wrist that had wrenched her away from gazing at a tapestry.

That serene smile as Lady Warstone had hissed, 'My son wants a word with you. Give him the respect of listening.' Then she'd turned to the hall and declared, 'I believe the child is stunned with her good fortune.'

Parting the laughing crowd, Ian had walked towards her so she'd had direct sight of the dais and Lord Warstone, her parents, and Beatrice, her sister, whose skin had paled to bone white. Her sister, who had spent weeks on her appearance, had had her fists clenched, lips pursed, and an expression of such venom that Séverine had looked behind her to see the object of her sister's wrath.

There had been no one there, and no one to stop her fate. The youngest Warstone son who almost smiled…she couldn't face him again. The rest of the crowd had displayed a mix of false delight and cunning malevolence. Spiteful glee and tittered words. Her only instinct had been to run, but Lady Warstone's grip had dug in. Only her innate good manners and a thousand eyes had kept her from crying out, but they hadn't stopped her eyes watering as she'd gaped at the man in front of her.

Ian of Warstone was stunning, charismatic. In royal circles he was coveted, revered, respected, feared.

His hair had a few waves in it. Enough to keep it away from a face carved by angels or the devil. A smile that was entirely too self-satisfied over conquests, but his eyes were the true draw. In all her reading, in all her gazing at tapestries or conversing with everyone and everything, she had never seen eyes like his. Grey with no warmth, no storms. Pale, like ice.

'Perfect,' he'd said. 'You're absolutely perfect.'

She hadn't known what that meant, not for weeks, or months, or years, but she'd understood eventually. It was a lesson hard won, but never forgotten. She'd been young, naive, innocent, and completely malleable in the hands of one who'd already been well forged. She was perfect because if his mother was the dagger, he was the sword at her neck.

Chapter Three

Months later...1298, still in France

'I'm sorry,' Henry said. 'I didn't expect such a woman to have the strength in her.'

Balthus ignored the servant riding beside him. Henry had been apologising for months, but as far as he was concerned he could apologise for a year and that still wouldn't be enough. It'd been almost winter when he'd surprised Séverine in the woodcutter's hut. Now the days were already getting longer. Would it be spring before they caught her?

Henry stretched his meaty fingers wrapped around the reins. 'Ignoring me? And how's that going to go when you haven't accepted my apology?'

Balthus had no intention of accepting any apology or excuse. Henry was supposed to have blocked the door, watched for any attacks, and, if a woman escaped, to hold her until Balthus came around. The task had been simple, direct. Henry was built like an ox. To get around him would be impossible, to subdue him, improbable. It was a solid strategy that shouldn't have failed, and yet Séverine had taken one of those branches in her arms and felled Henry with a strike against his head.

While Balthus had been rubbing his arm stump, feeling pity, pain, and ruminating on how to proceed, she'd gathered her two sons and disappeared.

'Perhaps I need to apologise more than once a day,' Henry said. 'That should do it. Hasten a return to friendship between us.'

He was trapped in a nightmare. 'It gains us nothing. There is nothing *to* hasten.'

'Ah, there you are.'

Where else would he be? He was on the laziest of horses tied to another plodding horse. Instead of being surrounded by mercenaries with trails of servants behind him, he rode alongside the worst kind of human: a servant who didn't understand his station.

He had no one to blame but himself for his companion, just like he had no choice but to ride like an infant. His lack of a left hand precluded ease of manoeuvring, but it was the constant pain, the frequent blacking out and falling off his horse that was the true indignity. When Henry had tied them together so that he could catch his master if he fell, Balthus couldn't protest.

Henry, on the other hand, felt it was his obligation to ease whatever awkwardness was between them by conversing.

'You know, you haven't said a word to me all day,' Henry said. 'Not one, and we've shared two meals already. I was beginning to wonder if some of the trees around here would be better company than you.'

They would be better company than him. Or at least safer because he felt like a desperate man with sword drawn, and if this jovial man kept up his congeniality, he would be the brunt of terrible violence.

'Talk to the trees, then,' he said. 'Or the grass, the insects, or birds, it matters not to me.'

Henry laughed. 'Oh, you'd like that while I slowly went mad. Maybe we could find some strays along the way. A pack of dogs would be nice.'

'To draw attention to ourselves?'

'My talking to trees would do enough for that.'

Balthus refused to add any more to the conversation. He needed to concentrate on easing the breath from his body, pushing away the arm pain aggravated by the minute shifts of the reins as he—

'How long is this supposed to take again?' Henry stretched his neck.

Weeks, months, years until it was accomplished, but what could he tell a mere butcher about obsession and thwarting a powerful enemy? How could he explain that to fail meant harm to thousands? Or that it was his own fault Séverine had escaped?

When he'd set out on this quest of retrieving his missing sister-in-law, he'd expected years to go by, not to discover her in the first location they stopped. Now that she knew he was close, she could make it harder to locate her.

All he needed was to ask her about a piece of parchment she may have taken from the old keep, and tell her that her husband, his brother, was dead. He'd needed to tell her and not jeopardise any of it. The irony was he'd told her none of it, and couldn't if he didn't find her again.

'However long it takes,' Balthus said. 'You

get paid regardless of whether you're here or at home.'

'Not complaining about the coin.' Henry gave him a sidelong glance. 'No man would... except those who aren't motivated by coin.'

This was ridiculous. 'You imply you're not motivated by riches?'

'I had a home, friends and a trade I loved. This is practically theft.'

Theft of his own servant. If his arm would give him any relief, he'd have travelled alone. It irked him that he needed someone. It irked that he'd chosen Henry even knowing, with certainty, that anyone else on this trip would be a far worse companion. How far he'd fallen!

His short temper was in part because of this impossible mission that was both a vow to a dead man and a quest. It wasn't even a vow he had made, but his friend and mercenary, Louve, who'd made the vow to his brother Ian as he'd died. That he would find his wife, and he would apologise for deeds Ian had done. That he would report that his brother loved her.

Louve had told his brother he would do so, but they both knew a Warstone needed to fulfil that vow. Because Balthus was the only Warstone without a wife, children, without responsibilities, he'd volunteered to find Séverine, who'd been missing for years despite the efforts made to find her. That impossible task was problematic enough, but to add the fact he had ulterior motives in finding her…

Even if she forgave him for reporting the death of her husband, she wouldn't forgive him that he intended to steal from her. Of course, she'd stolen from his brother first. That parchment. He didn't even know what it looked like, what was written on it. Nothing. Reynold had said he'd know it when he saw it. Helpful bastard.

So off he was on this quest, which wasn't his quest. Reynold was the one obsessed with obtaining the Jewell and dagger…the treasure. If nothing of this mad quest was his, why was he here? Because in a moment of weakness he'd said he would help, even though the whole mission was too unbelievable to be true. Yet here he was, because his parents and the King of England wanted an ugly gem called the Jewell of Kings, to which was attached the legend that whomever held the Jewell held the power over Scotland.

If it was as simple as locating the gem, all would be easy because some Colquhoun clan had it in their possession. Attack clan, obtain gem and be done. Except Reynold insisted that there was a treasure behind the gem and they now also needed some bits of parchment and a gemmed dagger with a hollow handle to find it.

This whole quest seemed a waste of his time, but he'd offered his help to Reynold, and meant it. Long estranged from his older brother, he wanted to know what a true family was like. Not his parents, though, who had an order for his capture, and no doubt wanted him dead by their own hands.

Add in the fact his left hand had been axed from his wrist months ago, his life, however short now, was full. Especially because, although his wrist wound had healed, by some twisted fate the agony of it had only increased. The end of his arm felt constantly on fire, the jarring of anything stopped his heart, his breath.

That made him short on patience. The way he was behaving right now was testament to that. He'd done nothing but rebuke Henry's every offer of help and ordered him about as if he was…a servant. In the past, he had never been cheerful or had friendships. He had never trusted anyone enough for that. His first and only friendship was with Louve, and even that he wouldn't admit to. However, he'd never been abusive with servants, even when his parents were around. He could afford the poor man some courtesy.

'You were not stolen. It is not outside the realm that I'd order one of my own servants to assist me.'

'Except I'm not one of your servants,' Henry said. 'You gave us all away, along with Ian's fortress, to that Louve fellow. Although since he's wed Biedeluue he's agreeable.'

The Warstone fortress owned and maintained by Ian of Warstone was a sizeable property. Ian's death, however, had left Balthus a probable heir. Except he hadn't wanted it. So, with some parchments signed, notarised and sent off to two kingdoms, it was now the property of his mercenary friend Louve, who'd married a servant, Biedeluue.

'You don't belong to anybody, according to Louve. This is merely a courtesy you do.'

'You didn't tell me what I was getting into. If I'd known I'd be in your surly company for more than a sennight, I would have brought all my knives instead of the essentials.'

Balthus turned on him. 'Then why did you?'

Henry looked down, a flush across the top of his ears giving him away. 'It looked like you... Never mind.'

Balthus refused to acknowledge that Henry pitied him because he'd lost his hand. He was almost grateful Henry looked away instead of answering a question that Balthus already knew the answer to. He was a mere excuse for a man, and absolutely worthless as a Warstone.

'It's done,' Balthus said. 'You need to concentrate on the landscape. Séverine had something in her hair. It wasn't red.'

'Ash, then, or soot, no doubt.' Henry wagged his finger as if it was of some import. 'I was watching the two boys in the field. They seemed happy.'

Clovis and Pepin were together. He didn't know what to make of that. His own parents had pitted one brother against the other since their births. They were united if anyone attacked the family, but amongst themselves they were more enemies than brothers. He was the youngest and always at a disadvantage, but he'd grown fast and had learned to look for weaknesses rather than asking to play.

His childhood had been one of opulent survival. He didn't know what to make of the boys' seeming poverty, or the fact that they were happy.

'I *am* sorry,' Henry said.

Here they were back to the apologies

again. True, he'd asked for Henry to help contain them, but he was the one who hadn't approached them properly. He'd been stunned they were there. Riveted that Séverine still had a hold on him after all these years.

'No apologies are wanted or needed,' Balthus said.

'It needs to be said,' Henry pointed out. 'You hired me to help find Séverine and the boys and tell them about Ian, and the woman conked me on the head and ran past me. Me!'

It was safer Henry only knew part of the mission. Balthus had not regaled him with tales of treasure and legends, especially as it could get him killed, so it had seemed prudent. As for Séverine's escape, at least Henry had the excuse that he had been bashed in the head with a log. Balthus's reason was only Séverine's beauty.

'What did the steward ever say to you when you made a mistake?'

'I got less pay, or a physical punishment, but that ended when I gained this.' Henry pinched the fat of his belly and jiggled it.

Balthus smirked. He didn't want to like Henry—his life wasn't safe for friendships.

'I don't have the coin of Warstone Fortress, so you had better enjoy that now.'

'Always food to find if you know where to look,' Henry said. 'It's fortunate for you I do.'

Balthus shifted in his seat, and his horse stepped sideways, jolting his arm.

'The boys seemed happy,' Henry blurted. 'Seems a shame to take them from the life they've found.'

Balthus rubbed his bandaged forearm to ease the pain. He appreciated the change of conversation, but there was no point. He didn't intend to know about the boys' lives. It was better they knew little of each other until the transaction was complete. He'd get the parchment, then tell Séverine she was free of Ian. As for his own soul... Balthus gazed at the useless limb bound to his chest. Useless agony.

Two words that summed up his entire existence.

'Fine, we take them from their life,' Henry said. 'These one-sided conversations are enlightening.'

'I didn't hire you for conversation.' Why did the man keep trying to converse with him? He could barely tolerate his own company. His arm wouldn't stop throbbing!

'What is a man of noble blood and heritage to do with a butcher as a companion if not for good conversation?' Henry exhaled. 'I have no sword skills, but I can tell you that you need to skin a deer starting at their leg joints. However, sometimes I wonder if you care about anything.'

Not when the pain overtook him. How was he to explain why he'd asked Henry on this trip that could take years? He simply didn't want to be surrounded by men who were proficient in what they did, not while he needed someone to help him dress.

Henry brought his horse to a standstill. Balthus had no choice but to halt his own mount as they were tethered together.

'I know my place in the world, and the world knows your place in it. Everywhere we go, a mighty Warstone enters a village, dines at an inn, and eats soup. You're the worst companion. Do you know what it's like, travelling with you?'

All too much, and he was sick of it, but there was something else Henry had said that alerted him. People knew who he was. 'We may need to split up.'

Henry eyed him. 'For what purpose?'

'To go from village to village and make some enquiries. Perhaps even find her.'

'How am I to find you again?'

'We'll know our destinations. If we don't see each other by the next full moon, we travel in the other's direction.'

'That's too long.'

'It'll take that long if the weather turns again.'

'It'll be spring soon, and how…how will the rest go?'

The rest… His disfigurement and the constant reminder that he wasn't who he had once been. With unexpected discretion, Henry helped him mount, ride, dress. He was grateful for that, but he wanted this farce over.

'There are four directions in which they could have gone. We need to follow with two.'

'I'm at your service,' Henry said.

'Remind me to remedy that soon.'

Chapter Four

A fortnight later...

'I think you pushed him too hard into the hole you had made, Mama,' Pepin announced.

'She did not,' Clovis said. 'How else was he to fall in the hole unless she pushed him? And it's a trap. Remember Imbert told us it took months to dig and line with smooth wood like that.'

It was the perfect trap, built inside a hut so no one from the outside could see it, and the truth of what she'd done in hitting Balthus of Warstone over the head and shoving him into it made her stomach curl.

After a few weeks of travel, they'd arrived at their destination. A small village where she had separated from the last of Ian's servants who'd left with her that fateful day. Sarah and

Imbert, the stablemaster, more friends than servants, had helped her enlist the others in the household.

They'd stayed together the longest until this village where she'd given Imbert coin to organise this hut and trap. Wind blasted against the sides of the thin structure. The rain had turned to snow then to slush. The weather was bitter and caustic. Even if they wanted to travel again, it would not be wise. She might have trapped Balthus of Warstone in the pit, but the weather had trapped her, too. It was just as well as she needed to know what danger he'd brought to this tiny village and to her.

'Tell me what happened,' she said.

'It was only him,' Clovis said. 'He's not the man you hit.'

'Mama doesn't hit!' Pepin shouted.

'Pepin,' she pleaded. 'Please.'

Glaring at his brother, Clovis added, 'He slowed the horse when he got into the square and dismounted. That's when we showed ourselves to him and ran.'

'He got lost then!' Pepin said.

'And Sarah saw us,' Clovis added.

Sarah, who must have immediately run to her to tell her to wait in the hut and prepare. So she had, right behind the door.

'What then?' she asked.

'I went to the woods like you told me to,' Pepin said.

'And a good boy you are for doing so.' The villagers were about so if harm came, he would be protected, but the woods was his favourite place to hide.

'I ran here,' Clovis said.

Clovis had burst through, closed the door and run around to the far side. Balthus hadn't fought, hadn't known he'd needed to fight because she'd cracked him over the head with a sturdy branch, pushed, and all that was left had been the sound his body had made when he'd hit the bottom.

Pepin peered over the smooth ledge. 'Do you think his legs are broken?'

What had she done? She'd hit Balthus on the head merely to disorientate him, but even that felt like too much the way he'd suddenly swayed, then she hadn't meant to push him so hard, but she was terrified it wouldn't work. Was it possible he'd broken his legs, his arms… his neck? She hadn't heard anything snap, but then she could barely hear anything over the roaring in her ears. With far more trepidation than her children's, she tried to see to the bottom of the pit.

It was as dark as night…which was her intention because enemies didn't deserve to see. But now she realised it was too dark.

She should be glad she'd hit and shoved him too hard. The entire family deserved pain, agony, and yet she felt ill. She needed to know if he'd survived.

'Clovis, is he still…breathing?'

Eagerly lying near the edge, Clovis peered down; Pepin mimicked him. She threw more kindling on the fire. Perhaps more light up here would provide more light down there.

Fear was closing off her senses… What would she do if the youngest Warstone was dead? Could any amount of hiding save her sons from the family then? And where was the servant she'd first injured?

'When you ran here, did you see anyone else with him?'

'No, Mama,' Pepin said. 'Did he ruin your hide-and-seek, too?'

'He's not moving,' Clovis said.

She'd go mad with this conversation reciting all her fears! She'd hoped this village would be a haven for approaching spring. She wished, fervently, that Balthus had never found her. She didn't want to run again. But there was no running from a dead Warstone in a pit.

Séverine jumped at the knock at the door. Froze when it opened until Sarah poked her head in and looked at the boys on their stomachs. 'Is he in there?'

Séverine nodded. 'Where's Imbert?'

'Doing a check and notifying everyone.' Sarah peered over. 'Who did you catch?'

'I thought you saw him.'

'It's cold outside and I kept my head down. It's dark down there, I can't see an insignia, so it's not Ian. A mercenary of his?'

Everyone's eyes were working better than hers! 'It's Balthus.'

Sarah grabbed the backs of the boys' tunics and pulled them away. 'You've got to run now.'

'He's too still. If he's dead or truly hurt...' Séverine said.

'Then they'll only hurt you worse. Get up, boys!'

The boys fought Sarah's grip until they were free. Clovis pulled down his tunic; Pepin looked expectantly at her. They may have known these servants all their lives, but their mother had the final say. She needed to be a mother to them. Now that the surprise of what she'd done had sunk in, a certain truth was becoming all too clear.

'I know that expression,' Sarah said. 'You

can't be soft when it comes to them, you must go. This was always the intention.'

'I know what they're like! But leaving an actual Warstone wasn't the intention. He's a complication. It was supposed to be a mercenary sent by my husband, one with the intention of dragging us back before Ian's parents. Or Ian himself, who wouldn't harm us.'

'Balthus is well known to be a favourite of his mother's, and intends to do you harm,' Sarah said.

She didn't know what he intended…he'd been reserved at the woodcutter's shed. No matter that moment by the tapestry where it had seemed they'd shared something, he was a Warstone, and she could only trust half of what he said.

'If I leave him, that's dangerous for you and Imbert.'

'His servants will take care of him.'

'There are no servants.'

'He's a Warstone, they're simply not here yet. His mercenaries are most likely burning the other villages as we stand here now.'

'He has no mercenaries. There was only one other man at my family's home. Even so, Balthus of Warstone is in that pit, and if he's harmed or dead, there will be consequences if I go.'

'Don't say it, child. Whatever you do, don't—'

'I'm staying to make certain he's unharmed. I need a torch to see if he's still breathing.'

'The only good Warstone is a dead one. You know that,' Sarah said.

'I'm going down there,' Séverine said. 'If he's dead, that risks all of us.'

Sarah huffed. 'I'm getting Imbert to talk some sense into you.'

Chapter Five

Pain was all Balthus was aware of before he could recognise where he hurt. His arm, his left knee. His head.

Shadows flickered, and there was the crackle of fire…and heated whispers between a man and a woman. The man's voice he didn't recognise. The woman's voice was familiar. Why?

A pain like thin daggers continually thrust into his left elbow, the rest he ignored. What mattered were those voices.

The man's was raised, the woman's whispered but urgent.

Something wasn't right. He opened his eyes. Above him, lit by firelight, he saw Séverine and a familiar-looking man, who was gesturing threateningly.

She shouldn't be standing so close to the

man, so near the crevasse into which he'd fallen. She was in danger.

'Move.' The word came out hoarsely and barely above a whisper. But the man stepped back immediately. Balthus couldn't see him, but he knew he was still there.

'Séverine, move.'

She turned her back to the man and peered down at him.

No! He tried to rise.

'Balthus,' Séverine said.

'Get away. Run,' he gasped.

Her brows drew in, but she didn't move. He couldn't hear anything but the clink of a door latch.

'Where does it hurt?' she said.

'Keep your eyes on him!'

'He's gone,' she said.

Where would he go? Her back was to him; she was too trusting. 'Step away, and I'll find a way up.'

She paused.

'Now! You can't fall in like I—'

'Balthus, how badly does your head hurt?'

It hurt like he'd fallen into a hole and banged it, except... '*You* hit my head, shoved me in here.'

She straightened, and he noticed the construction and the roof far over his head.

'What have you done, Séverine?'

'What should have been done from the beginning. It seems I've captured a Warstone.'

There was a bite to her tone, and something else that made little sense given her triumphant words.

'Why am I here? What is this place?'

She crossed her arms. 'Can't you tell? Your ilk has carved out hundreds of traps and created devices to contain and torture people, or have you never personally inspected any of them? I've seen them, it was what gave me the idea for this place.'

A well inside a hut. Until he inspected this further, it was indeed a trap.

'Now tell me, is anything broken, are you bleeding?' she said.

Concern. That was the tone he didn't expect from a woman who'd built a Warstone trap to catch a Warstone.

Maybe he could play to her softer side. 'I do hurt.'

'I don't care if you're in pain,' she said. 'I care if you'll be dying on me sooner than I'd like.'

Her words were harsh, but again something

was off. Did she care? No, that couldn't be correct; she had no reason to be concerned or care for him. He truly did hurt and couldn't think! He'd go mad within the year if the end of his arm didn't stop stabbing him so!

'Why don't you get a ladder and I'll crawl up so you can inspect me,' he said.

She huffed. 'You're well, then. That makes everything much easier.'

Careful to keep his left side hidden, Balthus stood. The pit wasn't large, no more than the height of a man and a half wide, but it was deep, and lined with finely sanded wood. Running his hand along the slats, he could find no purchase. This could be a problem.

'Let me up, Séverine,' he said.

'Or what?' she said. 'Why are you following me?'

'It's peculiar to have a hole in the middle of a hut.' He ran his hand over the sides. 'Why did you truly have this built? It's far too random to catch me.'

'How many mercenaries are on their way, or is Ian already here? Your servant isn't with you—where is he?'

There was a jest here somewhere if only the increase of pain, and the fact that there couldn't be laughter in his life, didn't distract him. He wanted to laugh, even if it was a pale version of the true emotion. The difficult aspect of this quest was to find Séverine. Years he'd been prepared to ride and seek. After all, she'd eluded capture by Ian…but now he wondered. How hard had Ian actually searched for her? Because he was finding her all too easily.

All he needed to do was tell her that her husband was dead and to find and secure a piece of parchment. Instead, she'd shoved him down a black hole to ask *him* questions. He could…stay.

Which had nothing to do with the fact he didn't want to end their time together, and everything to do with the very certain truth that Séverine had had this built… What else had she done in those years away? If he gave the reasons he was here, he might never know, which was unacceptable. And cooperating and not giving in to his impulses had never been in his nature anyway.

'You trapped me to gain answers? You could have asked me before you injured me.'

'You said you weren't injured. For a Warstone, you're not a good liar.'

'Why don't you let me up, and I'll show you what I am?' It was a weak bluff. He was nothing but weak.

She shook her head. 'I like you like this.'

'What do you think will happen when they find me in this pit?'

'Which *they*? From what direction are they coming?'

He could play this game. 'Does it matter who they are? Do you think my family or any of their entourage would cease looking for me? And yet you are standing there, waiting to be caught.'

'That's what you want to hear? *Farewell, Balthus?*'

Not in the slightest. He'd never talked to her for any length of time and in this way before. And, as much pain as he felt, he was loath to stop it.

Poorly dressed, her hair in a simple plait, the fire behind her cast shadows over her features, and yet at this angle he could imagine the length of her legs, pretend she was some angel sent down to absolve him of his sins... until he sinned with her.

How he resented Ian taking her away from him. She was to be his! It had wrecked him over the years to know she'd lain with his brother. He'd avoided that cursed house, and yet, whenever he'd been in residence, he'd craned his neck to see her gliding up a staircase or turning a curve in a hallway.

'If this is goodbye, I look forward to the riddles on how to escape.'

She pursed her lips. 'I don't play Warstone games.'

Oh, she didn't like that. Interesting. 'You ordered this built to trap a man, and your boys ran through a village slowly enough that I could follow them. I think you play games better than most.'

He didn't know why he was antagonising her. It wasn't the way to build trust when there was none between them. He'd expected, with Henry by his side, to ease her into some sort of agreement. After all, Henry was as affable as he could be, and perhaps she'd see he was different from Ian.

Different? He was an impulsive fool! Provoking her, imagining the length of her legs, what it would be like to lie with her. He wanted to get away from games, away from the Warstone life, and she'd just trapped him, and because it was her, he wanted to stay in it.

He'd never deserved her before and was now barely a man. 'Let me go, Séverine, and no one gets hurt.'

'Threatening me,' she scoffed. 'That didn't

take you long, though it is rather foolish, don't you believe?'

Threats were foolish when negotiation would fit much better. Either he was out of practice, having been in the company of non-Warstones while he recovered from his severed left hand, or the daggers of pain in his left elbow down to his stump were distracting him.

Sliding to the floor, he leaned his head back against the circular wall. Ah, his head ached. Perhaps, after he rested, after she left, he could find a way to escape. Perhaps—

'What are you doing?' she said.

'Resting.'

If he opened his eyes, maybe he could discern her reaction. If he could see her, he might see concern or indifference. What did he know of this woman?

What everyone else assumed. That she was a fragile flower who had been forced to marry his brother. The girl he'd caught dreaming while staring at a tapestry and who had seemed surprised anyone noticed her.

Except she wasn't fragile. She'd eluded his brother and hidden two growing boys for years. An impossible feat. Further, she'd confessed to constructing this trap, and she was pleased he was stuck in it. No, she wasn't to be underestimated.

Even if he had both hands, he couldn't escape this hole without help, but now he sat, and exhaustion was consuming his body. He hadn't lied when he'd said he hurt. Perhaps he could rest for a while.

'What's wrong with you?' she said.

He was physically and emotionally empty. Healing from a severed hand, immediately setting out on this journey to find Séverine. Grieving because of his brother. Angry at him still because Ian had tried to kill him. A few weeks out on this journey, and he was so weakened!

'Someone struck me on the head and shoved me into hole,' he said.

'Are you bleeding?'

'Again, inspect me yourself. Or lower a torch and do it that way.'

'I have, and it doesn't allow for the shadows.'

That had him opening his eyes. 'Why would you admit a weakness?'

'That's a—'

'I could hide a weapon along the edges since you shoved me in here with all my weaponry.'

'You won't harm me.'

'That's exactly what I'm here to do,' he bit out.

She paused. 'That was quite direct...even for one of your kind.'

'If I said anything else, would you believe me?'

'Why would you want me to believe you?' she said.

'Now, there is a question that has no answer.' If he told her anything, she'd think it a lie, but even so...why did he want her to believe him? That wasn't necessary to achieve his goal here.

He was so weary. Negotiating was the correct action to securing the parchment; being kind...a true brother-in-law would be the appropriate path to telling her about the loss. But what was right didn't feel like it. Why?

Because he'd wanted to make her suffer because she'd run away with his nephews and worry that bit longer? That would be his brothers'—Ian or Guy's—tactic. Because he had been curious? That was his brother Reynold's trait. That man studied everything.

Because he'd wanted to be around her for as long as he could? He couldn't say he'd missed her; he'd been in her presence for mere hours many years ago. He couldn't conceive of her smiling now, for why would she ever share joy with him? No, even that desire, one for which he yearned, didn't encompass the inexplicable reason he didn't blurt out the truth. It was a mystery.

Which fitted. Perfectly. He had been a mystery to himself ever since he'd broken away from his parents and sided with Reynold against them. Ever since he'd lost his hand, partly because of Fate, part foolishness, and no doubt to others a happy misfortune.

Is that how she saw him? As misfortunate? What would happen if he mentioned that day at the tapestry, would it somehow set this whole failure of a mission to rights? What if he just said he meant her no ill will, that he remembered how her eyes had shone as she'd gazed at the intricate colours, and that her boys had that same light in theirs when they'd run?

He opened his eyes, but she was gone.

'Séverine?'

Nothing but silence. Gone…she should be. Even if he mentioned anything good, nothing of any worth would come from staying in his company.

Chapter Six

Séverine didn't know why she'd stepped back and sat outside Balthus's sight. She didn't know why she hadn't answered him when he'd called out to her.

He wasn't well. His speech was slow, and he'd gone to the wall and slid to the floor. She remembered that scrape of a foot in the wood-cutter's hut. Had he been injured then, or only now?

When she'd shoved him, she'd been mostly concerned with her action taking him by surprise. She hadn't truly looked at him. But trapped, she had been afforded a glimpse of him she hadn't expected. As he'd walked, his palm rubbing the curved wood, looking for weaknesses, nothing of him had looked elegant and he'd favoured and hidden his left side, but there had been something tangible about him.

The shaggy darkness of his hair, the bluntness of a cheekbone, the fullness of his lower lip.

He'd changed much since the last time she'd seen him. Before, he'd looked much like all the other— No, even when she'd seen him that first time, he hadn't been like the other Warstones. When she'd turned and caught him staring at her, she'd reacted.

She'd been in the hall, standing farthest away from the dais and studying the newly delivered hunting tapestry, when she'd turned. The youngest Warstone had seemed as stunned as her. She'd been unable to look away, especially when his lips had parted as if he'd wanted to say something…significant. Then his mouth curved at the corner and…nothing. Séverine shook her head. It was all nothing. That moment between Balthus and her broke when his mother had gripped her wrist. She'd often think of it and wonder, but she'd never understood what it had been.

She did now. Because she felt that same arrested fluttering. Balthus, a man, was somehow that exquisite tapestry. Brutal violence with felled prey. The artist with colours and craft making violence beguiling, bloodshed magnificent. And some part of her traitorous self found the threads of Balthus intriguing.

More than that. When he'd looked up from the bottom of the pit, the paleness of his face, the black greyness of his eyes…it had been like looking at a soul trapped in Purgatory, *aware* he was ensnared there. It had affected her in some visceral way she couldn't explain, even to herself.

Was this lust, desire when she'd felt none before? No. It was confusion. Fear, perhaps, for her children. His words were games. He gave her half-truths, mostly lies. She couldn't trust him. He'd told her he was here to harm her.

Which…she did trust. So she'd stepped back. The words and the way he'd moved she could turn away from. She could almost ignore his beauty and despair, as well. But it was difficult to ignore for long that rough exhalation of his after he'd said her name and she hadn't answered.

It wasn't a breath of frustration or exhaustion— it had sounded like relief.

If there was one emotion Warstones didn't deserve to feel, it was relief. Moving to the edge, folding her feet under her, she peered down. Either her eyes were used to the darkness or the extra torches that Imbert had set up allowed her to see more. It was heartening to see that tic in his jaw. It couldn't have been relief; it was annoyance he was feeling. Good.

'You're still here?' he said.

'I won't trust you,' she said. 'It would be foolish of you to think I cannot harm you.'

'You left me with daggers and my sword,' he said.

'I have torches lit with fire. You may be able to climb out or not, throw daggers or not, but if you are a true threat to my sons, I will kill you.'

'Such fierceness, Séverine,' Balthus said. 'Perhaps this is the reason Ian left you at that minuscule keep.'

Was it common knowledge that her husband had walked away from her marriage first? And what did she care that he had? She hadn't loved him, though there had been times... No, she couldn't think that way, else she would be soft like Sarah told her she was.

'Don't mock me, Warstone, you know me not,' she said.

He shrugged. 'Then let me go, and we don't need to worry about knowing each other. It's best that way.'

Lies! 'Thus defeat the purpose of your following me?'

'When you leave for good, I wouldn't mind

some food, ale and a bucket to relieve myself in.'

'I'm not leaving until I have answers.'

'What would you say to that's the reason I'm here? All I'm wanting is to exchange information.'

'Is it not Ian who wants answers? Because giving him answers is simple. The answer's no. No, I'm not going back, no, he can't have the children, no, he can't have me.'

She watched as something flitted across his eyes, something darker than his surroundings.

'What did he do to you, Séverine?'

The concern in his voice! Standing, she almost shouted, almost swung a torch at him. 'Don't pretend, don't be kind. Remember, I lived with your parents. I know the monsters you all are.'

He was quiet again, but she practically felt the questions he burned to ask. He and his kind didn't deserve answers, and yet...

'Answer me this, are you truly hurt?'

He closed his eyes, kept his silence. That wouldn't get them anywhere.

'Do you need anything for the pain?' she said again.

'Do you ever think of that time at all?' he

said, a careful tone to his voice. 'The day of the announcement?'

Damn them all, and her heart, which felt like a vise in her chest.

'The day I was wrenched from my life, and your brother caused my sisters to hate me forevermore? That day?'

Legs stretched out, his head slumped forward, he exhaled roughly.

She couldn't see his eyes, his face. This man couldn't be defeated. He couldn't mean that moment with the tapestry. It had meant something to her because it had been the last truly peaceful moment she could remember. To him, a Warstone? It had to be just one moment of many. None of that was important.

'Are my boys in danger because you're here?' she said.

He rubbed his leg. 'If I say yes, you'll flee, and I'll only chase you again. If I say no, where would I be then?'

Stuck in a hole in the ground, but that wasn't the point. 'This isn't about you!'

'Given I'm in a pit, and you're free to do what you please, I beg to differ.'

She was imagining his defeated sigh if he was back to obscure conversations. Or perhaps his head was too injured for reasoning.

He made little sense to her, and for the villagers' sake, for her children's, she needed to hurry this along.

'Stop, just stop it. You're trapped, I could do what I want with you.'

'Yet you can't. I can banter in circles until I die of starvation. So, unless you do more to me than that, this is what we're left with.'

'You suggest I torture you? If you're like your brother, you've already been trained for starvation—and anything else I can mete out.'

'Which you knew, so the only point of this pit is to trap one of us to the death. Anything else would be foolish if you wish to keep your boys safe. Or you can come to the same conclusion I have, that it is about me, and you could let me ask my questions.'

'You've had plenty of time to ask.'

He inhaled, coughed a bit. 'Your boys are not in danger.'

'Until my husband gets here.'

He flexed his right heel, then his left. 'Your husband's not coming.'

'His men?'

'Only me, and you've delayed me from getting word to him.'

'What about the servant who travelled with you?'

'He went in the other direction in case you escaped that way.'

Likely a lie. No Warstone would be without servants and mercenaries. 'How were you going to meet up again?'

'We gave a designated time.'

'So, if I leave, he'll head this way and take care of you.'

'*If* he can find me. I only fell in here because I was following your boys.'

He sounded convincing, but then all Warstones had that ability...it was how they controlled kingdoms.

'How much of that was true?' She didn't expect him to answer.

'All of it,' he said. 'There, I've given all of it so now perhaps we can have an exchange and you can be on your way.'

'So...lies, then.'

'Why would I lie?' He looked directly at her. 'It doesn't serve me. You could truly leave, and I'd rot here.'

'Are you trying to appeal to my better nature when I know what you are?'

'My nature is yours. To the outside world we're family. Those boys share my blood, a truth you can never deny.'

No matter how much she tried to deny it, it

was the truth. It was also the truth that when she'd left Ian, he'd been much altered from the man she'd married a few years before. It wasn't only the cruelty and the control she looked for when she watched her children playing. She watched for their intelligence, their suspicion. For madness.

There had been times at the end when she hadn't been certain if Ian would harm himself or their children. Then, as if Satan himself had been on their heels, he'd led their small caravan to Forgotten Keep and left them.

All of that she could have dismissed. Why should she care where they were housed as long as she had her sons? But Ian's haunted gaze, the tender touch on her cheek…that last moment she'd seen him had made her question what she knew was truth. Her husband was dangerous and either he or someone else intended to harm them. He might have left her first, but all that did was give her the opportunity to leave him for as long as she could.

'How is he?' she asked.

Balthus shifted, kept quiet, and she regretted the moment of weakness.

He grunted. 'You don't want to know.'

Had her husband gone mad, or was he seeking vengeance for her humiliating him? Did he miss his children? Was that look he'd given her at the end one of regret? Perhaps she had gone soft. She had left him because he was dangerous!

'No, I don't want to know of him,' she said. 'I want to know if we're at risk. You keep finding us. How are you doing that?'

'I said no, and as to the rest, I don't know. Good fortune?' He adjusted his back against the wall.

'Why are you protecting your left side? You've been hurt. Do you need willow bark? Peppermint? A splint?'

When he didn't answer, she added, 'No deceptive comment? No misdirection?'

'Why do you keep offering assistance when you know I don't deserve any?' he said. 'See, you may think you're not a Warstone, but you're decent at traps as well as exchanging useless banter, which will get us nowhere, and I'm…' He shook his head, slowly…wearily. 'Let me know when you decide what to do with me.'

Closing his eyes, he rested his head back, bent his knees with one arm dangled on top. She was being ignored by her own prisoner and should leave. Her boys were important and staying here risked them. Except it was late afternoon, the weather foul. Spring was near, but it was still cold.

And there was something more here. His words were confusing, and not only for reasons that they were misleading, but because she sensed truth in them as well as frustration. As if he wanted to be believed, which was foolish on her part.

'Are you staying or are you going?' Balthus whispered.

Arrogant, as expected. 'It's late. A woman with two young boys is vulnerable at night.'

'Ah.'

'What is that supposed to mean?'

'Your being vulnerable isn't an attribute I would have ever given you.'

Odd, since it was what the rest of the Warstones continually thought of her…and never let her forget. Ian constantly kept her locked in a room or coddled. His parents had controlled her from day one. Just as this man was doing. She stood. This time she would leave.

'What if I need to relieve myself?'

'Shouldn't you be more worried about food or water?'

'I'd rather protect my boots and prevent tying them again.'

'Are you vain?'

He huffed. 'When I die of thirst, I don't want to look as if I have no pride.'

She didn't like knowing that he knew he'd die of thirst before he starved. The Warstones only ever suffered from their own parents. Ian had suffered though he'd mocked any of her comfort. Just as Balthus did now.

She hated that she noticed the differences and similarities between him and her husband, that she was comparing them.

She hated feeling any sympathy for this man, this Warstone. That family had yanked her from the life she'd been meant to have, and into uncertainty for the rest of it. Her children had to run the rest of their lives or else be subject to horrors and those seeking revenge. They'd be forced to become cruel simply to survive.

She couldn't protect them indefinitely. Her nightmare was that she'd fail them. This man had found her twice. Twice! He risked them all.

She grabbed an empty bucket.

'Fates!' Balthus said.

'You said you needed a bucket,' she answered as sweetly as she could. She could hear him scrambling from his sitting position.

'I didn't know you'd throw it,' Balthus said.

Had Ian known his wife at all? Or had this woman been created in the years away from them?

'Merely tossed it over my head,' she called out.

'And almost hit mine!'

Her smile at the tapestry and then towards him hadn't reflected this strength, but it must have been there because she'd fled a Warstone. So many questions that he wanted to ask her. So many answers he wanted to give and yet what would come of it? He'd asked if she remembered that time, and all of it had been about her and Ian. Nothing else was significant for her. Not her fascination and happiness over a tapestry. Not glancing over at some gaping man who couldn't look away from her.

All he had of her was this useless banter that would end, and he'd be left with even less than this. What had he become? All his accomplishments, the victories, the survival. He had been sent on this mission for legends to take down kingdoms, and mere moments in this woman's life beggared him into asking if she remembered a shared smile.

She was Ian's wife, and he'd avoided her for years. Now he had no lands, coin or a left hand.

He should continue to avoid her, and tell her the truth, so he could rot in this pit.

'Are you trying to find something else to fling?' he called out.

'Of course. I—'

A door slamming open, a cold burst of icy wind. 'Mama, Mama, you've got to see what I found—'

'Slow down!' Séverine said. 'The ledge!'

'Oh!' Pepin squealed.

Another slam of the door. The bottom of Clovis's leg as he hurled his body inside. 'Don't believe the little thief, Mama, he stole—'

'No!' Séverine screamed.

Balthus tensed at the bodies above him, at Pepin standing at the edge. At Clovis, who appeared fully because his body barrelled into Pepin's. Pepin, whose feet were no longer on the ground but over the pit.

Sweeping away his cloak, Balthus caught the tumbling boy.

Blinding pain, agony…darkness.

Chapter Seven

'Pepin!' Séverine grabbed the ladder and lowered it to the bottom of the pit.

'I'm in here!' Pepin said.

'Don't you hurt him!'

'I won't, Mama, I'm standing away from him now.'

'No, not you…' Séverine paused. 'Balthus?'

'He's not moving, either. We're staying still.'

'Hold the ladder steady, Clovis, until I get down.' Séverine adjusted the ladder to make certain it didn't slip. 'No, wait, go and get Sarah or Imbert, nobody else.'

'What are you doing?'

'I'm getting your brother,' she said.

'Pepin, climb the ladder!' Clovis yelled.

'No, stay there,' Séverine ordered. 'Clovis, your brother could be hurt.'

'That man's down there.'

'I think he's sleeping!' Pepin added.

'Clovis, leave the ladder and go. When you come back shine the torch down. Now.' She waited until Clovis dashed outside.

'Balthus, if this is a trick…' Séverine carefully lowered herself to the first rung. The walls of the pit were steep and the floors below could be slick.

'I've got it,' Pepin said.

The amused relief was instant at her son's words. 'Pepin, step back.'

There was the possibility Balthus could overwhelm her the moment she stepped down, or the ladder could slip. Two more steps. It was dark, but her son was there, holding the ladder. Enfolding him in her arms, she felt along his wiry body. 'Are you certain you are not hurt?'

'He caught me. He caught me. I didn't touch the bottom when he fell.'

'He was standing.'

She felt him nod against her stomach. 'He didn't catch very good, and we hit the ground. That's the only time I touched him, honest.'

'Balthus?' If he was going to overpower them, now would be the time, but he was curled on his side at her feet.

'Climb up now while I check on him.'

'I dropped my prize,' Pepin said. 'And I can't see anything down here.'

'Pepin!' She had no time for this. Glancing up, she saw no people, only the firelight flickering across the ceiling. She'd forgotten how deep this hole was.

If Pepin had fallen in and not been caught… Anything or nothing could have happened, but Balthus had purposefully broken his fall. What was taking Clovis so long?

Kneeling gave her a better view of her prisoner, but curled as he was, with his back to her, he did look asleep…or dead. She placed her hand on his chest, could feel the rise and fall of his breath. It was laboured, agitated. He was hurt, but where?

His temple felt warm but not feverish, and she winced when she felt the large lump on the back of his head, probably from her striking him before she shoved him here. Had he hit it again upon the fall? She could not tell, but the agitation of his breath didn't increase as she felt his head, and there was no blood. Carefully, just as she'd learned from the old healer, she felt along his neck, then down one arm, then the other. His breath hitched.

So did hers.

'What is it, Mama?'

Something was very, very wrong. 'Pepin, you need to go up the ladder.'

'I haven't found my treasure yet. I can't leave without my treasure.'

'We'll look for it later,' she said, but knew her son would continue to ignore her. What child would ignore the excitement around him?

Keeping one hand on Balthus's shoulder, something wavered inside her chest, similar to shock, more like horror. With a shaking hand she slid it to the end of his left arm, felt the soft skin become hard, tightly wrapped, then nothing.

Balthus was missing his left hand.

No longer able to kneel, she sat down hard, scattering dust, dirt, some pebbles across the floor.

It startled Balthus into consciousness.

Grey eyes locked to hers, but they weren't alert, they didn't see...

Her hand flew to her mouth and a choked sob escaped. Everything was wrong, but what could she say? She needed to say something.

'What's happened?' he slurred. 'Is the boy harmed?'

He looked over his shoulder at Pepin, whose eyes must have been as wide as hers.

'Séverine!' he snapped, his eyes clear. 'Are you hurt?'

What could she say? 'I'm well,' she said, brushing her cheeks with the back of her hand, rubbing her palms down her gown and doing it again. So many tears for a Warstone. What was wrong with her?

He sat up suddenly, blinked rapidly, swayed. He was going to harm himself! 'No, you're not, something is not right. Tell me!'

'No, no, Balthus, don't!' She splayed out her hands towards him as if to keep him down. 'The boys are well.'

A bang at the door! Balthus pushed himself to stand, his legs unsteady. Imbert came into view.

'You! You're Ian's man! Stay away from her!' Balthus put his hand and foot on the ladder.

'No, Balthus!'

Imbert's eyes snapped from Séverine to Balthus and he kicked the ladder to the other side.

Dislodged, Balthus spun on his one leg, patted his right thigh where a blade was held and grunted as if something stabbed him.

'No!' she cried.

His grey gaze shifted to hers before they went distant, and he crumpled to the floor once again.

Séverine's heart hammered in her chest. She was this close to losing her porridge. What had happened? None of it necessary, none of it…

'Séverine, get out of there now!' Imbert said.

'Mama, I think that man was trying to rescue you,' Pepin whispered.

Séverine spun towards her child, his eyes only on Balthus. Balthus, who had no left hand. Who had come round, seen her distress and tried to defend her.

'You're all right?' she said.

Pepin leaned in close to her. 'He doesn't like Imbert.'

No, he didn't. Half-mad with pain, Balthus had tried to protect them from Imbert. Something wasn't right. She needed to inspect him in full light.

'Imbert, throw something down here so we can get him up top.'

'You leave him down there.'

'He saved Pepin's fall!'

Imbert cursed.

'You've got to go up now,' Séverine said as gently as she could to her youngest. Not because she was worried for his safety anymore, but because what needed to happen, what she needed to say to Imbert, shouldn't be said in front of him.

Balthus's breathing was harsh, and under each exhalation was almost a deep moan. He was in torment, and a man in that much pain was unpredictable, but it was also telling, and something snagged at her thoughts because of it. Something she could do. If she was right, and brave enough.

'I can't go up until I find my treasure,' he said.

'We'll get it later.' She gathered the boy and gave him a boost.

He looked down over his shoulder at her and whispered, his voice part puzzlement, mostly awe. 'He's fierce, isn't he?'

Séverine watched Imbert hoist Pepin up, another little arm reaching out, showing Clovis was there, as well.

'I can feel you thinking down there,' Imbert said. 'I'm not helping you.'

Séverine climbed up. 'Pepin, Clovis, you, too, outside!'

Séverine crossed her arms, prepared to defend herself to this loyal man who would fight her over what she was about to say. 'We need to get him out of this hole. He's injured.'

Imbert exhaled. 'Injured or not, until we know we won't be under attack, he stays. Can't negotiate with his family if that man is free and can't have him running out and notifying any of them what we've done.'

Everything he said was true, and yet Balthus's actions had not been hostile. He hadn't attacked that day in the woodshed, he'd caught Pepin when he'd fallen, and he'd tried to protect her against Imbert.

Could Balthus be different from the other Warstones? Was it possible?

'There are new injuries, but there's another older one. He's bandaged up.'

'Will he bleed out?'

'I don't think so. But there's pain involved. If I'm correct, he's in nothing but pain.'

'What do you mean?' Imbert said.

It was only a suspicion, but now that she felt his arm, some of Balthus's actions were beginning to make sense. 'I came across this before when I travelled with the healer. Something under the skin. I can't be certain until he comes round again.'

'Then he's in pain, which I don't care about. My opinion stays the same.'

She should simply listen to him, but couldn't.

'Are you thinking of ordering me about like a servant?' he grumbled.

'When were you ever one to me?' she said. 'But I wish you weren't so stubborn.'

'Or right,' he said.

He *was* right. It was only the fact that Balthus had no hand that somehow changed him in her mind. Which was foolish again because whether he had one hand or two, he was still dangerous. Except…even injured like that, he'd saved her son from further harm.

Then there was the other matter of his missing hand. If she was right; he was in constant pain. What if…? It'd been many years before, but she'd seen a man suffer who'd lost a foot. The healer she'd travelled with had cut him again. The wound had healed differently, and the continual pain had stopped.

What if Balthus suffered from the same thing? What if she could heal him, and if he was different enough, she could sway him to her side? A risk, but a calculated one worth taking if it meant a better future for her sons.

'I need Sarah to bring me willow bark and a valerian tincture,' she whispered. 'Someone should have them. Buckets of water, more logs for the fire, food and ale, too.'

'I'll let her know.'

'And Imbert, when you come back, I need your blade, the big one, sharpened.'

'That I'll gladly do,' he said.

Chapter Eight

How much time had passed? Balthus was stuck in some bog pulled by the never-ceasing agony that circled through his body.

Every once in a heartbeat something else scraped against his dark sleep. Voices—a woman's, a man's. Children, which registered most of all. Children. Unharmed. Something about that was important.

His stomach turned, ached, and he rolled to the side.

'We've brought what you asked for.' A woman's unfamiliar voice. 'I also thought this would help.'

'He's still not stirring. I have to wait this out.'

'No, you leave him down there and you flee.' A man's voice, older. The voice belonged to Imbert, a servant of Ian's. A stablemaster.

'How can you think of leaving him? Something's not right, I think I know what it… Can't be certain until I… He needs to wake up.'

A pause.

'Mama, he's ill.'

'If I'm found out, what do you think would happen?'

'It wasn't supposed to be him!' A shushing sound. Quiet.

'Ian said he was the favourite of his mother,' Imbert said. 'She'll be looking for him. Even if I flee, if you set him free, none of you are safe. We knew the consequences and agreed to keep… Our plans depend that you flee to the next and the next and keep at it until they lose interest.'

'When have the Warstones ever lost interest?'

'Quiet! He could hear.' A woman's voice. Séverine's. She was there, just above him.

She was arguing with Imbert, as if they knew each other well. How and why was he here?

'Mama, he's definitely sick.'

That voice was Pepin's, which was clear. Everyone else was trying to whisper.

Séverine's voice was stronger now. 'He caught Pepin… Been injured. I think he hurts.

There's a chance I can help him, and us. We may be able to sway him to…'

'Never! Don't! He's in pain, you leave him in pain,' Imbert said. 'I won't help. I can't watch.'

'Come, Imbert, what if she's right?' That was Sarah. Imbert's wife.

'I'm going to do it,' Séverine said. 'Go now, but Imbert, when I've done it, I'll come and get…'

'We're leaving, then,' Sarah said. 'Come, boys.'

Heavy footsteps, a swish of a gown, a door closing.

Another blast of cold air, and he started shivering. He wasn't well, but this was better than the dark sleep. Better because she was saying his name.

'Balthus,' she repeated.

Her voice…he loved to listen to it. It was becoming clearer by the moment. He wished he could hear it forever, especially when it sounded concerned when she talked about him. Kind words for him. He'd have believed he was dead if not for the fact she would be as well. No, he wanted them alive, and well…he had found them alive and well. Thriving. Happy. He was here to ruin that.

'Can you hear me?'

He could. He could. He recognised all the voices now. Séverine, his brother's servants, his nephews. The one woman he wanted to love was right there. He could hear her gasp.

With soothing words to the half-delirious man down below, Séverine, with two buckets of supplies hooked to her arm, took the ladder down. She was relieved no one had heard Balthus's mutterings. A few broken words, sounds of discomfort and then nothing else.

Nothing but absolute torment would force a Warstone to reveal any vulnerability. Nothing but sheer determination would sustain a man to suffer a hand amputation and hide such a weakness from his enemy. All the more remarkable given the possibility it was a recent injury since he held it to his chest under the cloak as if it was still bound.

His left hand, which was significant, was gone. To test their loyalty to their mother, each son had had to hold their left hand above a flame. Over the years, a knot of scars would build. Ian had scars like these on both hands, and he'd told her the cause.

When she'd felt Balthus's callused right hand for potential injury, she'd felt no such scar in the centre as her husband had. Surprisingly, because his right hand was unharmed, relief had flooded her with warmth as she'd inspected his left shoulder and arm. Until she'd come to the wrappings and she'd tried to grasp the horrific truth of what she'd felt, and hadn't felt, beneath her fingertips.

Carefully, she set the weighty buckets down. He wasn't as tightly furled as when she'd rushed Pepin up the ladder, but he remained on his side. His breathing was a bit fast, but aside from that he looked like he was sleeping.

She couldn't see or smell a mess, but she wiped the wooden sides with the vinegar that Sarah provided on the chance it might mask valerian's rough clay smell.

As to the buckets' contents, there was some meat, bread ale, tea. She had to hope the amounts Sarah had provided were correct for the tea. Willow bark for the pain, valerian to make him sleep. Both would take some time. Nothing would last once she lowered the dagger and cut a bit more of his arm. There was nothing that would mask that pain.

Had it been an accident to his hand or had he done it to himself? Was her heart telling her something about him was different? Why else would she think he'd want to rid himself of his mother's diabolical love? Or maybe Sarah was correct, and she'd gone soft when it came to the Warstones. She didn't think it possible to forget what they were capable of, but how else to think, for one moment, there was a softness in him?

Still...what to do with him? What should happen? Whatever it was, she felt that Balthus's fate, and perhaps her own, depended entirely on what she did next.

Was she healing him because of that moment by the tapestry, or because he'd offered to help her with the kindling? Or was it strategic to woo him to her side? She thought about what the healer had done with the axe. The strength of spirit it had taken since there were no certainties.

She would have to make her own certainties and take her own risks, as she had done for years. This time Balthus was unknowingly along with her, but he got in the way of her protecting her boys. She'd do anything to protect her children, and that truth sealed their fates.

As for Imbert and Sarah, she'd made her position known to them. Sarah had the boys, Imbert would be ready with his dagger to come in and help. She'd do the deed, but he'd have to hold Balthus down when he woke from the tincture.

Sweat had formed on his brow and he was almost panting through whatever coursed through his body.

Vinegar soaked most of wood along the sides of the pit, and she futilely brushed aside stones and pebbles. It wasn't anything, but she could delay no longer, and knelt beside the man.

He slept despite the smell or her scurrying about, and part of her was loath to wake him because much healing happened when the injured slept. He didn't look injured or vulnerable. He looked like the finely honed warrior he was. Her eyes dipped along his sculpted torso, down his navel to legs encased in breeches that clung round his narrow waist.

His arms were free from his dark cloak. One hand had unfurled tapered fingers, elegant but for the ragged edges of his fingernails and calluses along his palm. His other arm, mostly wrapped in dark linens, displayed all the strength of the man, even with the harsh blunt end.

She didn't find it a weakness or something to shy away from. The strength was there, the man was there, and she imagined trailing her fingers along those tendons and veins, encasing her hands around him like linens. To feel the texture of him like that brutal tapestry she'd yearned to touch so long ago.

A clearing of his throat, and her eyes flew upwards. Grey eyes on her, questioning. Could he guess her thoughts?

Pale skin, eyes wide, her face a mixture of questions. Though he expected it, he didn't see pity there. Balthus didn't need to know how he felt to know he'd fainted from the pain again. To know she'd probably checked for injuries and knew his hand was gone.

But false concern hadn't been there as her eyes lowered and her gaze swept downward, settled along his waist and over his legs. He'd stayed still, but there was a part of him he had no control over when under her scrutiny. Before he embarrassed himself, he let her know he was awake.

'Don't move,' she said.

Easier said than done when her eyes were on his. Even so, it took him a while to settle the heat weaving through his blood at the sight of the blush across her cheeks and the vulnerability in her darting glance because he'd caught her inspecting him.

'The boy?' he asked.

'Pepin's unharmed.' She blinked. 'You didn't—'

'You have Imbert and Sarah,' he interrupted. He didn't want to hear what he shouldn't do. He hadn't performed with any great courage. It was likely the boy would have fallen on him anyway, and that reminder was enough to cool his wayward thoughts. Séverine couldn't have been admiring him.

'Don't talk of them unless you want another bucket aimed at your head. At this distance, I wouldn't miss.'

'It is interesting they are here was all I attempted to say.'

Balthus wanted to laugh at her response. Instead, he took stock of his state, and that of Séverine, with the front of her gown wet, her plaits loose. The smell of vinegar. Perhaps he'd been ill. That wasn't unusual.

What was, was that instead of shame or anger at his weakness, she had made him want to laugh. He needed a distraction from that errant emotion.

Carefully, he sat up and stopped when a sharp pain blinded him. 'Why not talk about them?'

'Not until you report what you intend to do with us.'

Her voice was no longer accusatory nor was it frightened. But something in her green eyes was different. No anger there but studying him all the same. What did she see? A weakened enemy or a man?

Now was the time to tell her he wouldn't do anything to harm her or his nephews. That he intended to set her free from his brother, and all he needed was a piece of parchment in return.

That was what he needed to say to her, but the pain wasn't ending. There was something else he needed to understand first, something that was just outside his thoughts. Was it the way she looked at him now? Or the fact she'd run away from Ian? Did she know the worth of the parchment she'd stolen?

Games, and he hurt too much to think. All he knew was that he wouldn't fully comprehend if he told her everything now in the condition he was in. He refused to believe it had to do with keeping her by his side.

'I think that's the question I should be asking you.' He shoved back and leaned against the wall. 'You're the one who captured me.'

'You kept following me,' she said.

He closed his eyes as the next wave of pain arced through him. He must have struck the limb or maybe he had damaged it more when he'd caught the boy. It would take time for the limb to stop spasming.

'It's hurting, isn't it?' she said.

He opened his eyes and took her in. Dishevelled red hair, freckles making her pale skin look dark. Sharp cheekbones, lips that were turned down a little.

He didn't like it that she wasn't smiling, that there wasn't happiness in those green eyes. But it didn't matter, she was still beautiful to him. Time had been kind to her in the years she'd been away, but it was all the harder on his heart to ever give her up.

Not yours. Despite Ian, there were too many obstacles. Lies. His parents. The legend. The fact that no woman would want a disfigured mate. Something she knew about now since her eyes kept flitting down his arm.

Despite what he said, Balthus was hurting. 'Your hand,' she said.

'I don't have a hand anymore.'

He knew what she intended, but still he pushed. Was he being protective or was he being a typical Warstone? 'Your arm where your hand was, it's hurting.'

'I fell into a pit. Twice,' he said. 'If you must

know, it didn't feel pleasant before or after it was chopped off.'

There was pain behind his words. 'Are you telling me we're not to talk about it?'

He looked around. 'I smell vinegar. Was I sick?'

'No, Pepin kept repeating it, so I brought some down and cleaned the area.' Tilting her head, she watched him carefully. She risked so much if she proceeded to poison him. Well, not poison him, but he'd see it as so since he'd take the tincture against his knowledge and will. All to carve on his arm… Was she being brave or foolish to think he was different enough to sway?

'I think Pepin kept repeating it because he was worried about you,' she added.

Balthus dropped his head, and his good hand fell to the floor, where his fingers splayed and then clenched.

Did this Warstone have emotions? Could he care?

'He was, Balthus,' she said.

His head whipped up then, and a muscle spasmed in his jaw. 'Are you attempting to tell me you are worried for me? You shouldn't be. My arm is healed.'

'Is the pain sharp, continual? Does it ever stop?'

His eyes narrowed. 'Are there villagers outside this hut blocking my escape?'

'When you hit your arm, do you momentarily lose the ability to think or see?'

He indicated with his chin behind her. 'You brought food.'

A change of subject. 'I did. I also brought some willow bark tea with buttermilk and honey.'

'Buttermilk? Do you think I'm elderly?'

Heat flushed her cheeks. He was a man in his prime and everything in her knew it. Even as she contemplated hurting him. Even while lying to him, she was always aware of their proximity. Of the familiarity of the way they talked, of his teasing tone right now.

'My son fell on you, and you lost consciousness... I couldn't wake you, and I thought it would help.'

'You want to help me.' He narrowed his eyes. 'Are we soon to be attacked? Are there villagers who are preparing torches even now to burn me alive? I know you are worried for the villagers should anything happen to me.'

'Why do you change the subject or try to distract me?' she said.

'How many other servants of Ian's are here? Imbert and Sarah weren't there at your family's estate with you,' he said. 'Come, these questions can't be worth your throwing a bucket at my head.'

Circles, they talked in circles. She was tempted to give him the tea now and be done with it. She was more than tempted to start answering the truth before he did and see what he'd do with it. 'They'd been with me for many years.'

'That's not an answer, and I observed your home for a week before introducing myself in that hut. So I can only assume they lived here, and built you this pit. Do the rest of the servants in this village live here, as well?'

'Why does it matter to you where servants are? I'm surprised you even notice them.'

He frowned. 'Are the other servants posted all over France? Did you have other traps made?

'Answer me this. Does the pain ever stop?'

'I'm used to pain, as you well know,' he said. 'We're raised with it.'

There, that was what she had been waiting for. That dimming in his eyes, that acknowledgement that he'd endured his parents' torture but hadn't exulted in it. Ian had talked as if it were the highest of honours. Balthus's voice, the agitation in his eyes before he'd masked it. No, he didn't think it an honour, he thought it a horror, as she did. He was trained to give nothing away, but his actions, his mannerisms told her all she needed to take the chance. To try and help him, to sway him to their side. He was different, and he just admitted to the pain.

Reaching behind her, she grabbed the buckets and set them before her. 'I'm hungry and thirsty and I'm certain you are, too.'

She wouldn't hide the willow bark tea, hoping he'd take that for the pain, but the valerian would be tricky. She knew exactly how much to use. But she also knew he'd smell and taste it—there was no covering that. The willow bark, buttermilk and honey would help. The vinegar saturating the walls, too. Was it enough?

He pointed to the ladder. 'You're leaving the ladder here and there's no one to protect you.'

'I'm taking the chance you're too weak to climb it.' His words had been somewhat playful, so she tried to jest in kind. When she saw his troubled expression, when she remembered why she shouldn't call him weak, a favourite word of his father's, she whispered, 'Balthus, are we past that now?'

His grey eyes were riveted to her before his brows drew in. 'Why, because I have no hand?'

'Because you saved Pepin, because until you knew Imbert was a friend, you tried to protect me. Because…you offered to help me with the kindling.'

He looked swiftly to the side and shifted. Torment was etched along the lines of his jaw, vulnerability in the shadows cast by his eyelashes.

Balthus wasn't like Ian, who could, unless asleep, keep any and all emotion away. She'd had to guess everything when it came to him. Balthus was different, and she noticed it constantly.

He was like a predator, hurting, and all the time they talked she noted the way he said certain words or tilted his head. The way he almost tapped his left foot as if restless.

Her…awareness of him was more than physical, more than simply about the way he moved. It was also in the words he chose. They were more open, raw, rough around the edges, and that bewildered her, coming from such an assured man. And still her awareness was more and yet simpler than that: because Balthus felt, he made her feel, as well. Alarming. Seductive, when she hadn't felt this way in a long time, or that she feared she hadn't felt this way ever.

He was a Warstone, and they were cruel to her. She shouldn't care that Balthus was in pain, or that she could help him. He was different, but it didn't mean he was different enough. Still, right or wrong, for her childrens' future, she'd take the chance.

Chapter Nine

Ever since he'd woken up, Séverine had been acting strangely. Balthus couldn't quite understand it. It was as if she was testing him somehow. Their conversation was confusing. Why care if he was in pain? Why tell him truths when she'd fought it for so long?

Did he have anyone to blame but himself for the way she acted? It was like an odd dance with one step in and twenty paces away. But the look she gave him now was different from before. It was as if something had settled inside her and it made him wary. She was lying about something, but he didn't know what. Her sudden ease with sitting next to him and the food made him oddly aware of his own nefarious actions.

He couldn't make it right with her even if he spent the rest of his life trying to. This was past the point of his impulsive nature, or the fact he didn't like to cooperate. It may be even farther than him simply wanting to spend time with her.

He needed to tell her the truth, but that was impossible without trust between them. If he simply told her about the parchment or Ian, she'd leave him here. Why would she stay? If he could build her trust, perhaps she'd help him find the parchment.

As for not telling her of Ian, that was both personal and strategic. Strategic because if she realised she had no enraged husband after her, she could run to her parents and gain their protection once again. His parents might fight for their grandchildren; thus, putting her parents in danger. Also, if she was within the confines of her parents' home, how would he gain access to that foolish piece of tree that Reynold wanted?

Then there was the personal reason he didn't tell her. Something that had nothing to do with her and everything to do with him. She thought herself married so he could at least pretend she was, thus forcing some distance between them. The longer he spent in her company the less he wanted that distance. It wasn't fair to his brother, he knew, but he was trying to do something good here…all to gain her trust.

Was that even possible when she ran from

Warstones? He knew his family, but she'd hinted that she knew them, as well. Had they harmed her? His questions kept increasing, as did his fascination with her. A dangerous combination the longer he stayed. No, he needed to approach the situation with caution. Earn her trust slowly, start with perhaps acceptance that he wasn't all bad. Time would benefit him here. When or if Henry arrived, he would help. Everyone trusted him. It was one of the reasons he'd chosen the butcher for the journey.

'Have we no longer mistrust?' he said. 'Would you believe me now if I said I wouldn't kill you? Or that you were safe?'

Wouldn't it be easier to blurt the truth, tell her he was worthless and a liar, that he meant to use her for some foolish legend? Oh, and that her husband had hidden her to protect her from his parents and himself, because Ian had been going mad and known it?

If he wasn't a coward, and said those words, she wouldn't throw a bucket, she'd throw hot oil over the pit. Still, he asked, 'I know little time has passed, but would you believe anything I say?'

Her body stilled, and he wasn't certain either of them breathed while waiting for her answer.

'I believe you when you don't tell me things,' she whispered.

Ian had underestimated his wife. If he'd picked her because he'd believed that she was malleable or naive, she'd proved that a false assumption.

'You believe me with my actions?' He waved his hand around. 'Is that because I haven't climbed the ladder or is it the way I shift my feet as I sit?'

She gave a small smile as if he'd answered her question. What had he said or done? Perhaps it would be wise if he simply stayed quiet.

'I think we should eat,' she said.

'Since I can hardly climb the ladder in my weakened condition, perhaps we should,' he said.

Her hands jerked in her lap and she exhaled slowly. 'That insult works with you as well as Ian?' she said. 'I presume your father said it to you all. Were none of us spared?'

He was starving, but that was not what occupied his thoughts. It was her bringing up her husband's name. It was the confession she'd made that the cruel words his parents used on their sons they'd also used on her.

'Was Ian there?' he said, adjusting himself. The rest of his body was settling after he'd crashed to the ground, but his arm continued to throb.

'Was Ian where?'

'When my father said that to you.'

She pulled her gown around her. 'It shouldn't matter to a Warstone, should it?' she said. 'Nothing of any import. Simply a typical day of harsh words and harsher deeds.'

At some point, most likely the day of the announcement, his family had wronged her. There was only he and Reynold left to make it right, and since he was the only one here, he bore the responsibility.

So be it. He was the last of the Warstones, who'd borne the brunt of not only the parents but the three elder brothers. His brother Reynold would say he had been protected from the true terror, but even the horror he had not seen had been felt. He was the stone on the floor that soaked up the blood spilt.

Sometimes, talking of those cuts and cruel words did little to help ease them. Other times, it helped to show understanding. She wanted to know of his pain? He'd tell her.

'My arm hurt when it healed, but…when it hardened over like this it became worse.'

She inhaled sharply, her eyes flashing to the ugly limb.

'It's a circle of pain that won't ever stop, isn't it?'

How did she know? His heart and his body were agony. And because they'd shared some words, he gave her the truth in one quick nod.

Her green eyes shone, and that glint of tears felt like truth to him. Before he did something foolish, he reached for the buckets, pulled the linens aside and handed out the food she'd brought.

Her brows drew in, but her mouth curved. 'I can't imagine Ian serving anyone. He wasn't kind to his servants.'

In this he'd answer truthfully, as well. 'I doubt I was. I had some men under me when I was out and about, but mostly I stayed at my parents' residence. I treated them as they had always been treated, though perhaps I was a bit kinder than Guy.'

'Guy dismembered cats,' she said.

'He favoured dogs.'

She lifted one of the leather flagons from the bucket, sniffed the contents and poured, then she did the other. 'Dogs didn't fare that much better, did they?'

He eyed the ale she'd poured into her cup, but with his eyes on hers he took the butter-milk and honey tincture. It was bitter. He never liked the taste of willow bark, but even this was foul.

'I'm told his death was over a dog,' he said.

She pointed her cup towards the wooden cup in his hand. 'You're drinking it?'

'I thought it might make me more agreeable.'

She blinked, opened her mouth. Closed it. 'You shouldn't be in pain, Balthus,' she said softly.

Yes, he should, but he believed that she wanted it differently, and stared into his cup to avert his gaze before she guessed what those words meant to him. 'So, is this what we're to do now? Talk?'

'You saved my son.' Her eyes slid from the wooden cup in his hand to the bucket and set her own cup down. 'A conversation and food seem hardly adequate as repayment.'

He shook his head hard; she'd have him begging soon for her forgiveness. 'You owe me nothing. My family... I wasn't there, but I can guess how they were, and there aren't enough lifetimes to correct what my family did to you.'

She wiped a tear from her face.

He watched more tears pool and one slip down her face before she wiped that away, too. 'Balthus, I...' Her eyes went to the buckets and around the pit before she straightened her spine. 'Why did he pick me?'

He took a deep draw and poured some more of the concoction to avoid pulling her into his arms. 'People notice you, Séverine.'

'Because of my hair,' she said, and frowned. 'I should have had it bound and covered that day. Maybe he wouldn't have seen me in the crowd then.'

He blinked. 'You think it's your hair people notice? It's unique, but—'

'My father's wealth certainly doesn't hurt.'

'There is that.' He yawned.

'Why were you looking at me that day? You wouldn't have noticed my wealth.'

He grabbed some bread, but he didn't feel like eating it. There was no wealth or power that equaled the way she'd looked at him that day. 'I thought we were talking of my hand?'

'Can you not simply say something straight for once?' she said.

He closed his eyes briefly. 'Why do you care about my lost hand?'

'I never said I cared. I am curious.'

She looked at his wrapped arm. 'Did...?' She plucked the roll in front of her, and clasped it in her lap. 'Did Ian do it?'

Ah, this was what she was getting at. Had

his brother, her husband, caused him harm? Did that mean she cared for him?

'It was my mother. It's not that she burned it to that point. It was merely in contact with the fire longer than usual and never healed.'

He couldn't believe he was talking about his life, but Séverine would understand, at least to a point, and hiding from her was tiring. He felt exhausted.

It was too much to add that he'd held it to that flame far longer than his mother requested to prove his loyalty, since it was in question. Ian, by that point, had attempted to murder him, and he'd begun planning to sever his ties with Ian and his parents and align himself with Reynold.

So, he stared into his mother's eyes, hadn't blinked, hadn't spoken, and destroyed his hand.

It had placated her long enough to conduct the rest of his scheme, and now he was here, talking with Séverine as he'd always wanted. He'd never believe that ruining his hand would be worth it. But for moments like this, with some honesty, some trust, and all her attention on him…he was daring to hope.

She even looked concerned for him. It warmed something in him. She cared for him, and maybe there could be something more? That was a step too far. Fool again! He didn't deserve her.

'You look ill from my confession. Perhaps it has been too long since you were under a Warstone roof?'

She shook her head. 'I never thought myself safe. Not once.'

'Running from us is infinitely safer.' He drank the rest of his buttermilk brew and set the wooden cup down. She poured more.

'I didn't make it very strong,' she said.

He took a bite of meat and bread. Neither tasted good, but nothing had for a long time.

'I didn't want to risk staying long in any location,' she said. 'But I missed my family and attempted to be with them for the rest of this winter.'

'You truly hadn't seen them for years?'

'You sound surprised.'

He shrugged and picked up the cup she'd re-filled. 'For my own family, it would be odd but agreeable, but for one such as you—unheard of.'

She rolled her bread between her hands. 'One such as me? Privileged? Coddled?'

'Loved. I'm surprised you held out so long.' She stayed quiet, and he forced himself to focus on the words and not the mesmerising way her hands moved.

'Ah, you did it for your sons' sakes. You left your husband for them, even knowing what could happen to you.'

'What did you think I left him for?'

'The usual reasons enemies do—to protect themselves.'

'I'm not an enemy, I'm family, remember?'

'All the more unusual for leaving us, then. Usually my family likes to keep family close.'

He liked this time with her. Liked the care he saw in her eyes, and her surprise when he'd mentioned love. He might never have experienced it himself, but he recognised it. She was loved, and in turn she loved her children. So simple for her, absolutely impossible for him... and yet he longed, nonetheless.

'Why isn't he here?' she blurted, then seemed to regret it.

Maybe she didn't want to talk about anything painful. Ian was painful for him. His brother had tried to kill him twice, but Balthus couldn't quite forget the times his brother had been almost good.

She tossed the bread to the side and brushed her hands. 'I'm not clever enough to avoid him forever. I'm resourceful and I've had good help,' she said. 'I can only think he purposely didn't try. He did leave us first.'

What to say? The only truth he could. 'Because I am the one who found you.'

Balthus didn't know why he did it. Maybe because he feared what he said was a lie or maybe it was the vulnerability in her voice. Her eyes beseeching, seeking comfort. An hour of conversation and they'd grown closer. Knowing that they shared some of their past. The fact that her eyes dipped to his lips before her tongue darted to her own.

But his hand was on her nape before he knew what he was doing. She stiffened, and he held himself still. His body felt strangely not his own as he asked the one question he knew he shouldn't.

'Do you ever think of that moment, Séverine? Of that time before?'

Her eyes widened; she shook her head minutely. He felt the hesitation there, but it wasn't enough. He needed certainty, he needed her.

Did she not understand? Did she truly not remember? Had his family, had Ian been so cruel that they'd wiped out all that was good from before? He refused to think that way. That moment was all that kept him sane. She must remember.

He squeezed her nape, brought her infinitesimally closer to him, closed his eyes briefly when her lips parted. 'In your father's hall, when you gazed at that tapestry, when I couldn't let you go from my sight until you were snatched from me. Tell me you noticed me, too. Tell me—'

A whimper, a cry, his heart soared when she relented and allowed him to tug her over to him. Her knees were suddenly straddling one of his legs, her hands going to his shoulders.

He was dizzy with the scent of thyme on her, the fluttering of the pulse in her neck, the way her skin felt against his bare palm. The fact her green eyes darkened; her breathing matched his.

'Do you remember, Séverine? Can you feel this, too?'

To touch, to kiss. To meld her body with his for however long she'd give him, for however much.

He had instigated the act to show her in the most primitive way that he cared; that he was hers, that he understood.

But did she? Waves rolled through his body, wanting him to crash forward. Bring their mouths, their tongues, together.

Her hand was against his cheeks, her eyes now full of tears. 'Oh, Balthus.'

But he needed, he begged her to come the rest of the way to him, to capitulate. She was the one with reason, he felt like a beast. All instinct, as his heart hammered and his blood pooled, slowed.

Another wave. He pulled away, shook his head.

More tears from her eyes.

He was tired. *Too* tired. He felt his body lose strength and he slumped. This wasn't because he had his heart's desire as she straddled his body.

The odd taste, he recognised it now. Willow bark and valerian, and a lot of it. Perhaps even something else! He would have known sooner if she hadn't distracted him with her conversation. With…her.

No!

And all this time she'd prepared to weaken him, to poison him, while he'd hoped to gain her trust and acceptance.

He would lose her again. Lose her and this time he was certain she'd escape. Henry didn't know where he was—he was stuck in a pit he had no certainty to escape, not with one hand. And…she'd given him a draught to poison him. He'd drunk cups of the vile brew which could have had anything hidden within its buttermilk and honey depths.

He'd prepared all his life to die by violence or deceit. To die by her hand, though, was a cut he hadn't been prepared for, couldn't. For how could violence come from a woman whose smile for him meant happiness? It was like seeing splattered blood on a butterfly's wings or flowers trampled in the mud. Impossible.

'Sleep now, Balthus,' he heard the traitor say. 'Sleep.'

Visions of the Jewell of Kings flashed, quickly replaced with Séverine turning from a tapestry, her smile of pure joy slowing fading as his brother had walked down the great hall towards her to repeat the words she hadn't heard. Words that had knifed through him both times he'd heard them.

And she didn't know. Didn't realise… Ian was dead. She'd betrayed him. Like everyone had ever done. Like everyone would ever do. Such joy in her smile and she'd struck the blade deeper than anyone.

'Séverine,' he choked out. She'd given him a lot of that vile concoction. Was this his path to death?

Absolute silence, though he could feel her

dark presence like a man who'd stuck his hand in a viper's bucket, or one who'd accepted a drink from an enemy. He wasn't certain he could, but he had to force words out. He might be lying to her, but she'd stabbed him. Turned the blade and sliced out whatever was left of his heart, of his soul. She'd *lied*. To him! He burned with an agony he hadn't thought possible given all the pain he'd endured. Was it because he dared to trust? All the worse, all the more, he wished for vengeance. Retribution!

'Pray!' he bit out past the poison taking him away from a life of redemption, past the anger that took him further away from the dream that this woman could ever care for him. 'Pray I do not wake.'

Séverine shook. Balthus had drunk enough valerian to make him sleep, but not enough. Nothing would ever be enough for when she sliced his arm again. He'd wake from that. Scream. Curse her name, and her children's, too. Probably have the strength to strangle her until someone forced him away.

His look of such longing seared with utter hatred in those grey eyes. He'd kept them fastened on her until he'd slumped heavily to the floor, and said so softly, so slowly, it didn't seem he was capable of knowing what he whispered to her. *There are worse ways to go.*

Her hands were damp, her body would not settle. He believed she meant to poison him. To *kill* him. All throughout she'd thought he'd taste it, would attack. That it wouldn't be enough and…

'He didn't even fight me.' She gazed helplessly at the vulnerable Warstone, this man who looked at her with almost wonder, who touched her, who intrigued her in a way no man ever had.

What had she done? It had started as a thought to sway him, but what if it went wrong, what if she had added too much valerian, and he died? Valerian shouldn't, but he was already wounded. His words had been rambling at the end. Something about Ian. Had he been about to tell her something new? Was her husband on his way here? Just outside the village, and would walk in to see his youngest brother impaired and in a pit?

Hands slick with sweat, knees shaking badly, she stumbled to the ladder, forced herself to climb up, to push open the door.

What had she done? What had she done?

'Imbert! Imbert!' she yelled.

When he rounded the corner, she pulled herself up. 'It's done. He's asleep.'

His crinkled brown eyes pierced hers. 'You mean to do this.'

'I need you to hold him down. He'll wake up. There's rope and stakes in the hut. We'll use those.'

Imbert paled. 'Wait…'

'There's no time,' she said. 'He's in the pit. It'll be fast, and then be over. Make certain Sarah keeps the boys away for the next week. The pit should muffle some sounds, but not all.'

He shook his head. 'He won't say anything. He'll be dead.'

'Imbert!' she said. Sound roared in her ears and she was the one who knew what she meant. 'What I will do will make him better. Think of how it will be for Clovis and Pepin to have a Warstone fighting for them instead of against?'

'I've known you a long time now, and if you believe it will be so, then we'll do it.'

Séverine felt no relief. None. Because it was true. And Balthus still needed to survive. Her plan would only work if he recovered, if he forgave her or understood. Only if…

Chapter Ten

Another cold night of sweats and nightmares Balthus couldn't walk off. Of crying out in his sleep and cursing while awake. He was still in the pit, his left arm was wrapped and bound to his chest, the rest of his limbs were tied down with ropes and held by stakes in the ground. Pinned like a bug, and just as comfortable. If he couldn't rest, he'd be damned if anyone else did. If he had to face all the ugliness of life, he'd make certain the rest of this village did, as well.

It had been a fortnight since he'd woken from this scourge, of fighting a fever that ravaged his body and his mind. If he had to suffer like this, he'd ensure that Séverine suffered like he did.

No, no one suffered like he did, especially her. He'd never once felt pity for himself. Not once. He was aware of the Warstone flaws and all the privileges. He may have longed for a true family, hearth and home. He may have wished fervently for happiness, but never once did he feel rage at how and to whom he was born, or what blood ran in his veins.

He knew why he suffered the most, though, because he'd gotten too close to his enemy. Believed in her smile and her chatter with her children. He remembered soft hands, a cool drink. Urgent, soothing words bringing him back from the darkness. He remembered her repeatedly asking if he hurt, as if she cared.

Before he'd tasted that valerian, before he'd woken up and felt the weight of a man holding him down, seen the blade in Séverine's hands, he had believed that there was good in the world. He had believed, been trusting! Him! He, who had been raised in suspicion and disbelief. He, who'd had further than most to go to trust!

He'd experienced pain before or thought he had. He'd held his hand to a flame, dislocated his shoulder holding a ladder's rung too long at his father's orders. His own brother had tried to kill him. He had so many dark experiences to compare to this time in the pit under the care of Séverine, but only now he felt suffering. Because she'd made him believe.

When he'd first woken up, when he'd been weakened the most, he'd thought his parents had created the monster she was. After all, what reasonable woman would slice off slivers of a man's arm? Even his own mother hadn't done such a thing. His father made torture painful but swift. His parents ordered massacres, but even those had been meted out like scythes to wheat.

Nobody had been tortured and then healed, only to be tortured again. For what secrets or vengeance? He asked, but Séverine refused to answer. A week like this since he woken from the last of his fevers. A week of looking at a woman whom he'd thought was every embodiment of joy, and she was all deceit.

A clang of metal and light single footsteps let him know the bane of his thoughts had arrived. The whispered words between her and the guard reminded him he was a prisoner.

The sun was just rising, but it was the flames from the fire above that allowed him to see that Séverine stretched her arms over her head. As a man, Balthus admired the curve of her back, the graceful curl to her fingers. Of course, any man stuck in a dark damp hole would look at her, but he knew his regard for her went far beyond revenge. This was some disordered blending of what she was supposed to be and what he knew she was. Between his loving her and now his hate.

For him, being this near Séverine after all these years fed his obsession like dry kindling to a fire. Now he wasn't certain whether the fire was controllable.

Faster, smaller shadows flitted across the ceiling, a slam of the latch announcing her boys had entered, too.

'No, out of here, both of you,' Séverine whispered.

'You've been here days and days.' Pepin's voice rang clear in the quiet hut.

'And I'll be here a few more. Where's Sarah?'

'Making bread,' Clovis announced. His voice was distinctive in its formality.

'I want to see him.'

'It doesn't matter what you want, Pepin, it matters what I say,' Séverine whispered. 'That man is danger, and you aren't to talk to him.'

'Why not?' Pepin said. 'He's in there. You're keeping him!'

Balthus almost chuckled at the loud whispering of the six-year-old.

'He's not an animal,' Clovis said.

Clever boy, although he felt trapped like an

animal. Whoever had constructed this space knew what they were doing. Weeks down here and the walls had closed in. Being pinned to the floor would break him soon. He'd be as mad as his brother Ian had been.

'Keep your voices down,' Séverine hissed. 'Neither of you were to follow me in here.'

'You asked us to carry these.'

'You did, now go.'

'Only a peek, Mama.'

Balthus closed his eyes, stayed as still as he could. He may want revenge on their mother, but the boys were innocent. Two weeks since he was carved on, another week of fever. Days of listening to them sneak in and hearing their chatter. It was sometimes amusing, most times it made him melancholic. Ian didn't know his sons like he did. Tied and staked to the ground in a pit in the middle of nowhere, and he'd spent more time with them than his brother ever had.

So he kept quiet and his eyes shut so as to not scare them. Their mother may have betrayed him, but his heart…his heart still wanted to hear her children.

'I still think he looks familiar,' Clovis whispered.

'Mama says he shouldn't,' Pepin said. 'But he followed us, didn't he?'

'Out, both of you, now.'

A scrambling of feet. 'Does he have my treasure? It's still down there.'

'It's not yours,' Clovis said.

'Boys. Go help Imbert.'

'Clovis, too?'

'Yes!' Séverine hissed.

Balthus's eavesdropping came to some use last night. The walls of this hut were thin, the relentless wind could be felt above his head, and he was almost grateful to be insulated by the walls of the pit.

From the broken words he could understand, some villagers wondered about Warstone attacks. Séverine appeared to have made herself a community, which pleased and terrified him. One or two people could escape a Warstone's notice, but a village wouldn't be able to. He hoped he'd simply misunderstood the situation, and not because villagers were preparing for an attack against his family but because they knew *to* prepare.

A slamming of the door reported the boys had left.

Balthus could hear the frustration in Séverine's exhale. The boys were getting brave, coming inside. He'd observed enough of people over the years to understand Séverine's conversation with her boys wasn't anything unusual. All she did was admonish her children for their actions, but they were confident enough in her love for them to talk back.

To be loved and cared for like that? To be disciplined and respected in a mother's loving tone? It wasn't any wonder why his heart wanted to hear their conversation; it was a wonder his applied reason, that she betrayed him, didn't put a stop to it.

'I know you're awake.' Séverine descended the ladder.

Her perceived happiness had haunted him all his life. Now her cold maliciousness would frequent the rest of his meagre existence. He'd never be rid of her, and she'd pinned him to the floor to ensure it. So he'd lain there doing what he'd done for the last week: staring at her beauty and cursing himself for never recognising the monster beneath.

'How do you fare today?' She gave him an efficient look, noting the blankets he'd shoved aside some time in the middle of the night, and the soaked pillow beneath his head. Today, unlike the others, she didn't offer to help make him more comfortable so the blanket painfully bunched in the small of his back, and the pillow that stank would remain. Good. He was tired of her false kindness.

'How am I?' he said. 'I'm pinned to the floor. Someone poisoned me and carved my arm. I'm feeling like you'd better not let me free. Ever.'

Other than a tenseness around her shoulders, she gave no indication she'd heard his threat as she set up the items on the floor. All routine, as if she was no more than a healer or a caring mother and he suffered a sore throat.

Instead, he continued to be trussed to the floor like an animal. He might now have blankets and pillows. He might be given food and drink and she might change his linens and test for pus, but for the arm bound at his chest, he was stretched on the ground like he was to be drawn and quartered.

At least before, when his hand had first been severed, he'd been surrounded by friends. He'd known the gift that it was and had treated it as such. He'd given away the magnificent Warstone fortress to his caregivers. Oh, there were other personal, political and strategic reasons to give such a stronghold to a loyal friend. Not wanting his parents to have it was one, but in the end, he'd done it because Louve and Biedeluue had been kind to him. And he'd wanted to change. He'd wanted to do good somewhere in the world, and if possible, to leave good behind.

It was one of the reasons he'd taken this journey to find Séverine, to gain her support and thus, because he trusted, here he was.

'Ask me how I am, then ignore what I tell you,' he said. 'Is this how we'll start every morning?'

'Until you've recovered.'

'Then I'll continue with my questions that I've asked every day and, of course, I expect you to ignore them as you always do.'

He hated that he sounded like a petulant child. The pain, her betrayal. What hurt most was that she'd asked if they were past the lies, and he'd hoped they were.

'Perhaps I'll just assume you ignore me because you can't remember all your lies.'

She flinched and tried to cover it with a shrug. 'Some of your lies may be truths.'

That was interesting. 'A phrasing my father often used. Spent much time with him, did you?'

She slammed down the empty bucket he recognised. The one he had to relieve himself in. At least he was spared the indignity of that in front of her, but sharing it with any of the villagers twice a day was another wrongdoing he tallied against her.

She knelt. 'Don't talk to me about that time.'

Even he didn't want to remember that particular past. He closed his own eyes tightly to rein himself in. He wasn't himself. His hatred was violent and yet, this close, day after day, she touched him, spread the poultice and wrapped the linen. Day after day, he felt her warmth, caught her scent, and his body reacted. Love. Hate. He was unbalanced!

If he had any reason, he should only revile her, but it only took him opening his eyes to know he couldn't do it. Her profile revealed the downward grooves at the sides of her mouth, the dark circles under her eyes. From exhaustion or emotion? He shouldn't care! She wasn't who his family thought she was. They hadn't realised when they'd forced her to marry Ian what malice lay beneath those freckles and abundant red hair.

'Preparing everything for the day?' he said. 'Wasn't my hand being chopped off once enough for you? Is this how it'll be, with me pinned to the ground, and week by week you'll slice off more of my arm?'

She exhaled roughly, turned her back and pulled items out of the second bucket. Soon she was pounding some ingredients in a mortar. The smell was foul, and familiar. 'That's Sarah's poultice for horses, isn't it?'

She stopped. 'It'll help with swelling.'

'For what purpose?'

She looked over her shoulder. 'To heal you, Balthus. I'm here to *heal* you.'

'Back to that again. That's a jest when you're the one who caused the injury. Why not simply slice my throat? I think I know why. I think you believe if you torture me long enough my family will find me. They'll know that every sliver of my arm you carved off was for every slight they gave. Violent, effective messaging, if I survive it.'

At the alarm in her eyes, a misshapen sense of victory coursed through him, and she turned to rearrange the supplies she'd brought. The same items she brought in every day. Honey, vinegar, clean linens.

Soon she'd untuck the linen, lay his arm against his stomach, and everywhere he would feel her touch. His body was healing and reacting. The ravages of fever were gone, and he'd gained much strength. It would only be worse today. If only he could break free!

'Stop pulling on the ropes, you'll undo all my work,' she said.

'I'll stop pulling on them the moment you let

me go. Given the secure comfort you've provided I'm guessing that won't be for a while.'

He wanted to stop his words. It was his vulnerability. The fact Séverine had felled him and now thought him less of a man. The truth that soon her cool fingers warmed his skin, and he shivered.

Her eyes flew to him.

'I'm cold,' he said.

She adjusted blankets around his legs. He'd have to kick them away again.

As if sensing his lie, she said, 'I'm not certain Warstones deserve comfort.'

Certainly not this one. 'You kept the fire going in the hearth at night.'

'For the guards,' she said.

'And rebuilt it this morning.'

Her hair and clothes were different today, clean with more colour to complement her bright red plaited hair. How did she have such hair like that? Her sisters were mostly brown-haired. The green of the gown wasn't of the quality of her upbringing, but something a bit finer and warm. He missed the dirt across her nose.

'Have you already eaten?'

The guard had shared food and conversation. Delicious food. 'I didn't know Sarah could bake like that.'

'Something you would know if you visited your brother and family.'

Séverine was right there, kneeling next to him. He couldn't escape, couldn't fight, he was at the whim of whatever she wanted. He hated it, but he hated it worse when she left. Some of the villagers talked, other villagers didn't. None of them compared to the torture and delight when she was next to him.

Today was different. Perhaps because the routine had been altered, but mostly it had to do with Séverine talking with him. He thought she didn't want to mention family, and here they were talking of bread, and his time at court.

He needed to remember her shoving him in a pit, poisoning him, and the agony of that blade when she'd sliced his arm. But already his body tensed in anticipation and need for her touch. He shouldn't want conversation with this woman. His thoughts should be on revenge. He couldn't trust her, yet if she stayed, he'd take whatever meagre bits she gave him.

Chapter Eleven

Séverine watched Balthus's careful expression. The resentment was there, burning steadily, but another layer of emotion, as well. He was wondering if she was playing some kind of game.

She was. He had some colour to his face. He lay there because he had no choice, but twice now he had stretched his legs as well as he could. The cut, and the stitches they'd made in his arm had held. Already the bandage she'd done the day before had no spotting, and enough time had passed.

'I returned home occasionally when King Philip granted me leave,' he said.

Kings of countries, and all their courtiers. Séverine knew he spent much time at Philip's court. So had her sisters, though they visited Provence, as well, the Marteldoises having closer ties to Provence. It been a long time since she'd cared for such things, and she didn't want to be reminded because Beatrice was well married now with no correspondence between them. They'd turned all their backs on her the moment Ian had taken her hand. If her parents hadn't rejoiced—

'I didn't see you, though. Perhaps you were hiding,' he added.

She had hidden. Balthus had rarely come to stay at Warstone Fortress, which had been a gift from his parents to Ian on his marriage. Lord and Lady Warstone, however, though inhabiting one of their smaller estates nearby, visited frequently at the fortress.

So Séverine had hidden as long as Lady Warstone had allowed it. When Balthus used to come, she could remain in her private chambers indefinitely, which suited her purposes.

Despite her marriage, she'd never stopped thinking of that moment at the tapestry when that strange warmth had unfolded between them. She hadn't wanted to see him again, terrified her true thoughts would become apparent, and the cruel and harsh treatment would become unbearable.

'Or perhaps I hid because I was in confinement. Does that satisfy your curiosity? Because I think that should be the end of the questions before I let you rot here.' She made her tone as haughty as possible to end this topic of painful memories.

'If I didn't know better, I'd think you didn't like me much.'

'The running away from your family should have been enough.'

'It was the family, and not particularly Ian who caused you to leave?' Balthus said. 'He would've liked that.'

Something of the way he talked about Ian made her pause; had he mentioned his brother in the past tense? Did that matter? Ian *was* the past, and she shouldn't care. 'Don't talk to me about him, or about your family.'

'I was under the impression that your carving on me had something to do with them. If not, there's no reason for you to be here.'

'We were meant to stay the end of winter and spring with my parents, and I'm here because you're injured…and healing.'

A muscle pulsed in his jaw at that. 'Doesn't mean you should stay in this village.'

'My reasons for being here are my own, Warstone.'

'You seem fierce when it comes to your children, and yet you risk them by staying here.'

'Don't talk about my children,' she said.

'Don't talk of your children or family. You say you want answers, but you won't believe anything I say, and by staying you risk an attack on this village,' he said. 'So, you're keeping me in a pit to simply taunt me?'

What was she doing? Balthus was correct… Sarah and Imbert were right. The moment she'd shoved him in the pit, she should have grabbed her children and run. She'd given the excuse that he might be hurt and, in truth, leaving a Warstone here would bring trouble to them. It didn't matter if Balthus remained alive or was dead, a massacre on these few homes was always a possibility.

But her staying here wouldn't prevent that from happening, just as trapping him in the pit wouldn't stop her from being dragged back to her husband and his family. Still, when Balthus had arrived at this village, she'd had to do…something.

'Again, I don't have to explain myself to you,' she said. 'You didn't tell the truth that you simply want to converse as family, and I told you I won't return. I think it's you taunting me.'

His eyes narrowed. She bit back any fears. Predators did this, but he was the one trapped.

'What made you push me into a pit?' he said softly. 'What made you poison me, and now talk of Sarah and her bread? I will be free of this soon. Then what?'

Heat flushed her cheeks. Did she want revenge, or to shame him? His family deserved it. For the moment she had been forced to wed, for the thousands of criticisms she'd received every day, for his parents threatening her children.

For Ian confusing her. The cruelty, the coldness when he'd been awake, and the soft words he'd spoken in his sleep. For making her feel something for him other than fear, and making the decision to leave him all that much harder.

'What do I want to do with you?' she said. 'I'll show you.'

Every word Balthus cursed at her were slices to her heart, every bit of his discomfort a weight on her shoulders. Any word she offered as explanation or sympathy he spat back at her. He refused to hear her anymore. Whatever shared moments they'd had before the knife had cut him were gone.

Her bruised heart hammered the discord continually in her chest, but it wasn't only the words he spoke now that haunted her. A fortnight of tending this man, of listening to his words while he'd been half-delirious with pain and fever. He'd muttered, he'd screamed, he'd revealed. Could anything he'd said during that time be true or trusted? Had Ian really tried to kill him? Where was her husband now? She'd asked, but he'd gone quiet. That frightened her most and she'd never asked again.

There had been other words, as well. Words laced with pain and such heartache. Did he love or hate her? He'd said both. The latter she could believe—it was what he'd said while he'd still been conscious before she'd tied him down and done what she had. But love? That wasn't possible. They didn't know each other. So why did his jumbled words affect her? There'd been nothing tender about Balthus since she'd trapped him in the pit. Fierce words, and promises of retribution. Her worry and *caring* for him made no sense. It had echoes of Ian talking in his sleep, and her heart pained her!

Now she was in the pit with Balthus alone. That was unusual. Most days since the fever had broken, she waited until Imbert or Sarah arrived. But Imbert was concerned in the progress to prepare the village for attack, and build new places for them to hide. No one wanted to travel while the weather was still bad.

And she didn't want to wait this morning.

Today she wanted to test the strength of his arm. To see if what she'd done had been successful.

Soon they would know. She merely needed to get through this. Just as she'd got through that day when Imbert had pegged him to the ground, and she'd held the blade. Balthus had already been rousing from their moving his body to wrap the ropes around him. When she'd made the quickest slash, he hadn't cursed or roared. But a strangled sound had wrenched from his throat as he'd thrown his head back, and the cords of his neck had strained. Panting, he'd swung his head wildly about until he'd seen her. She'd never forget the jarring shock in his eyes.

Aware that those same grey eyes were on hers now, Séverine moved the bucket to the side and knelt closer to him. This part of their day never got easier. It'd been like this every morning since his fever had broken. Harsh words, then this utter, eerie silence while he stared at her.

The pit provided no distractions except for him. As one day turned to the next, she only became more aware.

It was the heat of him, the sheer size next to her. She wasn't small, and he was supine and pegged to the floor, and yet to care for him she had to press her knees into his side. Feel his body expand with each breath, the heat, despite the weather, seeping up her legs and to the core of her.

It was the warmth of his masculine scent, the dark stubble against his jaw, and those eyes that watched her now with a deep hatred that made her hands tremble. She did everything she could not to touch his bare skin on any other part than his arm as she unwrapped the linen, but it was impossible, and her trembling made it worse. So the backs of her fingers brushed against his upper arm as she lifted the tucked end of linen to unwrap his arm.

It was only his arm, only her fingers, but it was his sun-darkened skin, the soft hairs that intrigued her. The tips of her fingers continually touching down an arm she knew was sensitive from the trauma, but the only indication that these brushes occurred were changes in his breathing or a fluttering of his lashes.

Whereas her…it affected her in ways it never should have. When she'd helped the healer, the injured party hadn't made her heart skitter in her chest or her body heat.

It was all the worse now because of what she had to do—to wipe yesterday's poultice away, to apply more with honey, and wrap it again. All while he couldn't wrench his arm away and prevent their skin touching.

Tossing the linen away, taking a small square of cloth, she cradled his upper arm to support it if any pressure she applied caused him pain. Despite his words and the defiant look in his eye, he never fought her. She wasn't fooled. Though he was tied up, the hardness in his gaze and his carefully stilled body let her know he was allowing her to touch him this way.

The short strokes of the cloth to take the old poultice away were efficient and light, yet she knew he was there underneath the thin bit of linen.

Scooping the honey to warm it in her hand, she pressed it to one part of his wound, then the other. Careful only to apply, not to rub. Everything should have been easy, but she felt awkward. Her hand dripping more of the honey through her fingers, down her own wrist, there were times she was clumsy and cupped too much so it drizzled languorously from her hand to his healing wrist, and as much as she willed it to hurry, it didn't. So the moment between them stretched like that sweet strand.

Sarah's poultice stank, but the viscosity was

liquid and required her to take both her hands and wash it over the thick honey in long gentle strokes.

The first few days she asked him if anything she did hurt him further, but he'd kept his silence, his eyes riveted on the rhythm. Once, twice, his nostrils had flared, and he'd looked away. When that occurred, she'd lifted her hands, waited. Again he'd said nothing, so she'd finished what needed to be done: guardedly wrapped the linen around his damaged linen. Again, careful not to touch his skin with her fingers. Again, impossible. Until, breathlessly, the task was done.

Like here. Now.

She clutched her hands in her lap. 'It's healing. The stitches are holding. They'll need to come out, but there's something else I need to—'

He'd looked away while she'd been wrapping, but at her words his head snapped back. 'We're done today? You'll leave?'

If he could have killed her right then, he would have. She saw it in his burning gaze, the tenseness of his body, his fisted hand.

'You can't keep me here forever, and even so they'll come for you,' he said. 'My servant knows what direction I went. He may take one look at this village, notice the walls you're building, and gather mercenaries. None of your preparations will mean anything. If anything, they'll make it worse.'

'How do you know—?'

'That there are walls being built, that they are preparing for my family to attack? Because I can hear everything.'

'We wouldn't be under attack unless you followed me here.'

'Oh, no.' His smile was not kind. 'I wouldn't be here but for you.'

The consequences of her actions were with her always…as was protecting her sons. Refusing to show him how much his words pained her, she snatched the linen that bound his damaged arm to his chest and the floor and wrenched it free from the spike.

His shocked expression was only matched by the pain she caused. As a person trying to heal someone, it was foolish. As a woman who had been plagued by this arrogant family most of her life, it was satisfying.

When she leaned over him to free his good arm, he said, 'What are you doing?'

It wasn't his tone that was the warning, it was the fact she felt his breath against the side of her throat, the vibration of his words in her chest that stopped her immediately.

Gone was the feud, this village, her fleeing. Gone was this pit and its reasons for being built—everything in her narrowed down until it was just this man beneath her.

Her belly over his torso, her breasts pressed into his side, her arm stretched to the other rope, giving his eyes, his mouth, access to whatever he wanted. And he felt…solid, warm. Her thoughts telling her to flee, her body wanting to sink, to simply rest on him. She flushed, hated herself, and wrenched the other rope free, as well.

He held still, his eyes roving from her shoulder, to her hand pressed to the floor, to her ear to her hip, before his eyes found hers, and he slowly lengthened his arms along the floor above his head.

What had she been thinking? Only wanting to prove a point, to rip off the ropes binding the other arm, she failed to heed the danger of her awareness of this man.

She shoved herself away and pushed back. Still kneeling, but waiting to see what he would do.

His eyes, the mistrust, almost broke her silence until she remembered who he was. How could she have any feelings other than hatred for this man? For his family and where he came from?

How could her body, even for one instant, want to…rest against him as if he was safe?

She may heal him of his affliction, and possibly it might soften him towards them to leave her time to escape, or it might not. But in the end she would escape. She and her sons would be free of the Warstones and this man who made her feel she had no right or a desire to escape, waited.

His eyes never leaving hers, he slowly sat up. When she didn't move, he looked above them, craning his neck.

'There's no one there,' she said. 'I expect them soon, but I don't know what's holding them up.'

'You've harmed me, and then freed me. Now you have no one to protect you?'

She was impatient to see whether if what she'd done had been successful. She wanted it all done so she could leave. Or he could.

'Move your hand,' she said.

'I'm not moving a cursed thing for you.'

Back to the words, and the anger. Back to his hatred of her. The first few days after his fever had broken, she'd tried to explain what she had done and why, but he had been feral with rage and mistrust. Further confirming that this man, though he seemed different, was flawed like all Warstones were flawed. Sarah was right that she couldn't trust him.

Though, in truth, she deserved his anger, and she'd never expected his full trust. This was about healing a man in pain. He'd be grateful, and she could persuade him to leave them alone. Perhaps he could tell her what he wanted with her and it would be over.

'Balthus, move it in a circular motion.' She laid her hand on his bound leg. His eyes narrowed at that touch. Flustered at his response, she returned it to her lap. But her palm still felt the heat, and she curled her fingers. This was ridiculous. She needed this over before she fell on the poor man. 'Please.'

His eyes on her, he rolled his good shoulder and then down his arm, circled his wrist and flexed his fingers.

She swallowed. 'Now do the same with your other hand.'

He jerked as if she'd slapped him. 'You're mad. That's what's happened.' Wariness gone, he yanked at the cords around one of his ankles, but she couldn't have that. Not yet. He didn't understand. She had to make him understand. She was a fool for untying him before that.

She laid her hand on his leg again. Again, it had the same effect. He stilled. This time his gaze stayed with her palm resting against his thigh, his brows drawn in, and he took in one uneven breath.

Taking in his closed expression, the width of his shoulders, the arrowing of his torso, and then where her hand lay. On his bound leg. On his thigh, her fingers almost brushing what was, most distinctly in the casing of his breaches, the outline of a man who—

She gasped, pulled her hand away.

His nostrils flared with something darker and more primitive than anger, and he flung himself away.

She was losing him! Séverine slammed her palm on his wound.

He roared, shoved her, and furiously unlaced one of his leg straps.

'Did that hurt?' she said.

'You're the devil,' he bit out. 'I don't know if it was before or after you married my brother, but your soul is bound to Satan's. Of course it hurt—you just struck a wound you made!'

He wrenched on the other rope, freed himself and stood.

'But did it hurt…really hurt?' She grabbed his leg.

His gaze snapped back to hers.

'Is it still hurting, like in a circle, never stopping?' She rushed the words out.

His eyes struck her, and he shook off her feeble attempt to hold him back, grabbed the ladder and hoisted himself up on the first rung.

Then stopped.

Pain lessening. Receding. Becoming nothing more than an ache, then diminishing even from that. Balthus pulled himself up to the second rung, his legs unsteady, his body trembling. Fighting what his body was telling him, what he didn't dare hope to realise. Aware that behind him Séverine waited, watched. Asked him again.

What was it she wanted? To know if the pain circled. He grabbed the next rung up. His mind begged him to run. To flee.

His body shook. Stopped him again, forced him to feel…not agony.

He fell to his knees on the floor.

Séverine cried out, but he felt nothing, more or less. No reverberations, though the impact stung the wound. It was still open, there was some blood at the end of his bandage. But there was no blackness around the edges of his sight, no sudden weakness. All gone.

'What did you do?' he whispered.

When he looked up, her green eyes were steadily on his, but the emotion behind them wasn't. She looked as wrecked as he felt. Tears shimmered, a frantic sort of worry, of something else he didn't want to name, but it was like…light.

'I tried to help you,' she said. She closed the distance between them. Her eyes on his, she raised his arm.

He let her. Her hands were gentle but firm. Secure. 'I may need to unwrap this again.'

Feel nothing, show nothing. Words of his parents, words of his brothers, words that he lived by, all torn to bits since she'd given him a tincture that made him sleep, and then sliced his wound, his weakness and shame.

When his fever had broken, he couldn't remember what he had been before he'd met Séverine. Rage, hatred, retribution had seethed. Lust, desire and something so carnal it had scared even him. He'd borne it all. Now this new emotion created by revelation, by disbelief and hope, felt like it would take down him, her, his entire world.

'You…' he swallowed, hard '…healed me.'

'I've been telling you.'

'But I didn't trust you.'

'I couldn't explain properly before. I still can't. There was a healer I knew, and a man had a missing foot and constant pain, and the healer cut it again and let it heal differently. The bandages were tighter, and she rubbed it often. Made certain there was movement every day...and then it healed. I know it was wrong, but I thought I would try it with you.'

'I wasn't listening.'

'There was no certainty. I don't blame you.'

'I—I don't hurt.'

'At all?' She ran her thumbs down his arm. 'I don't have the means to stitch it again or I'd take this off.'

'The ache is different.'

'You were cut before—' she said.

He shook his head. 'Before there was throbbing pain and something sharp in the background I didn't understand until it healed. But that sharpness intensified the more it scarred and never stopped. Now...that's not there.'

'May I?' She raised her palm, and he braced himself.

If this was only a few moments of reprieve, he didn't want it to end. He didn't want her to aggravate it, but she looked so eager, and he was half-delirious with need. Could it be true? He nodded, giving her permission.

She rubbed her palm over the end, gently, so carefully. The blood seeped a bit more, and she made a small pitiful sound.

He waited. He knew the agony was coming back at any moment.

'And now?' she said, licking her lower lip. His eyes went to that, and to the other signs that he wasn't dreaming this. He wasn't alone in his relief. Séverine felt this same wild freedom. Was that what had caused the flush to her cheeks, the rapid pulse in her long slender throat? That tentative curl to her lips that was almost a smile.

'It's... I'm wary,' he started. What was wrong with him? He was talking about his arm, not himself, but those emotions that seethed, rolled, were overtaking him. 'There's no...reason to this.'

'I know,' she said. Her expression was open, that hope he still fought beaming. 'You, your arm, suffered twice. The swelling is greatly down, there's no fever today, and now this. It'll take another full moon before you're truly well, and I should have waited longer to test it, but I think you're better.'

He blinked, swallowed. He couldn't take his

eyes off her. She shone so brightly it was painful to look at her.

Balthus's words… His grey eyes clear, glistening. One tear was trapped in those eyelashes of his. Fascinated, choked with something she couldn't name, she laid her hand on his cheek and caught it on her thumb, pulled it away and they both looked at that infinitesimal sign of vulnerability. Him with perplexity, her…with certainty.

Balthus *was* different. He felt. She clenched her fist around the teardrop to absorb it.

'I thought you had betrayed me,' Balthus whispered. 'I thought—'

She shook her head, frantic, suddenly wanting whatever it was he was thinking to disappear. 'No!'

He grasped the back of her neck, lowered his head, and laid his forehead against hers until their breaths were wedded.

'I thought everything I'd believed was wrong,' he said. 'I thought what sustained me was wrong. The promises you made all those years ago. I thought you'd lied.'

The same frantic pulse thumped in his neck that she felt in her chest. He wasn't making sense. These were similar to the words he'd said when the fever had overtaken him before.

She'd never made him promises before. And what about sunshine?

She didn't make him any promises now, but she wanted to. If only to give him something he needed. She laid her hand on his cheek. His breath hitched and he came closer, his lips almost touching hers. The joy he was expressing staggered her.

'Forgive me,' he said. 'Séverine, forgive me. I should never have—' He pulled away, eyes searching hers, fluttering down to her lips and back again. He was going to kiss her. Did she want him to kiss her? Her hand on his cheek slid to his shoulder.

'Balthus?'

His fingers on the back of her neck trembled, he groaned, her fingers bit into his tunic, tugging him towards her. But he held back and a tortured sound escaped her. It was a plea, and his eyes flashed with fevered longing before his mouth crashed down on hers. His lips firm, demanding. Utterly stunning.

She had to have more. To feel more. Wrapping her arms around his shoulders at the same time he laid his feet flat on the ground, using his legs to prop her up and lean her against him.

His bound arm was a deterrent between

them, but he used his body, as she did hers, to get closer. She straddled him now. Feeling the weight of her gown, the firmness beneath her that told her he was a man. One who had almost kissed her before. Wanting more, she shifted and slid her hips once and again, and Balthus wrenched away on a groan.

His breaths heated her lips. His eyes bounced across her every feature before resting on one curl, which he trapped between his fingers. She felt the sharp tug in her scalp before he released it.

Trailing his fingers across her cheek, rubbing a thumb on her bottom lip to pull it down. His expression pained, awestruck. Was he looking for permission? To acknowledge what was between them? Desire had been building between them since the woodcutter's hut. Lust fraying every time she'd unwound the linen. Permission. He didn't need words for that. It was the heat she felt between her legs, the swelling in her breasts.

The fact his eyes were so dark that she couldn't see his irises, when his nostrils flared, she'd had enough of waiting and tightened her arms to pull him in again. A quirk to his lips as if he was pleased before his hand gripped her hip hard and he yanked her against him to slam his mouth on hers again.

This time there was only him, the steady support of his legs behind her, the way his hand gripped and released her hip, her waist. A caress along her side, against her breast, which spilled over.

She knew he wanted to touch more, and her nipples ached for the scrape and pluck of his fingers, but she was loath to let him go. He knew it too and bit her lower lip, ran his tongue along the swollen seam—

A thump of the door latch, a blast of cold, heavy steps.

Séverine scrambled back, while Balthus stiffened. Neither of them could still their panting breaths.

'He's awake,' Imbert choked incredulously.

Balthus tilted his head up.

Knowing her cheeks were flushed, Séverine refused to look at Balthus and stood on trembling limbs.

'You freed him while we weren't here?' Imbert said.

'Not now,' she said, her voice so husky it was unrecognisable.

She hadn't had time to process her own feelings in this matter, let alone have the courage to discuss it in front of Balthus. A Warstone. One of the brothers from a family who bore her ill will.

And one she'd kissed. It had been the need in his voice, that tear. It was the way he'd felt to her, solid and safe. It was the fact they shared the same rapturous relief. He was different, and everything about him called to her.

'I've not harmed her,' Balthus said.

'You know that's a lie, Warstone,' Imbert said.

It was, but he wished with all his being it wasn't.

'I'll go.' Séverine picked up the bucket.

'He will, as well,' Imbert said. 'We have a guest who is asking for him.'

Séverine did look at him then. The closeness of what they'd shared was there in the flush along her neck, her lower lip wet and slightly swollen. How badly he wanted to press her against him again. He could still feel the urgent dig of her nails in his shoulders, the heat of her palms through the thin tunic. He clenched his teeth. He had to stop his thoughts, or he'd never make it up the ladder, and he was already having difficulty. His arm throbbed, but his weakness came more from the willing and demanding touch of this compelling woman than his injury, and his desire didn't stop abruptly because Imbert had arrived. Worse, he wore a short tunic because of his injuries so there wasn't any hiding his reaction to this woman.

When he got to the top, Imbert's glower could have felled kingdoms. 'I should have a dagger pointed at you.'

'You should.'

Imbert scoffed. 'And give you an opportunity to take it from me?'

Balthus shrugged. 'I'm injured and have only one hand. How fast do you think I'd be?'

'You could have no arms and I'd still never turn my back on you.'

'You used to.'

'What are you feigning?' Imbert said. 'You forget I performed tasks under your family all my life.'

If this man had still been his servant, his mother would have cut off his tongue. At one point in his life Balthus wouldn't have stopped her, but he would have regretted the loss. This was a man he could respect. 'Not all your life, and I'm presuming you're not under our roof any longer.'

'Do you think I would be?'

'You weren't that good a horseman. Why would I insist on you returning to your duties…

although your wife and her remedies would be convenient.'

Imbert called down to Séverine, 'Do you need any help with anything?'

'I'm simply getting the supplies in the bucket,' she said. 'Here.'

Imbert took the bucket and grabbed her elbow to help her up. When she got to the top, Balthus stepped back when every instinct begged him to grasp her hand and keep her by his side.

While Imbert set the supplies along the long table, Séverine patted down her skirts.

'The cut worked,' she said. 'He's…he's healing.'

'Now we have a friendship?' Imbert turned to Balthus. 'There will be no trust between us.'

No, he'd have to earn that, just like he'd have to earn his place in the future…whatever that would be. When he'd begun this, he'd known it would not be easy facing Warstones' atrocities and injustices. He'd made himself a target.

He wasn't innocent and deserved derision. What he didn't deserve, not yet, was kindness. He remembered some of his fevered talk. He certainly recalled each word he'd spat once the fever had broken. He'd have to apologise to this woman for several lifetimes. Everyone under this roof knew it, but now was not the time.

'Who came for me?' he said. 'Who are you handing me over to?'

Imbert crossed his arms and arched one brow. 'Interesting choice of words, and you don't look surprised, either.'

'All Warstones are relentless. It was only a matter of time before someone arrived.'

'Who is here?' Séverine's voice held a frightened edge he hated.

Imbert eased his expression. 'Not who you think, or you'd be gone already.'

At her nod, Imbert continued. 'A big man, rotund. Claims he's a servant of a man he wouldn't name. Goodness knows, he has no mercenary skills…or any skills that I could determine or test, which is why I wasn't here this morning.'

Balthus looked them both in the eyes to gauge their reactions.

'That would be Henry. My butcher.'

Chapter Twelve

~~~ ⤬ ~~~

Balthus followed Imbert down the same streets he'd followed the two boys those many weeks ago. There had been changes since then. The air was less cold and the roads more mud than ice. There was building going on, too: muddy trenches, and something that would resemble a tower when it was done. Balthus wanted to roar at them to stop. It wasn't enough and would only amuse either his parents or the people they hired. Worse, it would cause his parents and their guards to notice the tiny unnoticeable village, but it was almost too late for that. How fast could they tear it all down, and would they listen to him to do so?

'This is all going to have to go. They'll see this as a threat or some sort of challenge.'

Imbert grunted. 'With nothing, they'll have no protection at all.'

There wasn't an easy solution and it would take much thought.

'Where are we going?' he asked, though it hardly mattered. His thoughts should have completely centred on the villagers who flanked him, on the man in front who had once been in the possession of his brother's house and had now broken free. They should also have been on the man they had captured and held, a person Balthus believed to be Henry, but in fact, could be anyone from his family's home.

His thoughts should have been on fighting, escaping or controlling any of the possible dangers facing him. Instead, they were on Séverine, and the way her skin had felt beneath his palm. The wild beating of her heart, the shortened breaths, the green eyes turning dark, and the fact he'd held her against him and kissed her. He desired so much more, but all of that came at a price he didn't know whether he could or should pay.

'He's in here.' Imbert jutted his chin towards the closed door. The home looked similar to the one Balthus had been held in. Something of newer construction and, therefore, suspicious.

'I remember you well,' Balthus pointed out. 'You were a decent horseman. Are you still?'

'I don't want you here,' Imbert said. 'Did she tell you that you tried to attack me?'

'I don't… Your voice,' Balthus said. 'I remember your voice.'

'And you thought I was a threat to her when we both know the danger is you. But I am curious about why you reacted like that.'

He was curious too about Imbert's boldness with a Warstone. He rather liked it. 'You must have reminded me of a time I want to forget.'

Imbert tilted his head. 'It's a time we, too, want forgotten and yet here you are with friends.'

'It was inevitable that one of us showed up, though you've guarded her well.'

Imbert grunted. 'Warstone praise is empty.'

'Then take a thank you from a knight who knows when a debt is owed.'

'For keeping Séverine away from you all?'

'For knowing it was your hands that held me down when she did this.' His arm was bound, but he swung his elbow out.

Imbert frowned. 'That was also against my wishes.'

'It helped me, and you still didn't want it? Is this more protection for her or something else?'

Imbert crossed his arms. 'Where are you leading with these questions?'

Too much now. Somehow he had to convince these people to abandon the work they'd begun here. But something else pricked at his mind and was far more concerning.

'You built the pit. She paid you coin for that?'

Imbert's stare narrowed. Balthus almost grinned. Fear and respect were customary; he hadn't known he'd missed out on challenging conversations. Still, he was determined that Imbert shouldn't be too challenging. There were questions he needed answers to.

'This village isn't the only one that's protecting her, is it?' Balthus said. 'There are other places with similar traps?'

'You ask too many questions for a man who looks like a fly could push him over. You're grey, and there's sweat above your lip. Simply doing this much is pushing your boundaries. It won't take much to push you into another pit and pretend it was an accident.'

A non-answer was almost an affirmation. Balthus had hoped Séverine hadn't done anything as foolish as to create other villages like this. If she had, she'd need more than old servants protecting her.

'You want to know what my agenda is now?' he said. 'I have a feeling it's the same as yours.'

'Your death?'

'Her and the boys' protection.'

'You stay away from them all.'

'Is that why I've hardly seen or heard from Clovis and Pepin? Have they been ordered not to spend time with that strange man their mother shoved into a pit and then sliced with her dagger?'

'It was my dagger, and her decision to keep the children away, so I'd honour it if I were you.'

That…stung. He'd done nothing to harm her children, but his parents and perhaps Ian had done much to lose her trust. How was he to win it when he didn't deserve it, either?

He gave a curt nod to acknowledge Imbert's warning. 'As for everything else, I'll die, but it'll be for her first.'

'She's not your cause! What happened in the pit won't happen again. You're not worthy to touch her.'

'A Warstone never should.' Balthus knew that. But then, was he a Warstone any longer? He'd already broken away from his family, was already following Reynold's schemes to find the gem and treasure.

Balthus laid his hand on the latch. 'Are you going in?'

Imbert shook his head.

'If you think me a true Warstone, why not

kill me, fear me, or bargain with me? Is it only me who finds this conversation odd?'

'You're provoking and testing me, but it doesn't fool me. And it is odd because I have power here, and I'm not about to give it away. Why do you want to know about my horsemanship?'

'Would you believe I have a wager to stay on a horse in an upcoming race and need your help?'

'Did you place this bet after you lost your hand?' Imbert said, eyeing him.

He had with his friend Louve, who'd helped him recover the first time. 'Perhaps.'

Imbert huffed. 'Why do I believe that is not all? What more will you tell me?'

There was another reason to become a stronger rider. The building works here were only part of the problem. The other was finding out what Séverine had done in the six years she'd been gone, and how he could remedy them. He couldn't protect her if he couldn't ride. 'I'm still thinking about matters needing to be solved and the obstacles. All of that will need thought, so I'll stay quiet about the rest for now.'

Glowering, Imbert waved his arm for Balthus to proceed inside.

'Am I to open this door and get shot with

arrows?' he said. 'Or perhaps step right into another pit?'

'I think I'll stay quiet about it for now.' Imbert's lips twitched before he turned and walked away.

Balthus glanced towards the crowd of villagers in the street before he opened the door and stepped in.

'What happened to you?' Henry exclaimed.

Balthus hoped the newcomer was Henry, though he'd feared it was a messenger or someone worse. However, it was good to see the man, but how to tell him what had happened? He didn't understand it himself. Why had Séverine bothered to help him, and was she in as much danger as he suspected?

'That's a long story.' Balthus grinned.

'You've looked better,' Henry said.

He was better, but not well yet. Tiny tremors were weakening his chances of standing much longer, so he sat in the nearest chair. This was a simple unoccupied hut, no traps that he could see, but from Imbert's reaction he knew there were others elsewhere. Something he needed to discuss with Séverine as soon as possible.

'I am better.' Balthus watched Henry's reaction. 'You can mention it.'

Henry looked up in surprise. 'You're...displaying your arm, and it's bleeding.'

'I'm probably doing too much and will need new stitches. Do you have thread?'

Henry showed him his empty hands. 'It wasn't bleeding before—what happened?'

He did need stitches again, and more wrapping. Maybe it was their intention to make him better and then bleed out. His thoughts were still in chaos, but how could he go from the absolute agony of betrayal to relief and bewilderment to wanting a kiss from Séverine all in a matter of moments?

'It's bleeding because they chopped off more of my arm.'

Henry stumbled, bumped into the wall, which rattled the hut.

'Don't knock the place down, it's cold today.' Balthus looked towards the door, but no one came in. 'Isn't this odd, that they are allowing us this privacy?'

'Is it? I just arrived, and I'm wondering now if it was safe to do so. Did you tell me that they chopped your arm?'

'Séverine recommended it.'

'And you agreed?' Henry paled.

'No, in fact, up until a few moments ago I was intending to torch this village.'

'A typical Warstone reaction.'

Balthus flinched. 'I'm hardly Warstone anymore.'

Henry grabbed a chair and sat, his girth spilling over, and he widened his legs to brace himself. 'This is a long story.'

'I can't believe you found me.'

'I can't believe you're not surlier about it. I'm late, you know. It was the weather.'

Balthus shook his head. 'I missed the weather.'

'Missed the weather! Where did they hide you, some dark cave?'

'Something like that.'

'It stormed for a week and then the snow and rain made travel impossible. Then there was the fact I didn't truly know in what direction you'd ridden.'

'How did you find me?'

'They were building a trench, figured they were preparing for a battle.'

Balthus rubbed his forehead. This was exactly why he was so concerned. He needed to talk to Séverine!

Henry tilted his head. 'You're truly pleased you have less of an arm?'

'It's difficult to explain, and I don't know how it happened. I'm not certain even Séverine knows how it works. Only I have less pain. I don't feel faint, and thus far this week I haven't blacked out. Although I have done nothing but be tied down to the ground, so I can't test that theory.'

'With rope, like an…animal, and now you're grateful and feeling better.' When Balthus nodded, Henry added, 'I don't understand you Warstones, and before you say you're hardly a Warstone, please remember I wouldn't be grateful if *my* arm had been sliced.'

Balthus laughed. 'Fair enough… Now what?'

'That was my question to you.'

'I can't travel.'

'You have to recover.' Henry pointed to his arm.

That wasn't the entire truth, and for once he needed to start telling more of the truth. 'This village is now in jeopardy.'

'Your family is coming for you, and that's why you have to leave,' Henry said. 'Did you get the item you were supposed to get from Séverine?'

Balthus had only told Henry what was necessary. The rest of the time he'd treated him poorly. The fact this man was civil was because he was a better man. 'No, no I haven't.'

'She doesn't have it.'

'I haven't asked.'

Henry tilted his head. 'Because she didn't take the news of Ian's death well? He was trying to kill you when he threw that dagger. Did you leave that part out?'

'How—?'

'I wasn't in the hall when it happened, but nothing is a secret.'

It needed to be a secret. If what had happened in that hall had escaped the fortress and got back to his parents… 'It's complicated.'

'Because Louve threw the dagger?' Henry said. 'I did wonder why you didn't throw, but then, I didn't know how bad your hand was at that point. It wasn't as if we were talking then.'

They weren't talking now, and yet it seemed the entire world knew what had happened that day in the hall those few months ago. Warstone Fortress had been Ian's domain. He, Balthus and the mercenary Louve, a man who would call him friend, had already been circling the fortress to seek a way to break in. At that time the parchment was believed to be there. Louve had already found a way in as a servant. Balthus, when he'd seen his parents arrive for a visit, had decided to go inside with them.

It had been a strained visit where no one

had trusted their motive for being there. All the more for Balthus because Ian had tried to kill him previously.

But that last day, after their parents had left, Ian had seemed to break down. He'd thrown a dagger at Balthus, and to protect him, Louve had thrown a dagger towards Ian. Ian's dagger had missed Balthus…but Louve's had struck true.

Later, in the quiet of a chamber, they had discussed whether Ian had thrown himself into the path of the dagger aimed at him, wanting to end his life, but by that time Balthus's hand had been beyond healing and Louve, being the man he was, had chopped it off to save his friend's life.

It had worked out as best it could in the end. Louve now had control of Ian's fortress, and he had a feisty wife named Biedeluue. His parents had been well outside the gates before they'd been informed of their eldest son's death. They hadn't heard from them since.

When Balthus had healed sufficiently, he and Henry had taken off to find Ian's wife, Séverine, who, with any hope, might have still had the parchment that could lead them to a legend.

But Balthus had been in Séverine's care for

weeks now. If she had any coin, artefacts or treasures left from her time with his brother, he would have seen them by now. As far as he could tell, she lived like a peasant.

Balthus could feel Henry's gaze still on him, waiting for an answer he wasn't certain how to give.

'You *have* told her about Ian's death...' Henry enunciated carefully.

How to phrase any of this? His only thought was to touch Séverine again, to...be part of her life. Dangerous for her, but perhaps he could make it better until he had to go? Wrong, it was all wrong. She believed her husband was alive, she didn't know he was only with her to obtain the parchment to take down his family... although would she agree with that? Even so... to tell her of it would jeopardise her safety.

And yet he knew if he revealed it all, she would simply leave, and the mystery of her, what she'd been smiling at that day when she'd stared at the tapestry, how she'd found the strength to escape Ian would be lost to him.

If she knew Ian was dead...who was he to her? Nothing. A threat.

'I need to stay,' Balthus said. 'Can you do that?'

Henry straightened to his full height. 'We

left the safety of that fortress to avoid your parents, who are probably assembling a large force against us. You have been here weeks and you haven't told her of her husband's death or procured whatever mysterious item she is purported to have.' Henry kicked the dirt on the floor. 'Although wherever this item is, it seems doubtful it's here. Unless it's some stone, stick or a bucket of mud, because that's all I've seen since I've arrived. As for you not telling her of Ian's death, how do you think that will work out for you?'

Balthus rolled his aching shoulder. He might be sitting, and his arm might be much better than it had been, but time was still needed. 'I need to stay,' he repeated.

Henry tilted his head. 'Are you asking me to keep this quiet, to simply roam around this place that doesn't have a butcher and probably doesn't need my skills until you're ready to grow some courage to tell the woman what she needs to know?'

'I didn't say it didn't need your skills,' Balthus said. 'You still have your knives?'

Balthus took one look at Henry's smug expression and said, 'Don't say it.'

'You're not using my knives, but I am at your service.'

Chapter Thirteen

'How did he lose his hand, Mama?' Clovis said.

'Is it all the way off?' Pepin asked.

'He lost his hand. It's not hanging there.' Clovis kicked Pepin's shoe.

Pepin kicked back. 'If he lost it, where is it?'

'Boys!' Sarah clucked under tongue as she wove through the construction.

'They're curious, that's all.' Séverine carried two buckets of water to the workers. They were heavy, but not terribly so. When she'd first started, it had taken her two hands to carry one. There had been so many changes since then for her and her sons. Changes and skills she welcomed. Having Balthus here and him being a part of the conversation as well as village activity was unsettling. She wondered, not for the first time, if it was because he was a Warstone or because he was…him.

'We're all curious,' Sarah said. 'Do you know why?'

'I'll ask him,' Clovis said, dropping a bread loaf and picking it up.

'You'll do no such thing!' Sarah said.

'Why not?' said Pepin, who carried one loaf as if it were a stick, and already bits were falling off along the way. There were three dogs following behind them through the village streets, just waiting for their opportunity.

'Because a man is allowed his secrets,' Sarah said firmly.

Which was not what Séverine would have said, but she wouldn't correct her. Especially since she didn't know what exactly she would say. Warstones shouldn't be allowed any secrets. Balthus, however, had many, and for some reason she was giving him time. She could fool herself into thinking she'd waited because her demanding to know why he was here, or if he'd help her while he suffered was too soon, but in truth, there was a vulnerability about him that wasn't because his hand was missing but perhaps why his hand was missing.

'Who are they, Mama?' Clovis asked quietly, discreetly, as if he knew the question was loaded with secrets.

'Balthus and Henry!' Pepin announced.

'Henry's the one that Mama hit with the log. He says he's got a hard head, which is good, isn't it, Mama? Because I think Denise likes him!'

Séverine glanced around, while Sarah clucked.

'Quiet!' Clovis snapped. 'Mama?'

'They're men who came to help us, that's all.'

'Why'd you hit him, then?' Clovis whispered.

Pepin ran in front of her and whispered loudly. 'And why does Balthus keep staring at us?'

'Is he a good man?' Clovis said.

Her children! How to protect them and not lie? More difficult, how to tell the truth in a way they could understand? She couldn't, not easily. She also couldn't simply brush their questions aside anymore. Balthus was in their lives now so it was natural they'd have questions.

'I don't know yet,' she said.

'Why isn't it Father?'

Stopping, Séverine set down a bucket, and placed her hand on her son's shoulder. This was important and needed to be said. 'Clovis, bad people are after your father. I think he doesn't want them near us, so he stays away.'

That was what she liked to think. She didn't

want to remember Ian the way he'd been that day he'd left them. Mumbling to himself. His eyes unnaturally wide and searching and he'd been talking to shadows as if madness had been overtaking him.

'My father is strong, and could protect us from anything,' Clovis said. 'Maybe he's trying to protect us from him!'

Séverine's heart froze even as her legs carried her faster. Who was she to argue that? She didn't trust Balthus. Not completely, and in the ways that she did, how was she to explain that to a child? 'Even if someone...isn't good for us, sometimes they simply need help. Sometimes that makes the difference between whether they are trustworthy or not, if they are good or bad.'

'He looks ill,' Pepin said.

'That's because he's recovering, and still hurts.'

'What if he's bad, and you made him worse by pushing him in a pit?' Clovis said. 'What happens to us if our father kept him away, but you let him in?'

Part of her heart broke; there was so much anger in Clovis, and she feared her actions made it all the worse, but he had to know the truth. She may not know Balthus, but she knew herself. 'I will protect you with my life, Clovis. With my being, my heart, my soul. If he is bad, if he means either you or your brother harm, I will kill him myself. This I swear to God and you.'

Pepin nodded frantically. Clovis measured her words and gave her a single nod. Séverine took his acknowledgement.

Peril never waited for convenience. She didn't object to Balthus watching her boys. If they were curious about him, he'd be doubly so about them. But it was only a matter of time before the children or the villagers noticed the resemblance between Balthus and the boys. Imbert and Sarah knew the truth, but they wouldn't lie if asked a direct question, and Clovis was already asking questions, his eyes hardly leaving Balthus. She'd need to press him again on his intentions, and now that he was recovered and his companion was here, it was time.

They entered the place where building work was going on, handed out the supplies and took orders for whatever else she could. Her thoughts, however, weren't on the tasks ahead but on the knight and a man who'd come in to rescue him. Whom Imbert reported was a butcher.

It was too outlandish to be true. If that man wasn't an indication that Balthus was different from the rest of his clan, that man called Henry with no skills and a too jovial manner to be taken gravely, was.

She should take this gravely. Since she had last been in this tiny village, Imbert and Sarah had accumulated an array of tools that could also be used as weapons. They'd also purchased teams of oxen and ploughs. All of which were being used today to build fortifications that would help to keep the villagers safe but couldn't last long when it came to arrows and torches. Sarah and Imbert had to know that, and yet they pretended because she had kept Balthus alive, and she stayed.

'Where is he now?'

'Over there.' Sarah indicated with her chin. 'Imbert's following them around. Since they left that hut, they've been keeping themselves to themselves.'

Séverine's eyes followed where Sarah had indicated. The three men were walking away from the construction, all engaged in conversation, and were given a wide berth.

Henry was gesturing wildly while Imbert was listening intently. Balthus walked a few steps away from both of them. His arm was bound, and he cradled it in his other arm; he was also walking slowly. Still, she couldn't keep her gaze off him.

Unlike most days, today the sun shone brightly, the wind was crisp and blew his dark locks away from his face and allowed her brief glimpses of his profile. She craned her neck to see a bit more of his jaw, his high cheekbones, the curve of his lips. What was it about him? At first she could only see the similarities shared by the Warstone family. Over the days of caring for him, wondering whether he'd survive the fever, he'd just become…Balthus. It didn't mean she wouldn't use any advantage she may have. She still needed to persuade him to let them go. Still needed to know why he was here.

Except now he'd held her…and he wasn't anything other than a man whom she wanted to touch, to kiss.

'Mama, could we play hide-and-seek?' Pepin said.

'Ask your brother,' she said.

'I already did.'

'Clovis, help your mother,' Sarah said.

Séverine could hear the ensuing argument, but she didn't listen. Instead, she watched Balthus stumble. That wouldn't do.

Balthus shouldn't have heard her behind him, shouldn't have felt her presence. The entire village was a cacophony of hammering and shouts. But she was there, and he turned, cursed when he swayed, gave Henry a dark look when he reached out to steady him. Then he wanted to strike him when he gave a knowing smirk, knowing why he refused his help. Turning his back on the annoying butcher, Balthus waited as she came closer.

Her eyes in the sunlight were like the leaves on spring trees. The worry, the questions… the annoyance, however, were completely her.

'You're bleeding too much,' she said.

He had put his hand on the end to cover it, and the men who walked beside him didn't notice, but she did. He didn't know if that was because she cared, or because he was undoing her efforts.

'Given that you're the one who hit it, I thought you wanted it that way.' At Henry's rough cough and Imbert's outrage, he softened his words. 'I don't have thread.'

For a moment she looked as if she wouldn't help, and he thought fast about what he could say to make things better. He wanted to make it good between them…as if anything ever could.

'I do. Follow me,' she said.

Always. Though what he had said about her hitting it wasn't kind. Why couldn't he simply say something right?

He walked beside her, aware that her height was almost equal to his and her long limbs had a natural grace he admired, and wished the road was longer so he could watch her more. They entered a home next to the one with the pit. Inside it was vastly different. Lavish beds, quilts. Quality that she couldn't have travelled with, but must have been here before.

He wanted to ask if it was the old stable-master's cottage, but there were too many beds for that.

She caught him in his curiosity, flushed and rummaged through a small basket, pulling out thread and needle.

He sat and began to undo the linen. When she turned, he stopped.

'I'm probably undoing all your hard labour.'

She shook her head. 'No, it's not that, it's only... Before you were hiding it from me, and now you're simply uncovering it.'

He was. Disconcerted, he looked away. His whole life he'd had to pretend to be someone else; he almost felt he was displaying more of himself than an arm.

'I'm sorry.' She clutched the thread in her hand. 'I'm saying words that have little—'

They had more meaning than she knew. For him to simply forget his weakness, his disfigurement. For him to simply be…himself? The meaning for him was staggering, and difficult to believe.

He rocked his arm. 'You'll continue caring for it?'

'Every day. The bindings must be tighter, and you'll need the poultice with honey rubbed in deeply.' Her eyes widened, shone like summer's grass. 'Oh, do you not want me to tend it now? I'll need to show you how to apply the poultice without harming the stitches, and—'

'That's not it. I…' He wanted her to continue. Now that he was awake, he longed for the time they could be together even if it meant he would continually present his greatest flaws.

'You have experience and should tend it,' he said. 'I am obviously saying words that have little meaning. In truth, I probably muttered words when the fever was on me.'

She gave a knowing look. 'You weren't very pleased with me.'

He grabbed her wrist, which stopped both of them. 'I am sorry.'

'You will be sorry when you discover what

it was you said.' Her words were light, but her voice held a softer tone.

She looked down at where he his hand still clasped her wrist, then her gaze went to his. Eyes darkening before they fluttered closed. Before he knew what he was doing, he tugged, and she flinched.

He quickly let her go.

Looking down at the ground, Séverine berated herself for her conflicting reaction to this man's simple touch. All he'd done was wrap his callused fingers around her wrist, and yet the warmth, the tiny bit of friction, the slight tug towards him wasn't simple at all.

'We…we shouldn't have done that. Earlier, in the other hut. We… I'm married.'

She hated the hesitation in her voice, hated the inanely repeated words they both already knew. It was simply… When he'd realised that she'd helped him, Balthus's grey eyes had been full of utter relief, utter wonder, and when he'd touched her, rested his forehead against hers, it had felt right. Something good. And her stuttering words now were all wrong, even though they were the ones that made sense. Feeling anything for this man didn't.

'Nothing happened, that is…nothing that you should concern yourself with,' he said.

An odd choice of words. The way she felt, the way she'd acted was everything she should be concerned with. She was married! She was his sister-in-law.

'If Imbert hadn't arrived—'

'I'd have more than kissed you,' he said. She looked up. 'And most likely not even God would have pulled you from me.'

'That's blasphemy.'

'No, you healed me, a Warstone. If God wasn't involved, then the Devil was.'

Odd man. 'I wouldn't have been enough?'

The blaze of emotion, of utter stark desire, almost made her step back. No, it was enough to make her hold still…for him. Then he blinked, and when he looked at her again there was nothing noticeable in his grey gaze, and his lips gave a small smirk. 'Not blasphemy,' he said. 'Truth. Those two have been arguing over my fate for as long as I can remember.'

'I didn't think Warstones believed in the whims of fate; rather, they prefer taking it.'

He looked away; a slight tension tightening the corners of his mouth. 'Warstones maybe, but not me.'

Very odd. He was a Warstone, wasn't he? But then…hadn't she been arguing to herself that he was different? Oh, why was she wondering any of this? It wasn't the point!

'It's been almost six years since I last saw Ian, and even then...' She shook her head.

'You ran,' he said. 'Did he frighten you?'

Surprise ran through her at his wording, but it was the truth. 'Your parents, too. I wanted nothing to do with any of them. I didn't want them when they took me.'

'I remember you saying that when I first saw you.' He looked away. 'Yet you healed me.'

She had, and her argument to Imbert and Sarah was that she'd sway him to their side. Maybe he'd help, but why would he? And was that entirely the reason she'd attempted to free him from the pain? It was undeniable—she felt drawn to him, but not his brother. It was also a certainty that if he had kissed her, she would have kissed him back.

When he glanced at her again, she waved her hands for him to lift his arm, and she unwrapped the linen the rest of the way, then placed his hand on the last bit that held the blood.

'I don't even have to worry about you telling him.' She threaded a needle and set it aside. 'You all keep secrets. I won't tell him either, but I can't say he won't guess.'

But Ian and his touches had been very infrequent. He had never been cruel, always tender, as if she were something precious, but something had been missing, some fierceness, some urgency. Something she'd felt the moment Balthus's callused hand had squeezed the back of her neck, as if…she was everything.

That was what had been missing. She hadn't been Ian's everything, and he hadn't been hers. And this man wasn't either and could never be.

'And why you?' she said, pouring water over the area to see where it was torn. 'When no other man has ever?'

'Séverine, do you realise I'm right here?'

Balthus's voice sounded amused. She wasn't. She held his limb underhand and carefully made one stitch. 'Who else would I be talking to?'

'Only confirming. You seem agitated, and you are poking me with a needle.'

'I know you can take pain.' She glanced up. 'Sorry.'

His eyes were amused. They also looked soft. 'It's actually a compliment now. Before you fixed me, if anyone had attempted this, I would have fainted. I can take the pain now. You've made me strong again.'

She'd never seen his eyes like that before.

She didn't like the way that affected her, either. She went back to working on his arm.

His breath hitched.

'Felt that?'

He chuckled. 'Yes.'

'Am I offending your dignity now?'

His silence was heavy, so against her better judgement she looked up.

Chin dipped, the length of his lashes casting shadows around his cheekbones that shouldn't belong to any man. He seduced with his very presence, with the rough edges of his voice. 'When it comes to you, I have no pride. Whatever you want me to do or be… I would.'

Unexpected, the words pierced until she remembered who had delivered them. A liar, from a deceitful family. A man who had been half-crazed with pain yet had tried to defend her. A man who'd said he'd hold her against him and fight off God. A man she'd already told she trusted. She was another's wife. But Ian had left her, and long before that he'd scared her. Six years with no husband. A man with every resource hadn't found her, and yet his brother had? She shouldn't trust these men!

She narrowed her eyes. All those fancy words when they couldn't be true. She healed a man to persuade him, but how could she persuade a liar? 'Your brother is far more charming than you. His smile came easier. That helped when he told the world he'd be marrying me instead of Beatrice.'

Mentioning Ian was a far more effective way of halting his thoughts about holding Séverine than the stabbing of the needle into his flesh, which was still tender. She was killing him with her words, with her proximity. He should keep quiet and let her sew his arm. He should tell her the truth. What he shouldn't do was sit here with her kneeling next to him and listen to her tell him about his dead brother as if he were alive and, worse, as if she regretted his touch, while he burned for her.

But he didn't want to let her go. He didn't deserve her even if she wasn't married. He was wrong, desperately wrong to do this, but she took away his pain, and he felt...alive. Or at least like someone new. So for now, though he'd burn in hell for yet another transgression, he simply couldn't give her up.

He was a coward.

'What I don't understand, what I can never understand, is why he did it,' she whispered. Her hands were in her lap, her feisty umbrage from earlier gone. 'People said it was my red hair, that it shone that day. So for years I berated myself for wearing it down. My sisters have some red in their hair, but they have mainly brown hair like everyone else. Why me? But he never said anything about my hair. Not once. He'd…wrap it around his finger. And maybe to others that looked like he admired it, but his fingers were always clenching it, like it was a possession. *I* was a possession to him, and yet…' She shook her head.

'Tell me,' he said, though all her words were like points of a sword. There was some haunted bitterness there that he both wanted and didn't want to hear. She should never be full of anything dark, and if in telling it the knives inside him made holes in his heart… then that simply made more room.

'You tell me,' she said. 'I'm tired of my own thoughts because I never have an answer. He…' She shook her head, glanced at him, and then arranged the cups and spoons on the table as if to put them away, but there were shelves or cupboards. The hut had only one purpose: to trap, but oddly to heal, and bring him here with her like this.

Balthus waited, but knew Séverine wouldn't say more, and it wasn't his place to ask. Standing, he said, 'Thank you for this. You can't know what it means to not feel the pain…'

'I've given birth, Balthus,' she said. 'Twice.'

Startled, he answered, 'I guess you do, then.' Still laughing, he walked out the door and to the hut next to them.

'Where are you going?' she said.

'To see if everything is taken care of.' He opened the door to the makeshift hut that housed the pit he'd stayed in for weeks. He'd never get used to seeing the room from this angle. Walking around the small single room, he stared down into the pit, noted the distance of the small bed shoved against the other side of the pit and judged there was enough room not to kill himself accidentally.

Séverine stood in the doorway with her hands on her hips. 'How did that bed, those blankets, that torch, any of this, get in here?'

'Imbert and Henry moved some furniture in here for me. I suppose I took someone's bed, but this shelter doesn't seem to have any. I do have to admit having this giant hole in the middle of the floor is inconvenient. I wonder if I'll fall in and undo all your work.'

'You can't simply decide to stay,' she said.

'That's what I'm doing.'

'Why?'

'Because if you wanted me to go, you wouldn't have shoved me in the pit.'

'I fixed you so you could crawl out of the pit.'

'I could crawl out any time. You didn't have to fix my arm; in fact, you took a great risk to do so.'

'What about Henry?'

'Apparently, Henry is helping some people with game, and has become acquainted with a widow here.'

She looked at him in surprise.

Balthus laughed low. 'I thought so, too.'

Séverine looked around. 'I don't like it.'

'I don't want to keep climbing the ladder to sleep on the blankets down there. It's inconvenient and a waste of time and strength.'

Her brows drew in, but she kept quiet.

'We need to talk now. Why did you fix me? I know it wasn't only because I broke Pepin's fall.' Séverine looked behind her, but she did not close the door, and then he knew. 'You thought to…soften me towards you running with the boys.'

She straightened. 'I would do anything for them.'

He should be cross, angry. Instead, he was awestruck by this woman, who truly would do anything for her children, even carve up a Warstone. 'You took a risk, because it could have failed.'

'If it had failed, you'd be dead, so it wasn't much of a risk,' she said.

Balthus chuckled. He wondered again if Ian had bothered to get to know her. 'So you did it to help you protect yourself against the Warstones.'

'Your family,' she corrected. But Balthus had gone quiet. Séverine was done with silence. She'd had a lifetime of words that weren't said and so many secrets that there wasn't anything to tell anymore. She was still shaking from her thoughts, from the proximity of tending his arm. All week since she'd felt this awkwardness from the intimate time tending him. Now, even with the door open, she was all too affected by him. Every hair on the back of her neck was sensitive, her body felt too tightly bound in the clothing she wore. And now he said he wouldn't leave?

'Aren't they your family?' she said.

'Séverine,' he said.

'You say my name as if that's an answer.' She crossed her arms.

'You aren't at all what my brother thought you were.' He sat on the bed.

His words made little sense, but the way he said it did. More secrets that he didn't want to tell, but she recognised two other emotions.

Something like want and regret. She felt them, too. One more than the other, and that provoked a rampage of emotions she had no right to feel. She knew better.

Pointing towards a nearby chair, he said, 'Come sit, and keep the door open or not.'

'Won't someone hear?'

'What we need to talk about is hardly a secret.' He adjusted himself, winced. Already she could see the fatigue take him. He needed to rest, but she kept her silence. All the reasons she'd fled from him and his kind needed to be resolved.

'When Ian left you at Forgotten Keep, he left you with a full retinue, didn't he?' When she nodded, he added, 'I went there first. There were still some servants, but the walls, the floors…the home was bare.'

'It was under repair with so many people, are they—?'

'Still there. Still utterly loyal to you, a Warstone, too.'

Another odd phrase from this man who was far more open than his family, but he was still cut from the same cloth. And simply because she'd helped him with his pain it didn't change that they were essentially enemies. She'd run from his family, shoved him in a dark pit. He'd pursued her for reasons she still didn't know, but they couldn't be good because he'd never told her why. He was holding secrets he knew she wouldn't like. But what? She wouldn't know until they talked, until she, too, told him some truths. And she would do so without risking her children.

'It was under construction when we arrived. It wasn't that full.'

'But there were possessions, and when you left, people and anything you could travel with went with you?'

That was all true. 'Warstones have enough wealth. And I'm family, I should be able to travel with what I choose to take.'

'But you left them along the way. Are there other villages like this one? Servants you've left behind with coins, tapestries or paintings?'

'For their service to me, that is nothing new.'

He raised his brow, that was all. She stared right back at him. Trust him? Maybe only a little, but that look in his eyes when he'd realised he didn't hurt anymore, she believed in that. She believed in his silences.

'They needed the coin to buy supplies, to help set other traps, other ways of slowing down anyone pursuing us. Don't tell Ian. I don't want him harming those who are loyal to me.'

He frowned. 'You should have thought of that.'

'I did, but I…'

'You outweighed the protection of your children against Sarah's and Imbert's lives'.

She paled, stumbled toward the chair he offered and sat. 'Don't. I argued with them, and—'

'I apologise. It's brutal, but it was the right decision, the only path. Imbert and Sarah can protect themselves better than your children can. Or at least they can hide.'

She felt solace at Balthus's simple words. So simple and yet his words went far to ease her conscience, her heart.

'But, Séverine, I don't think you know what you've done.'

'I've built safe havens for my children.'

'No, you've started a war, one that my parents haven't seen. One that they'll never guess because it's not some mass of mercenaries headed their way or great political schemes from people of power.'

'I've done nothing but run from people who threatened my children. Do you know what they wanted to do to Clovis? What your mother said to me?'

'What did she say that day by the tapestry? When you didn't turn, when she grabbed your wrist, and made you turn while Ian crossed the hall towards you.'

She gasped.

'I told you I watched you.'

'Who are you?' she whispered.

He huffed out a breath. 'I'm not certain anymore.'

If his words on her choices gave her solace, these words gave her hope. It didn't make him safe, and it was a far cry from him helping them, but she felt she could trust him enough for now. 'It wasn't your mother's words that day, for all she told me was to turn around and honour her son as I should. I…hadn't heard the announcement.'

'I know,' he said.

'I didn't know it was for me, but I did turn as soon as I could.' Séverine didn't know why it was so difficult to tell the rest, it had happened so long ago. 'It was her grip on my wrist. Her face was so… I'd gone from looking at the tapestry to an expression on her beautiful face that I suppose was meant to be serene, but there was nothing there, and her nails dug and dug until my skin broke and I bled as Ian smiled at me, and people clapped.'

She wanted to say Balthus's expression had also been inscrutable, but it hadn't been. It had been full of rage before he'd regained control.

'Then I have news that may hearten you,' he said. 'The reason for my parents coming after you isn't the children. As long as you kept quiet, hidden, you would simply be another Warstone secret. But by planting servants loyal to you in various villages, you've established a mutiny. Do you understand? It's not only those servants you left, but those they've told, those here that are helping Sarah and Imbert. All silently rising up against the Warstones.'

'You keep… You're confusing me. You are a Warstone. I feel like I'm not… There are too many secrets.'

'And yet we've built some trust, have we not?'

Despite everything. 'I still believe your silences more than your words.'

He gave one of those warm soft smiles that were unexpected. The ones that made her heart answer despite her reason knowing better.

'What of Ian?' she said. 'How is he?'

He looked away. 'You didn't want to ask me that before.'

'Is it worse?'

He glanced at her. 'So you know.'

'Why do you think I left?'

He shifted. Was he uncomfortable with her questions?

'What do you care if his anger and his… madness is worse?' he said. 'You left him.'

'I won't feel shame for what I did.'

'You took his children.'

'It was them I was worried about.'

He exhaled roughly. 'I'm sorry. That wasn't fair.'

'It's the truth,' she said.

He winced and closed his eyes.

'Your arm. You're hurting,' she said.

He shook his head. 'I have to say more to you now. More I should have said instead of what I did. It's…complicated.'

'That I can understand.'

'No,' he said. 'This is… Ian tried to kill me a few months ago. Not by his own hand, but using a hired archer. There was never trust between us, but that…that changed the course of my life. You don't look surprised.'

'When I left, he wasn't the man I married, and even that man wasn't… I'm sorry. He's your brother, and I shouldn't disparage him, but—'

'He tried to kill me, Séverine. It's a truth

that I have a difficult time with. As a result, I approached Reynold.'

'He left your family long ago.'

'He did, but I remember him from before. He didn't trust at first, but eventually we came to an agreement to sever my parents' influence. To not allow them to gain any more power or wealth or—'

He stopped, she waited, and when he didn't say anything more, she said, 'There's more you're not telling me.'

He let out a breath. 'There's more I'm not telling you, but maybe silence is best right now.'

'Will it hurt my children?'

'No. But the building works here would. You need to tell them to tear it down.'

'I don't have control over what they do, or how they'll feel safe. Do you think they'll feel better if there is no wall?'

He exhaled slowly. 'No. And I'm staying. I don't know if that will help or hurt, but I can't do nothing. Why do you keep them away from me?'

'The villagers?'

'The boys. In the beginning I saw them, and then after that drink, nothing. I can't recall seeing them afterwards, either.'

He looked hurt, which couldn't be, but still. 'You weren't well, I thought to keep your privacy.'

His expression eased, but his brows still drew in. She wasn't prepared to tell him all the reasons, the words he'd said, the way she was acting around him. None of that she wanted her sons to witness.

When Balthus nodded, she let out a slow breath. Could it be this easy? She hadn't even pleaded with him about why she needed his insight on how to permanently turn Ian and his parents away or help them forge a future where they didn't have to run. She knew better than to not ask more questions, but fatigue was already weighing Balthus's shoulders down.

She was also scared to ask more now, too. If he offered to help; she'd take it.

'So you'll stay.' She stood and brushed her skirts.

'I'll stay.'

There was much to think on, especially as she risked the futures of her children and the people loyal to her. Especially as she was trusting a Warstone...who was against Warstones. Unfathomable.

'Regarding your arm,' she said, 'you'll need to keep it tightly bound to your chest for several more weeks. It's still swollen. I'd like to look at it, to see if it worsens.' When he didn't answer, she added, 'Balthus, it needs to—'

'I understand. I was simply imagining what that would mean.'

It would be more time she spent with him. More tense conversations where she was acutely aware of him.

'I could take care of it myself,' he said.

'I need to see how it's healing. The fever has only just broken. You need to eat and sleep more. When it's time, you need to move it more each day, and then bind it again to your chest.'

'Will horse riding do for movement?'

'Horse—? No! If you fall, the stitches won't hold. I can't say what kind of lasting damage that would cause.'

'If it's the falling, then we're fine. I mean to ask Imbert…that will take time…'

The next blink he gave was longer. She should go, but her feet didn't want to move. When his eyes were closed like this, she was able to watch him, notice his beauty, admire the masculine symmetry, and wonder why he intrigued her so.

Now that she knew him better, she should not have been as fascinated. When she studied tapestries, she admired their beauty first, then their composition, and after she'd learned the process, she usually moved on to the next. She knew there was no moving on from Balthus. He was a beauty who changed with seasons and emotions. She could study him forever, and then ask for more.

She'd hated the Warstone parents, was terrified of her husband, and somehow desired the youngest brother. When they touched she wanted more, when they talked she could sit by him forever. She just...wanted.

'Goodnight, Balthus.'

She opened the door, turned. His eyes were closed, he was already lying down. His breathing even, he looked asleep. She should let him be and yet some of his words she had to understand.

'Was that the truth, about whatever I wanted you to do, you would?' she said.

He turned his head, opened his eyes. They were mere slits of grey, but they were still piercing.

'Always.'

'Why?'

He swallowed, and she watched the rhythmic movement of his throat.

'Because Ian may have married you, and

you bore his children, but I watched you before he did,' he answered.

It was almost as if he'd claimed her that day; how she wished she had claimed him, too.

'At the announcement, I was teased about the four brothers for four sisters. Did you think that was what was to be?'

Inscrutable expression. Dark grey eyes. 'I had hoped.'

Chapter Fourteen

Out of all the challenges Balthus had faced in his life, mounting and dismounting a horse wasn't one he'd thought would be among the most difficult, but day after day it proved impossible. To defend Séverine, to protect her and the boys in any way, it was a challenge that had to be met. Higher ground in any battle was essential. If nothing else, they needed to have ability to flee or to send messages for help.

Séverine had brought a battle to her little family, whether she wanted it or not. There was always a possibility his parents would want their Warstone grandsons in the clutches of their bloodstained hands. Either to mould into something like Ian before the madness had taken him or to kill them so they weren't competition. No matter how many safe havens

Séverine arranged, eventually they would be found.

Either way, he refused to let her fight alone against them. He would be there. No, he'd be leading his parents and their forces away so they couldn't be near her or the boys.

That required him to mount and stay on a horse. It had been two weeks since Séverine had argued against him trying because he might injure himself. And he had, but not irrevocably. Mostly it had been because the recent deluge of rain had made the ground nothing but mud. He'd been filthy, bruised, but unharmed.

When he wasn't pushing himself on the horse, he had begun his sword and balance training, which included walking distances and using the branches of trees to pull himself up to increase his upper-body strength. Anything to gain more strength since he'd been idle for far too many months.

His reasoning didn't stop Séverine from chastising him night after night. The stitches had long ago come out. The wound was healing, but Séverine insisted on poultices and the linen wrap to keep it bound to his chest.

The limb didn't look any more repulsive than it had before; however, it continued to look unacceptable to him. There was always that moment before the last of the linen was unfurled when he expected his hand to be there again.

Séverine's actions were always efficient and quick, but he was still affected. He offered more than once to take care of it himself, but she refused. It was both glorious and torture to have her hands on him. But because his arm was the way it was, he kept his gaze away from her as much as possible. He couldn't bear to see her revulsion, which he was certain must be there because his was.

No, he was out of the pit, there was no more debilitating pain, but his life wasn't easy.

And thinking of Séverine's kiss or the way she felt in his arms? That way lay madness. He hadn't attempted to touch her in that way again, but she tempted him. However, since that moment they had rarely been alone. Either Sarah or Imbert hovered and played chaperones. He was both grateful and irritated by their presence. If he'd thought he was worthy of her, he'd have ignored the old servants and wooed her. He wondered constantly if Séverine thought at all about their kiss.

When he wasn't being thwarted by a horse, or by his longing for a woman who wasn't his, he attempted to win over Imbert, who held much sway in the village.

However, Imbert had many opinions on the best way to protect Séverine. Most of them were good…if Imbert had been surrounded by trained guards and had more resources. But there was nothing but simple supplies and simple men. Not nearly the force to bear a Warstone offensive.

All the while Balthus was well aware that this wasn't his battle. Not truly. And it was one that, had they known all the facts, they'd have shoved him in the pit once again.

He'd argued with himself about telling Séverine of Ian's death, and asking her for the parchment, but then he'd see her smile at a villager, or plait her hair, and he'd know he stayed not only because she needed his protection, such as it was, but simply to prolong this precious time.

Henry, in the meantime, would recite all the consequences, but kept his silence otherwise, and reluctantly accepted the excuses that Balthus's recovery and the state of the weather were good enough reasons to stay, but time was running out. Like now.

There was no point in delaying further. He needed to be able to ride a horse on his own.

The irony wasn't lost on him that if he were still in the bosom of his family, servants or a squire would assist him in dressing or mounting a horse. Now he had to rely on himself... starting with his own boots.

'I could help you with those.'

Balthus stilled at the young voice just behind him. Since his arrival, Clovis had tested boundaries but remained cautious around him. Both boys had, and Balthus guessed that if he could hear villagers outside the pit, the villagers and these boys heard that moment their mother had started slicing his arm, and every fevered curse he'd uttered since then. They had known he'd suffered.

Did he apologise? Shame wasn't an emotion he was used to experiencing let alone acknowledging, but the truth was he had frightened his nephews when all he'd wanted had been to be near them and their mother. They were a family, or what he'd hoped a family would be.

Something of the way Clovis held himself reminded him of his brothers. The watchful gaze that was utterly Reynold. He'd asked Séverine if the boys knew who he was and she'd answered no, but he hadn't asked whether Clovis had already guessed. He had to have noticed the colour of their eyes was nearly the same. The boy was too watchful not to wonder who he was. He was also *here*.

If Balthus turned, if he showed any reaction that the boy had acknowledged him, he might lose him. So he kept his eyes on his task, shoving on one of his boots. 'What could you help me with?'

A step forward. 'Your boots.'

Balthus stretched and thumped the heel in, then he pulled the lace up and tucked it into the top. 'I can put my own boots on.'

Another step and Clovis was in his peripheral vision. 'That way doesn't work. It's why you're falling off. You can't grip with loose boots.'

Balthus glanced up. Clovis's wary gaze swept across his features as if he was trying to understand him. He hadn't proven himself trustworthy yet, and he wondered how he could. But here was this boy, brave enough to talk to him on his own, regardless of his fears. What motivated him? Did Clovis remember Ian? His heart hurt when he thought that his brother was denied even these wary expressions.

Balthus huffed. 'I don't want someone else lacing them. It's why I do this on my own.'

'I saw your boot slip off before you fell. You won't stay on a horse without tied boots.'

He didn't know where this conversation was going. It felt as if Clovis wanted to talk about something other than laces and boots. Balthus was completely inept at conversation and out of his depth talking with children. Should he apologise and walk away? But the boy fidgeted with his tunic and Balthus held still.

'A man doesn't like to have his weaknesses pointed out to him.'

Clovis kicked some dirt at his boots. 'Neither do boys.'

Ah.

'Mama says that even if you're bad, I should be nice to you because you're trying.'

Balthus's heart skipped. Any breath he'd been about to take was gone. How could a boy know so much? These words…felled him. Mistrust from a boy who looked like Ian. That goodness from Séverine…

'Did you know me when I was little?'

Very brave indeed. 'Is that why you want to talk to me?'

Clovis pinched the bottom of his tunic and pulled it, but he looked at the ground and his cheeks had turned.

Perhaps that wasn't how he was to reply.

How did he know? The more he watched
Séverine and watched the boys play, the more
he knew she was right to have taken them away
from his family. At the same time he wished
Ian could have known them like this. Wary,
but brave enough to ask.

How could he not reflect on his own family,
especially when Clovis had asked if he knew
Ian? 'I did know you.'

'She won't tell me who you are.'

So the child had asked Séverine and she
hadn't told him. What had that taken from her
to deny her son that answer? Given the cruelty
of his family, probably nothing.

'You won't, either,' Clovis said.

That voice: he shouldn't have remembered
Ian as a young boy, but that tone, that victory
lacing every word, was almost familiar.

'I am Balthus, but your mother should tell
you the rest.' Balthus stood. Prepared himself
for the humiliation ahead, aware that he was
being judged by a boy of barely nine years.

'Mama has ignored other men who followed
us.'

There was too much significance in that
sentence, and he was far too ill equipped to
unravel it. 'I'm not your father.'

'I didn't say you were.' Clovis looked away then. 'I don't have a father.'

He did, and he didn't. The child was stabbing him with every regret he had. Had he ever been around a boy as young as this before? Never, but he was desperate to build bridges between them.

'I think we're both stubborn, though,' Balthus said.

'I'm stubborn?'

'You've insisted on showing me how to tie my laces, and I don't want you to.'

'Because you think you can't do it?' Clovis said.

Balthus was offended but wanted to laugh. 'You know other one-handed men who can tie laces?'

'I couldn't tie my laces when I started.'

Something ugly reared up violently inside him. It demanded he dismiss the boy. Some cruelty that wanted to shove or shout that he could tie his laces, that he wasn't a child. Balthus knew immediately what it was: Warstone training that fought against what the boy suggested. He'd shown enough vulnerability, weakness, softness in front of others. The boy wouldn't respect him unless he had a firm hand, harsh words and cold punishment.

But Clovis wasn't looking at him as if he was weak, he wasn't looking at him with fear or trepidation. He was looking at him like…he wanted to help. The emotion in his grey Warstone eyes was Séverine's warmth and goodness.

Obeying that, Balthus sat down and was rewarded with Clovis's half-smile. That smile was also Séverine's.

Pointing at his boots, Clovis began, 'First, pull out your laces and lay them flat on the ground, and hook one under your other boot so it's stuck and you're pulling only one…'

Tearing out the centre of a bread loaf at the small oak table in her hut, Séverine spun around as her boys entered and brought into her home warm spring air and the noise of clomping feet and happy chatter.

Her boys. How easily that sprang to her mind, but how could she not when all three wore similar grins on their faces? Balthus's smile…

Séverine hadn't seen Balthus smile since the pit, when Imbert had interrupted them. She could still feel the heat of his hand on the back of her neck, the words he'd growled against her lips. The way she'd needed, desperately, to be closer to him.

As if he knew her thoughts, his gaze swung to her. Feeling caught out, she swiped the side of her arm against the loose curl that annoyingly kept falling on her forehead.

'He stayed on the horse today, Mama!' Pepin tugged hard on her gown, jolting her to one side. Righting herself, she blinked at her youngest.

'He wobbled like this, and like that.' Pepin demonstrated, until all of them were laughing. 'But he stayed on!'

'I was taught well.' Balthus clasped Clovis's shoulder and they shared a look. Tears pricked Séverine's eyes, and she quickly brushed her hands against her apron and willed herself to be calm.

She was Clovis and Pepin's mother, but Balthus was her husband's brother. How many times did she need to repeat that to herself? Many, and it still didn't feel true.

'Food's about ready, and all three of you need to wash first,' she said.

Her boys ran right back out as if what she'd said was of no import. But to her it was. Clovis had dirt in his hair. Her eldest had, at least for a day, allowed himself to just be. Joy threatened to rip her apart, and she turned to face the table and the bread loaf. Just a few more tears and maybe Balthus would also leave. Once she was done with this part, she'd add butter and—

'Séverine, turn around,' Balthus said.

She couldn't—not just yet. Not when she was afraid he'd see what she was feeling. That whatever had happened today between her children and him had now added to the tumult of emotions their kiss had started. This had all started with her wanting to persuade him to help her...she hadn't gotten to that part, not truly. He stayed now, but for how long?

'I don't think so.'

'I need you to, I would like to say something. Please.'

She needed to stop pulling at the bread or there'd be nothing left for the butter. She turned.

His gaze was softer but no less intense. She wasn't ready and grabbed the table behind her.

'You gave me this day, you know that? By taking away the pain, by allowing me into your home, and to be around your children.'

He looked as overwhelmed as she did, and she grabbed the table behind her for support. Then gripped it as she felt her entire being leaning towards him. Wanting what they'd shared, wanting more. It was all wrong. Everything about this was wrong, he wasn't Ian, not her husband, as much as her traitorous heart wished he was. Whatever was happening between them or with her children needed to stop. Now.

'If you believe you can say a few kinds words to soften me towards you, you can think again. Just forget all that.'

He huffed out a breath and scuffed his boot across the floor. The same movement her children often made.

'No,' she said, not wanting to acknowledge that closeness either, and he looked sharply at her. His scrutinising gaze turned predatory and she realised her mistake.

It wasn't he who'd mentioned the kiss, or how they'd touched, or confessed that such actions affected him. She had by telling him to forget *all that*. He knew it, too.

Gone was the man with the wide grin and before her was the man who had kissed her devastatingly, who had touched her with need, desire, and had made it clear he wanted to again as his gaze leisurely took in her every feature, savouring her in a way she couldn't understand but was achingly aware of.

And her body responded. From her breath to her heartbeat to the heated pinpricks fluttering across her skin when his eyes darkened to almost black.

'Séverine, I see what is in your eyes, and we have no chaperones,' he whispered, his voice a little deeper and rougher than before. A particular rasp that flushed heat through her.

He'd noticed that, too.

A step towards her, and another. All the while he kept his gaze on her, until he was close enough for her to feel the heat from his skin, to smell the fresh cold air trapped in the wool of his clothes. To watch, truly watch him lay his hand on hers and still the last of her nervousness. Until she was nothing except a woman all too aware that the man that she wanted…wanted her, too.

'Balthus, don't— The boys will return and…' Why could she not get her words out?

'Then let me say something else,' he said. 'Thank you, Séverine, for the life you've *shown* me. Today meant much, and not only because I can ride again and have earned some respect from Imbert, but because I shared it with Clovis and Pepin. They taught me much.'

Relieved he'd decided to be courteous, she released the table behind her. 'The boys appreciate your time, as well.'

The corner of his mouth curved, and he

shook his head. 'Look at you. You think that is all?'

He reached out and pulled one of her locks and freed the crumbs caught there before releasing it to spring back onto her shoulder. She shouldn't have felt that touch, should have been embarrassed to have crumbs in her hair, but instead she had a mad desire to sprinkle more there, just to have her curls wrapped around his thick fingers like that again.

'If you think,' he said, very succinctly, 'for a moment I will forget those sounds you made when I held you against me, never want again the taste of your skin just behind your ear, and breathe the sweet scent I found there, you can think again.'

The door banged as Pepin tumbled in and broke them apart.

'Balthus, I'm hungry, get clean,' Pepin said.

Balthus look at him, but didn't move. 'I will in a moment. Can you see if the soup is done on the fire outside?'

Pepin skipped back out.

She shook her head at him. 'It's wrong.'

He bent his head to her ear. 'It's wrong, for more reasons than you know and I'm too much of a coward to tell you, but forget? Never.' He pulled back; his eyes searching hers. 'But do me this favour…let us talk tonight. You deserve the truth, even when it comes from me.'

'Do I need it?' she whispered.

His eyes darkened, a flare of heat in that grey. Like flint being struck and then gone. 'I do. Will that be enough for you?'

He seemed as surprised as her that she'd asked that question. It spoke of hesitation, of fear. It spoke of wanting to pretend a bit longer with him.

But she was a mother who needed to protect herself, her sons, and nobody should ever pretend with a Warstone. She deserved the truth. When he told her, maybe then she'd be reminded of their games and deceit and cruelty. Maybe then she wouldn't be seduced by his vulnerable searching gaze, his tender caresses, the way he'd kissed her as if she was everything to him.

'Am I to believe it when you tell me?' she said.

'No, it wouldn't be right for you to believe me now.'

'You're still lying,' she said. 'To me.'

He swallowed; his hand twitched as if he wanted to stop her from stepping back. 'Not… always.'

Here were the games she hated. 'Go and

get clean. I'll feed you, and tonight when they sleep, we'll talk.'

Something shuttered in his eyes then, but he turned and walked swiftly out the door.

Balthus strode past the boys with their bowls full of soup and back out to the little stream that bordered the village and the small woods. It was occupied by many villagers trying to get clean after a hard day in the mud, but he didn't care as he kicked off his boots, breeches, and yanked off his tunic. He left on his braies and the linens around his arm. Aware eyes were on him, he dived into the cold water.

It had been a victorious day. A day when he'd learned how to tie his boots and ride a horse. Insignificant achievements to most but that meant he had a chance to protect her. He still needed to stay seated longer and be able to use his sword, which might take months, but he'd do it to protect her and the boys.

He wished he could protect her from himself, but that time was quickly disappearing. He wanted her, and his body demanded it, but he wouldn't take her, wouldn't touch her again until there was some understanding between them.

She was terrified of his brother and ran from him. Ian hadn't been innocent, but while he'd been dying he had wished his wife to be told that he'd loved her.

Had his brother truly loved his wife, his sons? How could he, if he'd left them behind and defenceless against his parents?

Séverine was running and living a life never meant for her, but she was raising two children and faced odds that he could only guess at. And she did it while helping Ian's servants, by helping him.

He was a coward, but he could give her some truth. He could tell her about the parchment and legend. Maybe, if he was fortunate, she'd hate him for the reason he'd followed her. Then it wouldn't matter if he could never forget how she'd felt in his arms.

She'd be done with him, and safe. He needed to keep her safe.

'I thought I'd find you here.' Séverine walked up to the man slowly. He was in the stables, and there was hardly any light, but he was leaning against a railing used to hold blankets and stared at one horse in particular. Everything about him was relaxed, at ease with the world. The tension he'd been carrying for the last few weeks had gone. She had the urge to slide her hand against his lower back and rest her head on his shoulder. Instead, she stood to his left and matched his pose.

Then almost laughed. The horse he stared at was no doubt the one he rode. It was also the largest, strongest, most obstinate one she had ever encountered. Hardly anyone ever rode it, and for good reason.

'Did you get some food? I never saw you.'

He looked down at her. 'I did. Why did you think I'd be here?'

She was grateful he'd kept things polite between them, that he didn't mention why he hadn't returned after he'd stormed from her home. She didn't need games, or a man who kissed her. She needed to keep her sons safe.

'Because you Warstones always liked to celebrate your victories,' she said.

He looked back at the horse. 'It doesn't take much to impress you if you think staying seated on a horse is a victory. Should I let you know I can tie my own boots now, too?'

'Balthus,' she said. She was trying to ease the tension between them but somehow had made it worse.

'Ah, now it's you who acts like my name is an answer.'

Mockery when he deserved to feel some pride for his accomplishments today. Did she dare tell him that she was proud? It probably revealed too much of her admiration of him, but she couldn't allow him to think he was less of a man simply because of losing a hand.

'Your one hand isn't the reason you should be gloating over a poor horse,' she said. Sharply aware of his feelings and her own in this matter, she purposefully kept her tone light.

'You think I'm celebrating because of a horse?'

She had to tell him the truth. 'Many people get hurt, but some don't get up again. Some stop trying.'

His brows drew in. 'It's just a horse, Séverine.'

'And your hand is just the result of a horrific accident or something done to you on purpose. Something you haven't told me yet.'

'I don't—'

She waved him off. 'I don't need to know unless you want to tell me.'

He gave a curt nod, but his eyes held no answers. She'd thoroughly confused him. Did he not understand? Couldn't he see what she was doing, what anybody would if they just stood in front of him long enough? To realise that though he looked like a Warstone, he wasn't like them. He held secrets that were no doubt dangerous. *He* wasn't safe, but that, oddly, gave him strength, and in turn made him feel safe… at least to her. He wasn't the family she fled from. There was something true about him.

'Whatever happened to that hand,' she began, 'you still suffered horrible agony, recovery, fever, only to suffer it again. Then to look at the world differently, or enough to want to try it again? It's not the task, it's the man who's impressive. The victory is *you.*'

She knew instantly she'd said too much. His hand unclasped the railing, his fingers splayed as if he was reaching for her. His eyes widened then hungrily roved from the hair she'd ruthlessly plaited to her hunched shoulders to her hands clasped on the coarse wool blanket, then back again.

She could get lost in those eyes, and for that she needed to push him away.

'And it's probably gloating over a horse, too,' she said, her voice completely flat.

He cleared his throat, shifted his stance, so he was facing the horses again. For the longest of heartbeats neither of them said anything.

'Your boys are incredible,' he said.

She released her held breath, feeling relieved that he'd changed the subject.

'I watched them today.' His voice was a little hoarse. She wasn't certain she had one.

'Both of them?' she whispered.

'It was Clovis who helped me with my shoes.'

'Oh.' She tried to understand that. How could a boy help a man with one hand? And yet...she could see her son, with his serious face being exact on how to do it. What flummoxed her was that Clovis had helped Balthus. He'd been avoiding him.

Balthus gave a half-smile. 'Now, that feels like an answer.'

'Clovis helping anyone is an answer,' she said.

He turned and leaned his hip against the railing. The casual movement defined this man. He wasn't Ian. His shoulders were much broader, the ease with which he smiled much more ready, but the other emotions were there as well, like his vulnerability just now when she'd told him how she felt about his hand, his strength, about him.

He also let her see that he understood her.

'You're worried they'll turn into Warstones,' he said.

'Always.' It was a relief to say it.

'Even away from their family?'

She wanted to ponder on the use of his words. He was a Warstone and yet he wasn't offended, or threatened to twist her fingers because she didn't like their ways. The way he'd said the sentence was as if he wasn't a Warstone. She didn't know what to make of that.

'I am their family, but blood is blood, and sometimes that rules out anything else.'

His eyes eased. 'Clovis has mannerisms so like his father's. Does it make your heart ache?'

He did understand. There were moments when it absolutely hurt to keep them away from their father, but how could Balthus understand that? After all, he had the company of Ian whenever he wanted.

'It's when he straightens his tunic or his hair,' she said. 'Nothing out of place. I don't know where Pepin gets his mannerisms from.'

'You're telling me you didn't roll in pig mud while chasing a gosling?'

She laughed low. 'No, the moment I knew what a needle and thread were for, I was lost. I wanted to find the meaning behind everything. Even the simplest pattern could make something beautiful, and I was obsessed with wanting to find how that was possible. When

I learned to read, well…you can imagine what that did. A whole world of beauty to discover.'

Balthus stared.

At the warmth in his eyes, she flushed. 'I've told you too much.'

There was a curve to his lips, but he merely shook his head. 'I think I should warn you, then.'

A slight coldness slid down her spine despite his still teasing gaze. 'What?'

'When I was Pepin's age, I purposefully hit a hornet's nest simply because Guy said I couldn't do it.'

She laughed. 'Oh, I could so see Pepin doing that!'

He stilled beside her, his gaze nothing but burning, hunger and silence.

Glancing away, she cleared her throat, but she could still feel the tension in him, a vibration almost against her skin that sent goosepimples along her arms.

He, too, looked away, exhaled roughly. She also felt him shift just that bit further away from her. She was relieved, except she didn't like the sudden coolness where only heat had been.

Balthus was grateful for the railing he was leaning on. Humbled by the woman who stood next to him. There was a strength to her that could never be locked up. Had it been there all along or had her trials along the way brought it into being?

He ached, knowing she wasn't his, but also in part because he was certain his brother had never known his wife like this. He wouldn't have dared. It would have made him too vulnerable. A man could easily love Séverine, but for a Warstone she'd be a liability.

When he'd first seen her she had been studying a tapestry. Now to know she was always searching for beauty? No, if she was always this way, maybe Ian had had a hint of who she was when he'd locked her in that wreck of a keep. Maybe he'd wanted to keep her safe. If that was so, he wasn't his brother. No matter what madness had plagued him, he could never have let her go.

What must Ian have thought to rip out his own heart, to cause himself further pain, anguish, to accelerate his own madness to save the woman he'd loved and his own sons?

Balthus didn't have that strength. He couldn't do it. He knew he couldn't, because even if he had any goodness in him, he'd tell her that her husband was dead so she could have her freedom, the one that Ian had ridden across the country for and defied his parents for. For that was what had happened. He'd packed them away and set them up in Forgotten Keep against his parents' wishes.

Just thinking about her, about Ian, about knowing he could never truly be with her... to know she searched for beauty...that wasn't him. He was broken. It was too much. Too much hurt.

'I didn't approve of how you were raising them,' he blurted.

She jerked. 'Excuse me?'

'Taking them away from wealth, and their status. That neither of them knows anything about becoming a knight.'

The horse in front of them shifted as if it felt Séverine's agitation. 'I think I'll say goodnight.'

'Wait.'

She raised a brow.

'I was concerned you were raising them as servants.'

She let go of the rail.

'I was worried that when our life was thrust upon them again, they wouldn't have the skills to protect themselves from my parents or whoever set out against them.'

She frowned. 'Their father was supposed to

have done that, and never did. Further, there is nothing wrong with how they are being raised. Sarah and Imbert are good people.'

'No, I know that now. I have Henry, remember?'

Her anger eased, but he could see she was still waiting to run.

'Let me say just a few words.' When she stayed, he continued, 'You're not raising them exactly like Sarah and Imbert, either. You're teaching them how to read, write, their numbers. When they eat, their serviette is placed over their shoulder as all nobility does.'

'I don't need you to tell me how to raise my children. Who are you to do so?'

'I'm nobody, but I know what it's like to be made into someone neither here nor there. There are many nobles, but being a Warstone makes you different. Being the youngest that much more. I wouldn't inherit the world like Ian, or torch it like Guy. I wasn't to be anything other than a Warstone, which made me have no purpose. And even different for a Warstone.'

She leaned back against the rail. 'What are you telling me?' she said.

He grinned. 'You believe me now.'

'I think you know we're past that,' she said.

Such hope, but they weren't past it. He was still lying to her.

'Is this what you wanted to tell me about, my children?'

He shook his head. 'Grant me a bit more.'

'You shouldn't be granted any leniency when it comes to them.'

'I think I understood that when you ran away from us.'

Something flashed in her eyes before she looked over his shoulder. He granted whatever silence she needed, especially since that allowed him to simply look at her. Even for a short time. That bump on her nose, those lips such an unusual colour, her high cheekbones and the abundance of hair. She handled that hair several times a day, perhaps trying to control it. If he wasn't so fascinated by the way she did it, he'd tell her not to try.

'What is it about them, then, Balthus, about the boys? I... I wonder a thousand times a day if I did the right thing. I know if I died, they'd be at someone's mercy. They don't even know who they are, and Sarah and Imbert would keep them away, but in the end there's been the certainty they'd be with your family again. I was simply hoping to last long enough so they could know there's another way.'

He couldn't not touch her, and when his hand clasped hers, she jerked but he did not let go.

'There is another way of life. I'm just now realising that. You did well to take them away.'

'What does Ian think?'

He released her hand. Ian...her husband. 'I can't say.'

'Surely he's talked to you.'

'Hardly ever.' When he saw her expression, he continued, though he'd be skirting the truth. There was always a part of him that feared Ian had guessed his feelings about Séverine, and had purposefully kept him in the dark, but that was not what he could ever tell her. 'You know how our parents kept us apart. It's not as if we're close.'

She looked at his hand, then rested her own against the railing and looked at the horse, who was fast becoming his favourite. He wondered if he could pay someone for him. Then remembered that his purse wasn't what it had once been, but it had been...enjoyable to be with them.

The days he spent in the boys' company he found fascinating. Would he have turned out like this if he had been born to different parents? Free to run across a pig pen to chase a gosling, to laugh with the utter freedom of jumping into a pond? And their hair, dark like a Warstone's, but when the sun came out from behind a cloud, that highlight of red that was unmistakably from their mother was obvious.

But so much more shone through them than mere hair colour. It was her influence that allowed them to be happy.

'The boys will do fine,' he said. 'Swinging their sticks, helping in the fields, have made them stronger than most. And it has given them arms capable of swinging a sword someday. They may right now be between worlds, but you've given them the chance to choose which one they want. It's far more than they ever had before. You've given them a chance at happiness now.'

'Oh!' she said, then burst into tears.

Balthus clasped her to him, his damaged arm bound to his chest so he could only hold her with one arm. Her sobs shook against his chest, her tears dampened his neck. She clung to him as if the world was falling apart, and he held on. Just held her.

To be held like this. Not simply by a man but by Balthus. To be held as if it meant something, which she knew it couldn't, but she could pretend at least. It felt like he meant it. She was a mess, but no one had said the words she needed to hear about her children. However, no one could except a Warstone. She never would have expected it from her husband. No, if it came from any Warstone at all, it would be Balthus. The one who displayed emotions, and was rough around the edges but so full of merit it made her heart hurt.

The burst of tears was quick.

'I didn't mean… I don't want you ever to cry.'

She rubbed her face with her hand, pulled back. She'd soaked his tunic. 'It's not you.'

'It sounded like it was. I said some things, and—'

Resting her hand on his chest, she patted him a few times. 'What you said was thoughtful, that is all.'

He clasped her hand against his chest, hard, and his expression changed. Nothing about him was any different. It shouldn't have been, and yet something altered. Grey eyes locked on hers, his hair waving down and covering one of his ears, the ease of his posture apparently in a state of relaxation, but he seemed tense, ready to pounce, as if the slightest provocation would alter him from a man who was comforting her to revealing his true nature. Not safe. Something dangerous.

No, something fierce and significant.

She couldn't blink. There was a tightening her chest, and the hand pressed firmly against his heartbeat grew damp. His eyes tracked her reaction, and he blinked, let out a long exhalation and released her hand.

She wanted to lower it, tried to, but it was almost stuck until it fell back down to her side.

Strange man, strange reaction.

'Sorry,' he said, a hint of remorse and too many other emotions he seemed to want to express. 'I've never been told I was kind before, at least not by someone who meant it.'

After her conversations with his mother and father, she knew what he meant. 'I did mean it.'

His eyes never leaving hers, he shook his head. After a moment when time seemed suspended, he cleared his throat and leaned against the horse blankets on the rail.

His stance was much the same as it had been when she'd entered. It was a bit darker, the horses far more settled, and she could hear no more sounds from outside except for the occasional scurrying of animals or perhaps it was some trees in the cool night wind.

It was odd that they had this time to themselves, without her children or interruptions. Her life hadn't been quiet for so long. When she allowed it to be so, the danger of her predicament usually encroached. But that had no place here.

Because of this man, no doubt. Whatever she feared from her husband's family, he was part of it. So the consequences of her actions were already here.

'I need to tell you something that you won't like.'

All the heat left her, and she braced her hand on the blankets. 'What is it? Did Henry send a message and Ian will be here tomorrow?'

'No.'

'What have you done?'

'It's what's already done.'

His eyes were serious, though his stance was casual. She didn't find it endearing, and instead of wanting to slide her hand around his waist she wanted to shove him away and flee.

'I don't like it when you do this.'

'I'm not withholding anything. Nothing new… But it's a reason I'm here.'

'I should check on the boys,' she said, although why she said it she didn't know. She needed to hear what Balthus had to say. She suspected it had something to do with needing to ensure they were well.

'They're safe for now,' Balthus said, 'What I have to tell you won't harm you...at least immediately.'

She blinked. 'Are you going to harm me?'

'Never.'

'Ian?'

A twist of something in his eyes, and he shook his head. 'Not my parents either, though I can't guarantee with them. It's why I've stayed.'

'I thought they'd protect me because of the boys, their grandchildren.'

'They might have once, but now it's uncertain.'

'Because I ran,' she said.

A muscle clenched in his jaw. 'In part...'

'What is that supposed to mean?'

He straightened. 'You are trusting me.'

His tone was incredulous, and perhaps at other times she'd feel sympathy for this man who wasn't used to trust, but not now. 'I'm trusting you less and less as this conversation continues.'

He pushed off the blankets and leaned his hip against the rack. 'There's no easy way to say all this. My parents want something the King of England wants.'

'The throne?'

He chuckled. 'True, but something else. You know how King Edward is obsessed with King Arthur and the Holy Grail, Excalibur and everything?'

'I don't blame him, I love those stories, too.'

'There are other tales he's obsessed with, as well. The Jewell of Kings.'

He looked at her as if she was supposed to say something, but she didn't know what it could be. 'It's an ugly gem.'

'Yes, but Reynold believes that it, along with the dagger it's hidden in, plus some pieces of parchment, perhaps even a map, leads to a treasure.'

'A legend with a treasure...' she said.

'Reynold's been studying it and believes that the legend, that whomever holds the gem holds Scotland, actually has other meanings. That it hides a treasure large enough to control countries.'

'That's unbelievable. I've never heard of all that.'

'You wouldn't have. I don't think it's common knowledge, although soon it might be.'

'Wait, are you telling me you think this legend, like King Arthur, is true?'

Balthus shrugged. 'We want it in our possession, not our parents'.'

'We? Your brothers are…going against your parents on this?'

A muscle spasmed in his jaw and he looked away. 'Against the King, as well. We believe that that neither should have such power or such treasure.'

'How long has this been going on?'

'Before you left. Reynold's been working on the tale for years,' he said. 'Are you believing me?'

'You're frightening me, and the ramifications are severe. But pardon me if you think I'll believe it safer in Warstone brothers' hands than in the King of England's.'

Balthus exhaled. 'Reynold wants to gather all the information, treasure, gem, dagger, and then…bury them.'

She almost laughed. 'That's convenient as it's already buried. I haven't heard of any such… You're saying that it's true, that the gem is out there.'

'Oddly, none of it is in our hands, but we know mostly who has the items. Reynold's been writing letters trying persuade a certain Scottish clan...the Colquhouns...to our side.'

She took a step back. 'I see why you believe I'd be harmed, but you said you wouldn't do so. Even having this information puts myself, my boys, in harm's way.'

'I know, but you're part of the solution.'

'For whom? You, the King or the War-stones?'

He grinned. That rakish smile, the fanning of lines from his eyes and the grooves in his cheekbones went straight to her centre. 'Clever.'

'Compliments will get you nothing. Tell me.'

'When you fled Forgotten Keep, you took several items.'

'Anything that wasn't pinned down.'

'Were any of those items books or pieces of paper...perhaps a map?'

She stepped away then, clasped her arms around herself and began to pace.

Balthus knew not to lay a hand on her or say another word. He'd pushed her enough, but he silently willed her to understand the importance of what he'd told her, and that no matter how he felt about her, this part of the mission couldn't be compromised. His heart, his life...

those were forfeit anyway, but he needed to do a good deed for Reynold, and he wouldn't fail.

'You told me that you had other villages along the way that you paid in coin and in certain items. To make traps.'

'You told me that was dangerous because I was subverting your parents' control. All the while you're doing it.'

She paced again, obviously frustrated at his comment. She had a right. It wasn't fair, but it was also the truth.

'You're cold?' he said.

'We've been here a while.'

They had, he found it odd that they'd had this opportunity, but he begged all the heavens to make it last. Looking around, he found a smaller blanket and handed it to her.

Sweeping it over her shoulders, she glared, and paced again. 'I've told you enough.'

'We're supposed to believe each other again.'

'But to tell you where these villagers, coins, traps and items are puts me and them in jeopardy.'

'They're already in jeopardy.'

She adjusted the blanket. 'Enough! Do you honestly believe I have it?'

'Ian had it.'

'All those artefacts he oversaw packing himself. If it was in Forgotten Keep, then he purposely put it...' She paled.

'My brother wasn't unintelligent...except for underestimating you.'

'I don't have anything here...a few coins... but it's not safe to travel with items anymore. Not without protection and...' Her eyes were wide and incredulous. Annoyed. 'Is that what your chasing me about the country has been about? Some foolish legend?'

'At least you know of it.'

'Your parents weren't quiet about it,' she blurted.

'My parents.'

Her eyes widened. 'Your brother.'

That was worse. 'Which was it, my parents or my brother? Neither is safe. What are you not telling me? If any of them told you about it, then you are in danger. They'll do anything to stop you.'

'It's nothing that you need to worry about.'

He stepped closer to her. 'It is.'

'Why?'

There was only one answer to this. The wrong one, but one he couldn't seem to help. He took another step closer. 'I think you know why.'

'Because I healed your arm?'

He shouldn't push it. He shouldn't, but he would, because he always wanted to. 'Think a little after that.'

When there was a slight flush to her neck. He wanted to bury his nose there, scrape his teeth, and taste the heat.

'You mentioned it,' she blurted.

That pulled him up from his actions and his thoughts. 'What?'

'When you were feverish. You mentioned many matters actually. I did say you might regret it.'

He felt the blood drain from his face. 'What else did I say?'

'Words. You weren't coherent. I…kept everyone away when you were like that.'

He'd thank her, but her voice, the way she held herself was so careful. Her worry told him what he should have guessed. 'Ian told you, didn't he? In his sleep.'

She pressed her lips.

'He used to sleep talk. We all knew this weakness of his.'

'I don't want to tell you…that's…'

'Did he say anything more personal than what I confessed to you when I was recovering?'

'No.'

'What I said was personal, wasn't it? Not about a legend at all.'

She fully blushed. It was he who should have. He'd been obsessed with this woman all his life. Judging from her trapped expression, she was begging him to change the subject, but there was only one conversation he wanted to have. He took a step away from the blankets and towards her.

Her eyes widened.

'I'll help you,' she said.

No. She wasn't escaping from him that easily. He took another step.

'I think I know where it is. I put all the books and scrolls in one place.'

'That's good. When do we go?'

'A few days. I think the others understand why you want them to tear down the wall but support the trenches. It may take more instruction, however, and...'

She shifted as if wanting to take another step back. It only heightened his need to possess, to chase her. They were closer, but not close enough. She clutched the blanket around her shoulders; all he wanted to do was rip it from her.

'Séverine,' he warned.

She straightened her shoulders, lifted her chin. 'I don't want to talk about it.'

A half step more and he caught her gently at her nape. He was aware of the way her eyes had darkened, the slight panting of her breath through her lips that had parted a bit more. The way he could feel, under his thumb, the fluttering of her heart.

The way she smelled of thyme and sunshine.

His own body reacted, the flush of heat, the palm touching her nape suddenly damp, the thundering of his heart. And his breath that wasn't anything as light as hers.

She didn't move. She didn't move when everything inside him wanted her not to. She quivered under his palm as if his just standing here…breathing with her…was something affecting her as much as he was affected.

Could she be as affected?

'Can't I say now what I didn't intend to then?' he asked. 'What I said when I was feverish, when all I felt and heard was you. When you called to me and pulled me from the dark?'

'No,' she whispered, immediate and sure. But there was a tremor behind her rushed voice, a flutter of her lashes, the tug inward of her lower lip. Minute changes in her wide green eyes, a pleading, but he knew they were not because she wanted him to heed her blurted denial of what was between them but because...because she felt the affinity between them, too. Because as much as he wanted to say the words to her, so there was no doubt how he felt, there was a part of her that wanted to hear it.

Her gaze roved his expression from his eyes to his lips, lingered there before stuttering back up, and he knew with certainty that Séverine wanted him, too.

'Very well.' He cupped his hand to the back of her nape, tilted her chin just so...just *right*, and kissed her. When she leaned into him, darted her tongue against his, he tightened his hand, stepped between her legs. And he kissed her more. A long-awaited kiss of years of want and wonder, of weeks of acute need. He drowned in the sensations, the length of her against him, lean, long limbs stiff with surprise, then pliant, wrapping around him, one hand gripping his arm, the other biting her nails into his shoulder. The sensation of kissing her, his tongue stroking hers, deepening the kiss before tearing free and pressing hot kisses on her lips, nips from his teeth, tongue. Just needing a taste of her, to saturate the emptiness inside with the thyme in her hair, the sunshine clinging to her skin. The scent of her, the one he'd never realised had haunted him, that he craved.

'Say no,' he growled. 'Tell me to stop.'

In the periphery was the shifting of horses, the smell of hay, of old wood damp with rain, but his world had narrowed to her. Stealing his arm around the small of her back, he pressed close, frustration at the distance forced by his bound arm, by the clothing they wore.

Her arm wrapped more tightly around his shoulders, and with a low primitive growl he splayed his fingers lower yet to feel the curve, the sway, to gain more purchase to press her tighter yet.

A sound of want from her that poured lust hotly through his blood until he was a man consumed, and he noticed too late the shift away of her hips, the tips of her fingers rasping a release of his collar. Alerting his body that she was pulling away.

Desperate hunger compelled him to duck his head, to grasp the last moment between them. A flick of his tongue against the delicate spot beneath her chin, a nip to her ear. One slow meaningful kiss to the corner of her mouth. She was beautiful, her cheeks flushed, the scrape of his stubble marking her delicate complexion, her lips swollen from the pressure of pulling her tighter.

Balthus stepped back, just when Séverine did. His hip hit against the blanket rack and he leaned against it for something to steady himself. Waiting for her to strike him across the jaw, to hurl the words they needed to hear, to watch in agony as she turned away to leave him behind.

Her breath was shallow, as quick as his own that sawed through his lungs. As he tried to cool his need for her, his eyes greedily soaked her in. Slowly, never taking her eyes away from his, she unlaced the ties at her side. He shuddered, her lips curved, and her gown dropped. He swiped a blanket off the rack and threw it to their feet to add to the one that must have fallen from her shoulders when he first clutched her close.

Grabbing her wrist that clenched her chemise, he raised the limb to his lips and nipped along the curve to her elbow, pulling her closer with each taste, ducking his head and inhaling along the delicate cords in her neck. She took advantage of their proximity, and her featherlight fingertips played with the linen tied at his neck, then danced along his collar bone, his shoulder, palming flesh that mere weeks ago had been in agony.

Her movements were slight, nothing more than brushes of one finger, then another that dipped into the hollow of his throat and then behind his ear. Touches that he felt everywhere until they spiralled, heat heavier and heavier until his desire pooled lower and slowed down. While he secured her arms around him, thrust his knee between her legs, and lowered them both to the floor, his balance secure, perfect, because she was in his arms.

Still, he relished the widening of her eyes, the slight whimper of her worry that the movement would hurt him somehow. The only way it would was if she stepped away again, and he would ensure that wouldn't happen. Not until she was his in some permanent way.

Shuffling her chemise up and over her legs, his weight over her, his mouth once again capturing her lips, the sounds she made as his hand travelled from her thigh, over her hip and to her belly. To circle a finger around her navel and then trail it between her breasts.

He tugged on her lower lip, pulled it into his mouth and suckled gently as he trailed his fingers under her bunched chemise up over one nipple and then the other. The frustration built for her as her hips rocked, for him as he wished his other limb to be unbound so he could anchor them together. To feel, not only see, the tension in her body grow. Groaning against her lips, he shifted his own weight so that his body was there for her to rock against, to ease the ache he created.

And she did, stopping and shuddering as she realised what he had done. He hissed out a breath as he ripped his mouth from hers and kissed everywhere the chemise didn't cover, his hand roaming and caressing her breasts, pebbling her flesh.

'Balthus!' she cried, her hands caressing his shoulders, her nails scraping across his linen tunic.

He cursed as his hips went forward, and he lost his balance. Until he had no choice but to go forward or pull back. Needing her permission for either choice. It was her choice. His choice was hers.

'Séverine, tell me.' He bit and swiped his tongue along the curve of her ear.

With a knowing gleam in her eyes, she shifted until she was completely under him. His reason scattered; his need increased. Dropping his head into the angle of her neck and shoulder, he helplessly thrust once, twice. Unable, unwilling, to stop the instinct that she yield to him. Raising himself up on one arm, he gazed down at the woman who'd captured his imagination. His heart sprawled beneath him, and he murmured words of her strength, her beauty, and his frustration at her chemise that thwarted his touch. But he shook his head when she gripped his tunic.

'Not yet,' he murmured. *Not ever.* As much as he wanted her, he didn't deserve her. This time was for her.

He sat up, and gradually, achingly, let his eyes roam down her body where her legs were sprawled around him, where she was wet and wanting.

'So beautiful,' he said. 'Whenever you blushed, I wondered about the colour of your flesh here.' He circled his thumbs around her plump lips. 'Never in my imagination did I imagine how exquisite you'd be.'

Letting his hand wander, he stroked along her inner thighs around her hips, a pattern he repeated with no shape or purpose other than to touch, to feel. Her own hands suddenly sneaked under his short tunic and swept across his stomach, causing the muscles to contract, his balls to tighten, and on a strangled moan he stopped her questing touch. Shifting his weight away from her hands, he cupped one knee and raised it to her hip, opening her up even more. Her breath hitched, her hands dropped to the blanket and clutched there.

Then he smiled.

Séverine both feared and exulted in Balthus's burning grey gaze. Wicked, tender touches. Callused gentle caresses. Her body didn't know how to react. To stay still and beckon or move to demand more. All she knew was that she could deny this man nothing. For to deny him would be to deny herself, too. Never could she have expected this from him. Never this night near horse stalls on rough wool blankets as he released her leg and smiled more. Then, with more light than darkness, he cupped her other knee and bent it towards her chest, too.

When he released that leg, she kept it still and his predatory smile grew. 'So good,' he whispered. 'So perfect.'

His gaze fell heavy between her legs and everything around her sharpened. The stars seen just through the loose slats along the back wall were brighter, the colours on the draped blankets more vivid. Never had she felt like this, never had she been touched so that her body reacted. Only with this man with his every touch telling her of his searing need and deep ache.

He shifted down, dropped his weight.

'No,' she said.

'Yes,' he rasped. The shocking need in his voice kept her still as he feverishly kissed her belly, his hand caressing her splayed legs. Wide circles on her heated skin, until his touches turned lighter, his kisses slower, languishing. Lower. Tender presses of his mouth, beckoning flicks of his tongue.

She tugged at the blanket, pulled at his tunic. Yanked on his hair. He lifted, his eyes narrowing on her, his lips slick from kissing her, his cheeks flushed. He looked as if she had ravished him.

She swallowed audibly, unsure what she meant to say. To tell him to stop or to continue? Keeping his eyes on hers, he dipped his hand between her legs and pressed his palm against her mons. A needy whimper crossed her lips and a wicked look gleamed in his eyes.

'I'll stop if you mean it, Séverine. Do you?'

Partly. The act was unbearably intimate, then he flicked one finger against her slick folds.

'That's unfair.' She huffed a shaken breath.

A wicked, knowing smile as he did it again. 'Yes or no?'

A frisson of unease went through her. He wanted her to make a decision feeling like this, wanting this? And knowing she—? No. She didn't want to remember. She didn't need to, it had never been like this. Eyes searching hers, his smile dropped; his hand stilled.

She grabbed his wrist. 'I want this, I want—'

With a gentleness and strength that was entirely Balthus, he lifted her to his mouth, and began again. Lengthened caresses, vibrations from his words, his thumb circling, pressing. The feeling— She moaned. 'It's too much, no, I want—'

'Your pleasure.' He licked, licked again. 'Yours. nothing more.'

'I want you.'

He grunted against her flesh, sawed his tongue, her words seemingly setting him off, spiralling and tightening her body until she only wanted release. 'Give me this,' he demanded.

This wasn't right, this wasn't all she wanted. She wanted to see…utter joy in his eyes. That look they shared, that touch when she didn't push him away. That communion when he rested his… Then there was no room for argument, no voice for words. No thought except Balthus and his demand, his pleas against her thighs, against the fold of her skin, against— She released on a keening cry that he swallowed up with his kisses, with his words of adoration.

Each easing of the tremors and shudders in Séverine's glorious body Balthus felt to his very marrow. Her eyes tightly closed, her breaths stuttering out of plump, damp, kissable lips. Her entire body was radiant with sated desire. He memorised the patterns of freckles against her cheeks, the fan of her lashes suntipped honey-blonde on the ends, the wings of her eyebrows that mimicked the fine lines framing eyes that darkened to unfathomable depths the longer he kissed her.

When she opened her eyes, they sparked like stars, her lips gently curved; she was a woman loved, and he hoped she felt it. In silence they continued to touch, her with a hand on his cheeks, him with circles around her hip. The angle was awkward, with his bound arm preventing him from fully holding her. But he didn't regret it, not when it was she who wrapped him in the linen.

With her, he didn't feel disfigured. He felt...

'What are you thinking?' She playfully

swiped a finger between his brows, and he eased himself up.

He didn't want to think at all. Thinking meant he'd remember that he was still lying to her…as he lay against her, like a husband with his wife. Like he'd always wanted.

Like he was sure Ian never had. If he had, and had basked in the soft wonder on her face, how could his brother have ever left her? If there had been moments like these, why would she have run? He knew he wondered not out of anything spiteful or jealous but because… because it frightened him. Because if Ian and Séverine had touched, kissed…if it had felt like this between them and still it had fallen apart, then what hope for him? He had no wealth, no children, he lacked a hand and a way to touch her as any other man could.

And there were times when Séverine hinted that even six years ago Ian's madness had plagued him, that perhaps he'd been cruel. The servants left at Forgotten Keep hadn't said much, which had told him they were still loyal to its mistress, but what he did know was that Ian had raced to the location and left the next day. He'd left his wife in a keep needing work, in a place away from anyone she'd known. And she still needed to run?

'Tell me of my brother. What he did to you, what happened to make you escape.'

She gasped, sat up abruptly, her eyes stricken.

Too late.

For him, he knew his brother was dead and gone. That what they had shared, while unsanctioned by vows, was not wrong. But she didn't, and he might as well have slapped her. He should have been spouting tender words, more tender touches. Finding some way to prolong this encapsulated warmth in this shored-up stable.

Instead, he'd hurt her.

Pulling her legs out from under his body, she scrambled for her clothes. Her breath in pants.

'Séverine—' he began.

She sliced her hand through the air. 'Don't say my name as if it's an answer or a question. Don't say anything.'

He stood with her, gathered up the blankets while she dressed.

There was no warmth in those green eyes, no pliable rest in her body. Her shoulders were tense, her hands curling as if she wanted to strike him. He deserved it.

'We'll travel in a few days to the abbey, which is also in France.'

'The abbey?'

'The one by Forgotten Keep. It's where I left all the books and parchments and scrolls. They should still be safe there.'

He folded the blankets on the rack. 'I'll tell Henry to travel ahead. To scout for danger.'

'He's not to go to the abbey.'

'No, just the keep.'

'I'll give him a token, so they know he's from me.'

He wanted to say so much, but this generous woman was closed to him once again. And that had nothing to do with being Warstone or an enemy and everything to do with his own failings.

Chapter Fifteen

'One of us didn't return to their bed last night,' Henry said.

'Could you say that in a more resounding voice? The children didn't hear it.'

Henry raised a brow. 'Do you want them to?'

No. He pulled Henry away from the village and out near the woods in the cold morning to keep as much of this conversation private as possible. It would be noted he hadn't returned until late, and everyone would see he was now having a private conversation with his butcher. There was nothing to be done about that.

'I have some matters to discuss with you.'

Henry shook his head. 'I don't want to know.'

'All those weeks on the road where you were begging me to talk so you didn't have to have conversations with trees and now you want quiet?'

Henry crossed his arms. With his considerable size and girth, it just pushed his stomach out. The man was like an ox; Balthus was glad he didn't have to train him.

'I want quiet because I like it here. There's this widow who has the veriest set of—'

Balthus held his hand up. 'That has nothing to do with—'

'It has everything to do with it. I should never have got tied up with the Warstones.'

'You were raised at Ian's fortress.'

'I was too young to know any better. I do now. If you tell me what you want, it'll all be about some task that'll take me away, and I'm not interested. I was better off when I was simply your butcher who tied your boots,' Henry said.

When Henry's face darkened, probably in an apology he didn't want, Balthus said, 'I was better off when you weren't a man who tied my boots because your pay was double.'

Henry let out a bark of laughter.

Balthus did, too. Of all the certainties in life, having this man as a friend would never have been conceivable until now. Therefore, it made what he had to say next all the more difficult, but it was necessary. 'I have to tell you for *their* sake.'

At Henry's reluctant nod, he began the tale of the Jewell of Kings, the parchment, the mission, and what needed to be done to obtain them. That he had to travel with Séverine and her boys, when at any moment his parents could seize them.

When he was done, he gave Henry a moment as he paced, rubbed his face, let out growls that were expressions of frustration, disbelief. Until the wide man stood before him again.

'I'll never understand matters like this,' Henry said. 'The certainty of our foolishness makes nothing better.'

The insolence! But Balthus welcomed it. It felt better than the reserve and fear he'd been treated with all his life.

'At least I know where you stand,' he said.

'Why are you telling me any of this?' Henry said.

Balthus had asked himself that a dozen times. Henry was still a servant. He had no compunction in using his skill as a butcher. He wasn't the mercenary Louve, who wanted to save the world. Henry, out of all of them, could be free.

'I'm telling this because we can't travel like you. You can get there far quicker than any of us.'

'And I need to arrive at the keep before you to see if it's safe.'

'I can't blindly travel to a place without knowing if I put them in jeopardy.'

'Ah, you care…and you trust.'

He wouldn't deny it. 'If there was any other way…'

'I know you don't feel comfortable sending me on ahead, not because you feel I can't do it but because you fear something would happen to me. And yet you can't go ahead yourself because you'd put the woman and boys in danger.' Henry chuckled. 'You risk me because you more than care for them. I see how you look at each other. Know that when your back is turned she watches you like a woman in love. I know she wasn't near her home either last night. Which brings us back to the fact you're a fool because I'm guessing you still haven't told her about Ian.'

Balthus couldn't. If he did, he'd lose her. The only time he could have… No, at any time he told her it would be the end. She'd fled from Warstones, and when she knew she was released from her marriage vows, she wouldn't have anything to do with them again. He was selfish, and a coward. She shouldn't have anything to do with him.

'It's none of your concern what I have and haven't said to my sister-in-law,' he said.

Henry snorted. 'Since I'm about to die for some task you've given me, I say it is my concern.'

This was the hell he'd brought on himself by bringing a servant from whom he had no secrets.

'She loves you, but you'll ruin everything when she finds out you've been withholding the truth.' Henry stepped back, exhaled slowly. 'You don't plan to tell her.'

'Again, what I tell her has nothing to do with you, butcher. We need to ride to the keep; she needs to go the abbey to find something my brother needs. I'll be on my way then.'

'Do you intend to send her a letter afterward and have a messenger report it?'

He hadn't thought that far ahead, but what other choice did he have? He didn't think he could face telling her now. After he'd seen how she looked at him with warmth and curiosity in a way she usually reserved for beautiful things. To know what kissing her, touching her was like, and to see it fade. To see it disappear and change to something like disgust. He wasn't ready to let her go.

Henry crossed his beefy arms. 'You're worse than a fool.'

Balthus narrowed his eyes. 'Will you do what I've asked?'

'Why, yes, my lord. I'm a servant and have been ordered to—'

'Don't say it.'

For once Henry didn't.

'Don't jest. I told you more than most because I don't want you underestimating them. You do need to fear them.'

'Them? You're no longer a Warstone?'

He didn't know what he was anymore. The longer he stayed with Séverine, the more time he spent with her boys…he didn't recognise himself.

But he should for her sake because she was running from Ian and from all Warstones. She didn't want her boys to turn out like them, and she was right to protect them. The crux was…he was one. And he was still lying to her. Now too cowardly to tell her after what they'd shared. He didn't deserve her, no matter how much he longed to be someone else. Someone who had beauty she wanted to find.

No matter how much he longed for her.

Chapter Sixteen

Séverine no longer questioned riding beside Balthus, the boys weaving between Imbert and Sarah, all on the way to return to a place she'd sworn she'd never go to again. Her life wasn't a question of whether something was wise, or safe or correct. She'd passed those barriers long ago when she'd run away with her children, run from her husband and hidden from the rest of the family.

She could never pretend she was simply weak or distressed or a victim to fate because during those six years of running she'd set up havens and traps to protect herself and her children.

If Balthus was correct, she was also creating small forces who would defend her and the children. Her! So far she come from that fateful day when she'd been snatched from dreams of living in the abbey near her home.

Even if she wanted to return to that life, she'd lived too much to sequester herself now, and her children still needed her.

She needed... Balthus.

She'd never been kissed or touched like that. Wanted. She'd been taken from her life and then forced into Ian's, only then to be set aside again. She'd never felt married while she'd lived under Ian's roof. Now she'd been away six years, running, hiding from a man who scared her. A powerful, wealthy man... who hadn't found her. Had he even looked for her? From the moment that Lady Warstone had clutched her wrist, she'd felt like a possession tossed between Ian and his parents. In fairness, she'd felt safer with Ian, but only because he'd kept her locked away, even from himself. With few visits and even fewer times he had lain with her.

In the end and until that day he'd left her, the idea of being safe had been a tenuous one at best. Like standing on moving sand that eroded to the pounding waves of the sea of his parents' control.

She shouldn't have done those things with Balthus, and there had been that moment when it seemed he'd braced himself to receive her umbrage. But ever since she'd heard his feverish words, seen the light in his grey eyes when he'd felt only relief, she'd wanted him. So she'd taken off her gown. She thought he understood what was between them. Thought he felt it, too. But while the warmth they'd shared still coursed within her, he'd struck her with the truth: she was his brother's wife.

Hurt. Embarrassed certainly. After all, if that was how he saw her she shouldn't have throw herself at him. And why wouldn't he? It may have been six years since she'd seen her husband, but for all she knew, Balthus had seen him within the last few months.

Had he truly broken away from his parents and bound himself to Reynold's cause? If so, why trust her with that truth and then mention Ian? Was she also part of the cause because she'd broken away?

Did she want to be? It was too unbelievable to be true, and yet she believed him. She couldn't imagine such a life, facing danger, fighting, all over chasing a treasure. That was a life as far from studying books and tapestries as could be. No, that wasn't the life for her or the one she wanted for her children. She'd never understand this family. She didn't want to…but her children were at risk. She must help.

So though she wanted to stay away from Balthus, she rode beside him. Worse, they rode toward a keep she hated. All to obtain a parchment which could, perhaps, defeat his parents. All those moments she'd felt a closeness with him, had he…lied? Had it all been to seduce her so he could get the parchment? The irony of it wasn't lost on her. Hadn't she healed him to use him? She could see now that was a foolish belief.

Thus, he'd get his parchment and instead of forming some alliance with him, she needed to stay away from danger and disappear once again.

'Why is your family the way they are?' she asked. 'Why do they do what they do?'

Balthus slowed his horse and looked over at her. His expression was inscrutable. Nothing in his grey eyes gave her any indication that he'd heard her, let alone understood what she was saying. She wasn't certain she understood what she was trying to convey. Her family had noble blood, they wanted wealth and power, and she couldn't say their marriages and schemes were not conducted in order to gain more of both. But they were also generous and gave to the arts, to the villages and the abbeys. They were generous with their children up to a point. She hadn't wanted to marry a Warstone, but even they couldn't refuse such a good match. Still…

'Why have there been no *consequences* against them?' she added, because that was what she truly wanted to know. There were consequences for everyone who ever came into contact with them, and yet they never suffered.

Balthus rode quietly beside her. As her questions continued, his gaze slipped past her shoulder and out to the trees beyond. Not to avoid her, though; she knew that now. There was much under the surface when it came to him. No, in the little time they'd spent…since that moment in the stables, there were fissures in the darkness he cloaked himself in that allowed her to see a truer Balthus. But once this was over, what then? Nothing. There was no future for them.

'I don't know,' he said. 'I'd like to say there were books written by my ancestors, or that my parents regaled us with stories of their childhood that would explain what they do. I don't even know if one was more deceitful than the other and by being together they grew worse, or if there was a horrific event that made them that way. I do know our wealth spans generations on both sides, which leads me to believe the roots were planted long before they bore their sinister fruit.'

That kind of familial history she could believe. How else to have as much as they did if it hadn't been acquired over generations. How else to be so adept at planting massacres and chaos if the roots weren't already corrupt?

A cry pulled their attention to the right where Clovis and Pepin rode behind two of the villagers, both with their willow sticks that they pointed to each other. From Clovis's mutinous expression it was clear Pepin's stick must have struck. From the expression of the men they rode with, it was equally apparent that the game had lost its appeal.

'They never stop.' She sighed. 'I keep hoping that perhaps they'll grow out of it, or Clovis will realise Pepin is younger, or Pepin will stop competing or…something.'

'I think that is typical in any family,' Balthus said. 'My parents had intentions for us, but there were rare instances where we were siblings like Clovis and Pepin. Once there was this hive. I don't know who challenged whom or why anyone would rise to it. We were all laughing, even Guy, who was running into the lake because the hive focused on him.'

'He likely deserved it.'

Balthus chuckled. 'No doubt. I do wish... I do wish I had been kinder to Reynold, who is different, but I didn't appreciate it then.'

'You're younger than the rest. How could you know?'

'He did. I, however, never questioned a mother holding her sons' hands to a flame, or a father forcing their guards to hold the inside of a ladder until time was called or their shoulders dislocated. Depending on his mood, he'd either grant mercy to the poor soul or spear him through the gut. I'd like to say the ones who got the swords had other weaknesses, so they were no good as Warstone guards, but that wasn't so. I watched good men die at the whims of my father, who affectionately helped with the fitting of my first coat of plates.'

'You're saying you can't hate them, though you have allied with Reynold,' she said.

He looked around them. 'All of this is new. The betrayals, the— I don't doubt that as the years continue there will be enough deceit to bury me in hate for them. There's enough they have already done...'

'Your hand.'

'That truly was my doing to prove my loyalty to her. I held it too long.'

'There's something else you're not telling me.'

'Weeks went by with it not healing. When I saw her again, she held my hand as if she cared, and then broke my fingers while it was still wrapped.'

What could she say? She loved her family, she tried to instil that love in her children. She was horrified but not surprised. 'I'm sorry.'

'Again, I was only aware of the unusualness of my household when I was old enough to know better, but I did nothing as I was a Warstone who gained from their games. You may feel sorry for me, but I had a part in their cruelty.'

Ian had been aware of their cruelty, had hidden her away, but he'd frightened her all the same. Balthus didn't, but he might be different around his family.

'They are cruel,' he said.

'I know.'

His hand gripped the reins. 'Did she ever…?'

'That day she grabbed my wrist was the last time she ever touched me, but there were threats when I was carrying Ian's children. I feared for them. Do I need to fear for their future again? I'll go to the abbey, exchange coin for the books I left, but afterwards what certainties do I have?' She knew she'd hide again, but she couldn't do it for long.

Balthus sighed. 'You've eluded them for years and taken their grandchildren. They've been under the impression, I was under the impression, that you were terrified in some hovel in some other country. But instead you've been right under their noses, going from village to village, spreading their wealth freely without expectations, and have gained trust and loyalty.'

'That was only a few people, some servants I asked for help, and they gave it. They love the children, and saw how Ian treated me…and… Why are you looking at me like that?'

'You don't understand. I've tried to tell you. You left two servants of a Warstone household that are no longer loyal to Warstone but to you, and not only that, you give them wealth and an order to create a place to hide away from Warstones or their guards. No two servants could build enough on their own, so they encourage and trust a few others, and so on. You may have left Sarah and Imbert here, but it was the whole village who protected you from me, wasn't it?

'Do you think they have family and friends they told?' he continued. 'Of course they did. You created an army that at your mere word would rise against my family.

'In the meantime, their own sons are collaborating against them. If we gain the power of the Jewell of Kings, that'll keep them in check, and then…time will do the rest. They'll die, and their legacy will be over.'

His words. Resolute determination. Unfaltering conviction, and that visceral rawness he carried with him. That no matter how much he had to scrape to carry out these deeds, he would.

And for once Séverine thought she saw a sliver of light at the end of this for her and her children.

'They're your mother and father,' she said. Under all the plotting and cruelty, that was what affected her most.

'Though they are the grandparents to Clovis and Pepin, it changes nothing.'

'But…'

'Say it.'

'Ian is loyal to them. I remember you from before…you are loyal to them.'

'I cared for them as a child would any parent. My parents and the people who support them must be defeated.'

'Your brothers?

'Any betrayal by them that you worry about for the future…has already been done. I am not a good man, Séverine, though…' A muscle spasmed in his jaw and his raw grey eyes stayed on hers. 'Though I wish I could be.'

Too much.

Balthus turned away from her, his gaze elsewhere, his attention on their surroundings, but it was too much. Not only for the relationships around her, but for this man and his family. For Ian her husband, too, she had to remind herself.

But Ian had become… He wasn't true to her anymore. She'd never wanted to understand him like she did Balthus, but, further, he had never revealed himself. An inexplicable sadness settled against her heart because although it was the logical decision to go against the Warstones, there was a sense of loss there, as well.

Though what Balthus, Ian, what her children had lost was lost long before they were born. That loss of…love. Looking at the man who rode beside her, she wondered if he knew what it even was.

Chapter Seventeen

Another day to travel, another day of lying to the woman he loved. The further they rode, the further he knew he wasn't worthy of her, the more he tried to create barriers to keep himself away from her. And…as wrong as it was, it was Ian, her husband, his dead brother, who was the last barrier.

She'd been a dream, a fantasy to him all his adult life, and over the last days of knowing her he'd given her his heart. That night in the stables when he had been permitted to hold her, it had been everything and not enough. Wrong and yet right.

He'd ruined it by mentioning his brother, and yet he'd saved them both because he had. He needed to stay away from her. He wasn't worthy of her. Even if he wasn't lying now, he'd lied in the past, killed, was cruel.

There wasn't enough forgiveness in all the world to wipe his soul clean. And he wouldn't, shouldn't soil Séverine's soul by trying. And her boys. Whether because he felt the tension in his mother, or because Séverine was desperate to keep the boys apart, Pepin rode with Séverine, almost on her lap.

And because he was desperate to spend more time with them, he offered to take Clovis, which immediately didn't go well.

'I don't see how this helps you.' Clovis took Balthus's hand and swung himself up.

'With balance. Your teaching me how to tie my boots will only get us so far.'

Although whether Clovis was pleased with that decision, he didn't know. The boy held himself apart.

It was time to have his own horse, and he knew it. The village hadn't had enough horses to spare, though, so the boy rode stiffly and awkwardly with him.

'Where's your family?' Pepin called out.

'Pepin,' Séverine warned.

Balthus didn't need to be warned. Though he'd had the conversation with Clovis, it was still Séverine's decision.

'I have a mother,' Balthus said.

'Does she like playing hide-and-seek, too?' Pepin asked.

His mother liked her games, but that wasn't one of them. 'She...hates fruit,' he answered.

'Is she our grandmother?' Clovis said.

He felt that question as well as heard it. From Séverine's wavering eyes towards him, she had felt it, too.

'She can't be our grandmother,' Pepin said. 'We have Mama, and Sarah and Imbert.'

'Sarah isn't our grandmother,' Clovis said.

'I have brothers,' Balthus offered, but only because he was desperate. He realised immediately his mistake. How could this conversation be so hard? A few moments of travelling, not even time for a midday meal, and already he wanted to hand them to someone else.

'Where are they?' Clovis said.

Gone. Balthus looked at Séverine. She looked worried but resigned. She was coming to the same conclusion as him. How much to tell? 'Far away.'

'Why aren't you with them?'

'Because I'm here,' Balthus said. 'I miss them. My mother loved my eldest brother, Ian.'

'Why did she love Ian?' Clovis asked. His voice was too keen. Did he guess Balthus was talked about his father? Perhaps. He had mentioned he knew him.

'He was the first. My father loved him, too. He didn't like fruit, either.'

'I won't like fruit,' Clovis said.

Séverine made some noise of discomfort.

'Sorry, Mama,' Pepin said. Then he looked at Balthus. 'I have a hard head.'

Balthus chuckled.

'Is this man our father?' Clovis blurted.

Utter silence. Balthus held his breath.

'Why would you say that?' Séverine's voice wavered.

'He keeps following us. Our father would follow us.'

'He's not,' Pepin said. ''Cause Mama pushed him in a pit.'

'But she wrapped his arm,' Clovis said.

He needed to change the subject. Something safe and yet trustworthy. Something that wouldn't be about his family, or any feeling of belonging or that he wanted to be these boys' father.

'I forgot I had something of someone's,' Balthus said.

Clovis craned his neck to look as Pepin shouted, 'What is it?'

He realised his mistake too late. While riding, he couldn't get into the pouch attached to his horse without a hand.

'It's in this pouch here.'

Clovis looked down at the pouch. 'You don't have anything.'

'Oh?' he said, enjoying teasing the boy. It made the time and effort of searching a dark pit worth it. 'It's about this round, this flat and—'

'My treasure!' Pepin said.

'Careful!' Séverine said.

'Sorry, Mama,' Pepin said, a huge grin on his face.

'It's not your treasure,' Clovis said.

'Yes, it is. I dropped it in the pit.' Pepin looked at Balthus. 'That's where you found it?'

'Right there in the darkest part.'

'It's not yours because I'm the one who found it,' Clovis said.

'By the stream!' Pepin said. 'That doesn't count. There are loads of stones by the stream. The one you found is different.'

'How can a stone be a treasure and you two fighting over it?' Séverine said. 'Is it made of silver?'

'Your mother doesn't know how to skim stones, does she?' Balthus said.

Clovis snorted and Balthus grinned. The

boy may have more of his mother in him than he'd thought.

'It's very, very rare,' Pepin said. 'Clovis didn't like it that I found it first. Do you skim stones with friends?' Pepin asked.

It went quiet and Balthus realised the question of friendship was aimed at him. A few months ago, he could never have envisioned this much happy conversation. Neither could he have imagined that the answer to the question of friendship would be positive.

'I have a friend,' Balthus said.

The boys went quiet, so did Séverine. It was surprising to him, too, that he could announce such a thing. Other than his family, he had had no close ties with anyone. It was also surprising to talk of friendship, but Balthus would confess to a thousand odd things as long as they kept away from anything important.

'His name is Louve. He used to live in this place called Mei Solis.'

'An odd name,' Séverine said.

'Very. He didn't name it.' As if that was important as to whether they could have a friendship. If Louve knew he was having this conversation, Louve would think *he* was odd.

'Where is he now?' she asked.

Ian's home. Hers, if she had stayed. 'Warstone Fortress.'

Séverine looked at Clovis, and Balthus tensed, but the boy didn't say anything, and Pepin had lost interest. Did they not remember or know their name? A feeling of loss hit him. To have family, and not. To desire to claim them, and he couldn't.

'Why do you talk in the past when it comes to your family?' she said.

'Pardon?'

'You always talk about them in the past. Not now, but often.'

He must have when he'd talked about Ian, and she'd noticed. 'I'm away from them.'

He could feel her eyes on him, so he kept his gaze ahead. Watched their small group travel. Big enough to be noticed but too small for anything defensive. Imbert with no skill for fighting and him with only one hand and who would easily tire if attacked. He'd vowed he'd protect her and on their first venture out, he was a poor example.

Would they make it to their destination or meet enemies along the way? How long could he stay in her company and hide the truth from her? Once he had the parchment, if she did possess the parchment Reynold wanted, he needed to leave. His mission would be accomplished.

His good deed to prove to his brother Reynold that he was trustworthy would be complete, and yet... The more time he spent with them, the harder it was to think of leaving. It was also more difficult to keep the truth from her. It wasn't lost on him that what he was doing wasn't good for Séverine or her children. That by fulfilling the vow to his brother, he'd break any vows he made to her.

Chapter Eighteen

Despite the cool evening air, Séverine woke up feeling restless. The travelling was tiring, but sleep eluded her. She didn't question why. Tomorrow they would arrive at the outer village of the Forgotten Keep. Once they crossed over the last hill and through the next small forest they would see the abbey near the keep.

She would be back where she'd started six years ago.

Something poignant kept pinching her heart that had everything to do with the man who travelled with them. The one who all day looked both settled and lost.

She didn't think Balthus's reaction had anything to do with the way they were travelling, which hadn't eased the journey. She thought her holding Pepin would somehow keep a more orderly procession, but Clovis rode with Balthus and Balthus near her so they weren't separated at all. It had all been natural, though. As if the four of them riding together was meant to be.

Dangerous thoughts when Balthus wasn't here for her or the boys but for some ridiculous mission rife with games, power and control. All the traits she loathed when it came to Warstones.

But she wasn't prepared for the boys' questions and what they'd do to her heart. Neither was Balthus, and it half amused, half terrified her. She didn't know what he would say. She didn't want to lie to her children, but she didn't know if Balthus wanted to acknowledge he was family.

In her own mind, she could hardly call him a brother-in-law. Did he feel like an uncle to Clovis and Pepin? No. In the moments they'd shared he'd felt like their father. One whom she knew...and didn't.

Who was Louve, and why was he at Warstone Fortress? Where was Ian? Was he looking for them?

And Balthus... She didn't watch him as an enemy. She watched him as a woman did a man. In some deep part of herself she'd noticed it from the beginning; it was the way he held himself. The elegant mantle that his brother wore as if it were inherent, he wore like a cloak he could easily, and often did, discard.

There was something more impulsive and raw about him that she achingly wanted to touch. But her restlessness came from the way he'd cared for Clovis today and had so carefully answered her boys' questions.

Tomorrow, if what she'd left at the abbey was what he needed, he would leave. Her restlessness increased, and she knew she cared. That, despite his words in the stables, despite the fact that he was a man whom she should only mistrust and hate, she couldn't stop thinking of him. She needed to talk to him. Perhaps he didn't need to leave alone. She hated the dangerous games he needed to play, but she still needed to run, which had its own inherent dangers. Moreover, he had severed ties with his family so perhaps the risks were less. Maybe tomorrow wasn't all there would be. Maybe they could find a way to be together.

Tonight, Balthus was keeping watch at the outer part of their circle, far past the other watch guard and the farthest from the fire. When he'd volunteered for such a shift, she'd worried about him because he was still recovering. However, if there was one trait about the Warstones...no, that comparability had ended long ago. The fact he undertook the hardest task hadn't anything to do with Warstones, who would have bludgeoned others into doing it for them. Balthus sat up in the middle of the night in the cool air because it was his turn. It was simply his duty to do so and he did it.

Before she knew what she was doing, her feet took her to the last place she'd seen him. What she found was a man sitting and leaning against a tree, sound asleep. It was as startling as finding snow bells through ice. Just as beautiful and unexpected. Hardy and yet…vulnerable, if such a word could be applied to Balthus. His black hair slashing downwards and long lashes casting shadows against his cheekbones and jaw. The tightness to his jaw, the quirk to his lips that made her heart quicken was instead softly rounded. She wanted to kiss him. To wake him and watch his eyes open. Wanted to know if the kiss would proceed to more.

However, if she woke him now, he might not be pleased he'd slept. Ever vigilant, she could well imagine him berating himself on his weakness. Maybe she could even tease him a bit.

Where were these thoughts coming from? She had no right to tease or wake him with kisses, and wasn't she angry with him? After the stables when he reminded her of Ian, and…

no, there had been more shared between them since then. And now he was weary because he pushed himself to protect her and the boys on this journey. How could she hold herself back from this man? A tender part of herself opened up to him, and now she wanted to soothe him.

He was beautiful in that masculine way that was impossible to describe. He still reminded her of that brutal yet riveting tapestry, the one that if she studied it, she'd have an idea of the weaver's skill. With him, she wanted to be closer. Days with him, weeks, she'd touched him in a way only a healer should, but all the time she'd admired the way he was made. Then he'd kissed her, kissed her again, and his touch? It had been her unravelling.

Now he slept, and something daring wove through her. Would she heed it? Lifting her skirts ever so carefully, she stepped towards him and still he slept. He'd pushed himself so hard, all to help her, to defeat his parents, to answer his nephews while still respecting her need to hide. And that, again, how he was with her children, was all it took for her to make the decision.

She stepped closer still and knelt.

Balthus's dream was infused with rolling waves of languid heat…pleasure. A persistent revolution guiding him that he willingly followed, uneasy until a gentle weight straddled his lap and iron bands of need tightened. With a heavy arm, he clasped the source against him. A desirous anchor of soft breath against his neck. A feeling of completeness, of needful desperation. The heat above him damp, and he drove towards it once, twice. A hot gasp, a woman's quiet cry, a grip against his thigh. Nails biting through his skin, breaking him from the cocoon of warmth to the cool air of night; the cold wet grass, the unforgiving tree he leaned against. To the scent of thyme escaping from long red tresses tangled and trapped by his arm. To Séverine, placing damp kisses along his neck, just under his chin before his scruff started, trailing to behind his ear. The length of him a hard bar between them. Insistent as the beating of his heart.

He looked wildly around him, at the quiet of the woods, the faint spark of a dying embers where he knew the camp was. 'I slept? Is there danger?'

'Nothing. No one. Only me.' She pressed closer to him. 'Don't stop.'

Something rumbled and broke. He searched her eyes, which were dark, but her lips were full, her gaze slumberous. On a groan, he captured her mouth, their tongues exploring, tangling, pressing tighter. Showing his need and desire for her with his every breath.

Séverine settled on his lap, his bound arm trapped between them, a sting of pain that he ignored as her soft flesh gave to his. 'I want… I need you.'

'I know, you've told me when you were sleeping.'

He cupped her head in his hand lifted her eyes to him. 'How did we get like this?'

'I meant to wake you in a different way,' she said. 'But you talked.'

He never talked in his sleep. As the youngest brother, he would have heard of it. All the others knew about Ian, and yet… Was it her? What did he have to tell her so badly he could only say it in his sleep?

'You listened.'

'You said some words that you said before. They didn't make sense then, but I think…you talked about me.' She patted his arm. 'I laid a hand on your arm and then you tugged me.'

'You were kissing me.' It had been a dream, but it wasn't. They were memories now and needed fast clarification. He was already losing control, his mind snagged because his body didn't want this conversation…only her.

'I was.'

'Because of what I said,' he clarified.

'And what you do,' she whispered.

He had been asleep when she'd approached. Very little made sense with her in his arms, the slight dampness of his neck where she'd kissed him, the fact her fingers were gripping his tunic, ready to tear it off. Her fingers mimicked his own, which were buried somewhere near her hip.

'Tell me what I said.'

She shook her head. Did it again as she lifted herself and slid down.

Lust slammed through him.

'Move, Balthus. I want to kiss you more.'

No. Something wasn't right. He hung his head, his chest heaved. 'You're undoing me.'

She slid her hands along his shoulders, his skin damp with sweat under his tunic. 'I know. I want you.'

He wished he knew what he'd said, what he'd done to gain her affection, but he could guess. He was obsessed with her so was it any wonder that he talked to her while sleeping?

But there was more that needed to be said—must be said. 'Séverine there's—'

She rested her hand on his chest. 'Secrets. I know. It doesn't matter. Tomorrow we return home. We don't have to know them, not now.'

She tightened her arms and legs around him. Her rushed words and the urgent rolls of her hips enflamed and called to every need to possess. He stilled himself, aware that his breeches and her crushed chemise were the only barrier to him burying himself in her.

Staring into his eyes, she rolled her hips again. He grunted and gripped her hip hard. She trembled in his arms, and he wanted every single one. Crushing her body against his, he felt his own body pulse against her heat.

He couldn't last like this, he had so little control. One hand could free him and—

He had to do the impossible. Must, even knowing the magnificence of holding her would end before the sun rose.

'I can't keep this secret. We can't.'

Séverine tried to still the deep fluttering inside her; attempted to ease her hammering heart and slow her breathing. She could do nothing about her trembling as she looked up at Balthus's tortured expression.

She knew he wanted her. It was physically evident in the tension of his body and his words. When she'd knelt by him while he'd slept, he'd turned to her as if he could see her with his eyes closed, and he'd spoken to her. They hadn't been feverish, disjointed mutterings, but whole thoughts on what her children meant to him, what she meant to him, how hard it was to let her go, but he needed to. And the more he'd talked the faster his breathing had become, as if his words hurt him.

So she'd rested her hand on his arm to soothe him, and on a harsh groan and faster than she had been prepared for, he'd gripped her gown and dragged her over him. Not even then had he woken, but her body on his had agitated him. When he'd whipped his head back against the tree, the cords of his neck had strained and he'd let out a growl of such feral desperate need, she had been lost. He was in pain because of her; she would end it.

Now his gaze was unfathomable but vast, *forever*, and it included her. The swelling in her heart was all too comprehensible: she loved him. Loved Balthus of Warstone. The brother of her husband.

No matter how much this moment meant, it wasn't enough, and she would only ever want more. She didn't want a life without him, but here he was reminding her that that was how it would be.

Foolish hopes of a future together!

Because she was married, and as much as she knew that what was between them was right and good and everything, she couldn't keep it. No matter how much of forever he showed her in his tender gaze, in his gentle touch, in the whispers of breath against her temple, there was no running away with him.

Everything in her that wasn't gentle unravelled within her, and as her own heart was crushed in her chest, Balthus's steady grey gaze wavered as if at any moment she'd disappear.

It wasn't she who would be gone tomorrow. It was him. It was them. Then she wept.

Balthus had never felt true life before. Oh, he may have been born, learned to walk and breathe. Learned the ways of childhood and of becoming a man. He may have felt some camaraderie with Louve, some familial affection when he'd approached Reynold in his courtyard and asked to be a true brother. But his heart and body had only been mimicking life. His lungs pretending to draw in air, his heart to beat. He'd never been alive until Séverine had placed her hand on him and said... always.

That word meant far more than a word whispered across tongue and lips. Always meant something he'd never granted himself. His false life wasn't meant to last for always, nothing of his soul was worth forever. But Séverine gave that to him, gave him life and always, and he succumbed to it all. Took her kisses, the weight of her heat against him, though he knew it was wrong.

And he knew it as Séverine's gasps and tears revealed the lies.

'It's Ian, isn't it? You've sent him a message, and he'll be there at the keep, waiting for us. What have I done? What will become of the children? Of us? Ian will know.' She choked. 'I can't run from him forever, and he'll know. They always know!'

Her sobs were distressed, her words frantic. Balthus gave useless murmurs in reply, inadequate pats as he wrapped her body in his loose cloak and pulled her closer to him. Soaking them both in her tears.

'Stop. Stop. Séverine, there's no need for this. There's only us. Ian's not there. There is no message. He is not coming, neither is he a threat. Not now, not ever. Ease your heart, my—'

She abruptly pulled away. 'What did you say?'

He rubbed her back. 'You worry about your husband…but you shouldn't. Not anymore. Not ever again.' Balthus breathed in deeply. Braced himself and told her what he should have told her that first day. 'Your husband, my brother, is dead.'

It was the cold that reached her first. As if her entire body had been plunged in a winter lake.

'What did you say?' she said, and even then she was certain she wouldn't hear him properly. Not through the terror and roaring in her ears. He couldn't be saying what she thought.

'He's dead, Séverine. Ian's... There was an incident at his fortress some months ago. It wasn't an acci—'

She ripped her chemise free from his legs and stood to her full height. 'This is...true? Not a game?'

He stood with her. 'I should have told you.'

'Told me what... Warstone. That a man I have fled from for years is no longer a threat? That your brother has been killed? That I am a widow?'

'All of it. Any of it.'

Rage shook her limbs. Séverine raised her fist and struck him. The fact his face exploded with red did little to ease her embarrassment that she had been duped, and that her husband was dead. Or her rage that it was this man she'd given her heart to who was the one who'd shamed her.

'I thought you were different. I thought you weren't a Warstone, with your games and lies.

Why didn't you tell me? To prove that I have no moral code? That I attack men in stables while they're sleeping and can't keep—'

'No!' he said. 'To keep me away from you!'

She stepped back, shook her head.

'I am the one with no honor. I'm the one who needed to remember a man, a good man, is the one who deserves you.'

Madness! 'Ian wasn't good. Ian tried to kill you, left me in that keep and abandoned his children. He hasn't even searched for me. I know it, or he'd find me like you did and...' She gasped. 'How long has he been gone?'

'Ian loved you.' He rushed out the words.

'What?'

'Those were his dying words,' he said. 'To tell you he loved you and hoped that you were safe. That he mourned leaving you and the children, but he did it because he had to. Because he wasn't...he couldn't trust his parents, or his own thoughts and deeds.'

'You go too far.'

'It's true. He said as much as he could to Louve. The rest...the understanding, that came because of what happened when he died.'

'You act like you were there. Did you kill your brother, Balthus? Twist a blade or stir a potion to fell the father of my children?'

'I played a part.'

She raised her hand to strike him again. When he waited for it, she cursed. 'Tell me.'

Her tears were gone. Sorrow was there, biting at her heart, but now rage ruled her. Secrets. How naive could she have been? She'd thought she'd grown up since being away from the Warstones. Had congratulated herself that she could carry two whole buckets! It was laughable. She didn't have strength of heart or will. This family always won with deceit that far surpassed any of her so-called cleverness.

He shook his head.

'Tell me!' she demanded. 'Who did it, and why. He was my husband. How far do your lies go? Are your parents even alive? How did I not know any of this since I've travelled the entirety of France and Provence and I have all these people loyal to me. People you tell me I can command to overthrow the Warstones. Do they even exist?'

Balthus stepped back again, his body half in shadow from the trees, half in the dim light from the moon. 'My parents are still alive, they truly do want this legend because the King of England wants it, and if we're right, they know it leads to a treasure. They can't have more power or wealth. Reynold and I have a tenuous agreement. I still need to prove myself to him. To do that, I vowed I'd find you, and obtain the parchment he believes exists.'

'If I have it,' she said. 'I have possessions, but there's no certainty whether...'

'Ian told Louve what he'd done. That you and the legend were hidden in a location no one knew.'

'So even the reason of him loving me and taking me to Forgotten Keep was a lie? It wasn't me or the children he wanted safe; it was some foolish scribbles.'

'He...lost more of his control after you were gone, Séverine. I can see it no other way than he broke his own mind to save you.'

'Is this your attempt to make me feel shame when it's not me but all of you who are to blame?'

'There's only two of us against our parents now.'

Ian was gone. No, she couldn't think about him and finish what needed to be said. 'You are truly making an alliance with your brother.'

'I know it is as unbelievable as a legend with a treasure, but it's true. I approached Reynold and we made a pact to end their reign.'

'And do anything to do it, including lying to me.'

'I didn't lie to you because of the treasure,' he said, then turned and cursed.

This was worse. 'You were to tell me immediately. Let me guess. You were to ask me for it when there was some trust between us. After all, what if I had sided with King Edward in the six years?'

'That's not the reason I waited.'

She laughed, but it was bitter, because she felt that thorn. 'I know that because it was apparent to you I hadn't sold myself over an elusive scrap of felled tree the moment you saw me carrying kindling.'

'Séverine, I waited because I—'

The thorn turned to a shard. 'You care for me? Lies! All of it. You have no feelings because if you did, you would know how much this hurts me.'

'They're flawed, I'm flawed, but—'

'True? I won't believe you again. Now tell me what any widow deserves to know.'

He exhaled roughly, rubbed his arm as if it pained him. She felt no pity for him. She only waited.

'He wasn't well,' he said. 'In the hall of the fortress, with witnesses, he threw a dagger at me...and then Louve threw a dagger towards him. Louve's dagger struck true, but—'

'Louve again.'

'A mercenary who is aggravating, but he made company with Reynold.'

'And somehow with you, as well. Thus, he's at Warstone Fortress because Ian's dead, and he's holding it safe while you find me to get this parchment.'

It was more than that, and he didn't know how she'd react. She had run...but there were her children. 'Reynold and I never wanted that estate and signed it away to him. My parents have their own estate, Warstone's was completely Ian's. Naturally, it should go to his children, but...'

'You did what?' she said.

'You ran,' Balthus said. 'We couldn't leave the estate vulnerable to our parents. Of course, it hasn't been sealed by France's king yet, and it may not be, but we've delayed—'

'You gave my sons' inheritance away to a hired sword?'

'Yes.'

'How far do your schemes go?'

'Séverine—'

She shook her head once. 'No. I won't believe your feeble apologies, either. Have no concerns, Warstone, you'll still obtain that parchment, and I'll gladly hand it over. When I do, I never want to see you again.'

Chapter Nineteen

It was the rushed whispering of her boys that wrung her from a sleep stretched with anger and despair. She could feel their presence at the doorway long before the smell of warmed wine and fresh buttered bread wafted into her room from where they stood. They'd arrived at Forgotten Keep long after the sun had set the previous night. If it hadn't been a full moon, and the fact someone had lit a lone torch at the entrance to the small keep, they might have ridden past it. In the end, it had been Sarah's horse that had seemed to know where to turn on the path.

The moment she'd called out, the guard, who must have been half-asleep, lit more torches and alerted the handful of servants still living there. It was a chaotic but comforting greeting. Much could have changed since she'd run.

Warstones could have razed it to the ground or the servants she'd left could have been slaughtered by her angry husband. The fact it was all still here with more repairs done was almost too much to bear and more tears fell.

Exhausted, she'd done what she could to assist, which wasn't much for it seemed as if the household had been mostly prepared for their arrival though they were earlier than expected. So the moment the boys had been cared for, she'd found her own bed, and fell on it. Now, if the light was any indication, it was well past time for prayers and breaking her fast. Rubbing her sore eyes and damp cheeks, she called out, 'Come in, boys. I'm fine.'

Sitting up, she brushed her gown down her front in a vain attempt to straighten herself while Clovis carried the tray and set it on the table nearest her, and Pepin shifted awkwardly. Watching their hesitation broke her heart and she waved her arms to bring them closer. Pepin shuffled forward, but Clovis stood as still as an ice crystal on an icicle. Snatching the bottom of his tunic, she yanked him to her. He gave only a sign of surprise, not protest. A heartbeat later Pepin leaned his weight into them, and she opened her arms a bit more to gather him close.

It was one of the sweetest moments they'd ever shared as the little family they were, and all too brief for when Pepin wriggled, Clovis jabbed back with his elbow, and Pepin kicked out.

'Come, you two.' She tried to sound firm, but their familiar rivalry fortified her heart more.

Séverine released her children, who scrambled back and stood before her. Their legs were tangled in her gown, their hesitant expressions a bit less solemn.

'I've worried you.'

Pepin gave a quick shake of his head, but Clovis said, 'You've been worried.'

Séverine's breath caught. 'Here I thought I was being clever not showing you.'

'You're clever, Mama.' Pepin glared at Clovis. 'Mama's clever.'

Séverine braced herself for the fists to fly and for her to intervene, but…

Clovis looked like he wanted to argue but didn't. His discomfiture, and the fact he did not straighten his clothing or hair after she'd ruffled both, made something odd happen in her chest. He was growing up. He was young, and had far to go to become self-sufficient, but in the time with Balthus, he'd changed.

'Clovis doesn't believe I'm not clever, Pepin, it's just sometimes difficult to hold feelings in.'

'Like yesterday,' Pepin said. 'You had feelings everywhere.'

'I did.'

'We heard you from the courtyard, too. You cried in your sleep.'

Oh!

'Is it all right now?' Clovis asked. 'Will you be all right now?'

She gave a small smile to let them know she was well. 'I was all right before, during and most definitely afterwards. It was only a bit more than usual.'

Seeing their still-concerned faces, she added, 'You've never seen me that way before, have you, but many people need to cry.'

'See, Clovis!'

'She doesn't mean you.'

'I mean... I mean both of you.' She patted the bed. 'Here, come and sit.' When they did, she continued, 'We've been busy all your lives, haven't we? Always moving. But we never spoke about it.'

'Clovis moaned about it!' Pepin pointed out.

At Pepin's comment, Séverine put her hand on his legs and he stopped.

'He was right to object to it,' she said.

Clovis shifted next to her, and she clasped her hands in front of her. 'You would have been right to complain, as well. All your lives you've met children who didn't move from home to home, who knew their friends for years and years. Were you envious of them?'

Pepin shook his head, but as she kept her gaze on him, his eyes got bigger and shone with tears.

One look at Clovis's expression and she knew he had felt similar longings. 'Did you ever wonder why we did what we did?'

'To play hide-and-seek,' Pepin said. 'Loads and loads of hide-and-seek.'

'So Father never found us,' Clovis responded.

Séverine started.

'How did you—? You don't remember him, do you?' When Clovis shook his head, she added, 'But you heard about him from Imbert and Sarah?'

'They whisper about him all the time,' Pepin said. 'And we ask.'

Of course they had.

'Is he bad?' Clovis asked, his chin jutting out.

'No, he's not. She wants to see Father! Don't you, Mama? He hasn't caught to us, like Balthus.'

She couldn't do this. She couldn't. Her eyes were welling up and her children were blurring before her. She dropped her face into her hands.

'Pepin, be quiet!' Clovis said.

Séverine rubbed her face. 'No, no, we need to talk. We haven't talked, it's just that you're my children and…'

She looked at their worried faces. This wasn't what they needed. They needed her to be strong for them when she told them. When she said what was absolutely necessary and not one word more, they needed to know she was there for them. She was there as she'd always been and would always be.

But how to tell them their father, who they couldn't possibly remember, was dead? They'd care because they were starting to feel the loss of a father in their lives.

'What your mother is trying to say—' Balthus emerged from the doorway '—is something that it is my responsibility to tell you.'

Séverine straightened, pulled her children in close. She didn't like him being here, but wouldn't say anything to her children. All morning he'd checked the reinforcements of this small keep. Much work had been started and mostly done, but more was needed if they were to stay here for any period of time. He hoped she wouldn't stay. It wouldn't take much for his parents to find this or add it to their strongholds since they'd potentially lost the Warstone Fortress.

'I think I'm the judge of whether something is or is not your responsibility.'

'Yes,' he said. 'But this is something I would like to do.'

'I owe you no favours, Warstone.'

'Neither would I ask them.'

'Mama?' Clovis said.

Séverine turned to her sons. 'Balthus is your uncle. Your father's brother.'

'You're family?'

Balthus knew by the look in Séverine's eyes to keep this as simple as possible. 'I am.'

'Why didn't you tell us?' Pepin said.

Balthus eyed Clovis, who didn't look surprised like his brother. 'Because I had terrible news to tell you and didn't know how to tell it.'

Séverine gasped, and he knew he was going further than she wanted, but it needed to be said. Truths needed to be told. He'd learned his lesson.

'Is that why you were shoved in the pit?' Clovis said.

'Yes, your mother guessed.'

'He's dead,' Clovis said, turning to his mother. 'Our father is gone, isn't he?'

Pepin wavered, and Séverine grabbed him immediately. Balthus wanted to hold them all.

'Yes, he is,' Séverine said.

'He never made it,' Pepin sobbed. 'To find us.'

Séverine stroked Pepin's hair, soothing him, and Balthus broke down. Striding over to the family, he placed his hand on Clovis's shoulder, but the boy wrapped his arms around his waist and Balthus almost fell to his knees.

When Balthus opened his eyes, he saw Séverine's gaze on him. He wished he could understand all the thoughts in her green gaze. Wished he could sit on the bed next to her and hold her. Wished his arm wasn't bound so he could hold them all closer than he already was.

But even with all those wishes and wants, he didn't deserve them, and she knew it. She brushed Pepin's face and looked into her son's eyes, then she grabbed Clovis and brought him to her side.

Balthus felt the loss of warmth.

'We'll make it through this, but there's much to talk about,' Séverine said. 'Can you give me that?'

Looking as brave as any boy, Clovis grabbed his brother's hand.

'Now, go off and explore.' She pushed them away gently.

Balthus tried to smile when Clovis looked over his shoulder at him before he closed the door, but he knew it was a weak attempt to ease the boy's concern. They were young, though, and good. Séverine saw to that.

Séverine made a sound and straightened her shoulders. 'Do your parents know of this keep?'

'They might now, but Ian wouldn't have left you here if they had. He was trying to protect you.'

Something crossed her face he couldn't quite discern. Was she disappointed this keep was discoverable? If so, did that mean she was contemplating staying? She had to see it wasn't adequate yet for protection and, though well hidden, if it had inhabitants, they were bound to build enough of a community to draw even more wandering families.

'Thank you for allowing me to tell them,' he said.

'Clovis has got close to you.'

For him to earn his nephew's affection was humbling, but from Séverine's expression and tone, it worried her. Yet another reminder that what they had, if anything, was fragile and he'd ruined it by not telling her about Ian's death. 'He's young. There will be others after me who will hold his attention. There's an old watch guard. He'll have the skills to teach the boys swordplay and how to squire.'

Frowning, she looked away, clearly conflicted regarding that information. He was as well, for he wanted to train, play with and watch her sons grow into men. He wanted to— No, it had been his own deeds that had caused this rift, and one he couldn't apologise enough for.

'I'm sorry, Séverine.'

'For what?' she said. 'Their father being dead and now they've inherited positions that kings will attempt to control? Or for ripping me out of the life I wanted in the abbey? That life is so far away now... Do you know I haven't been able to attend church daily let alone the three times a day I did? I was always too scared I would be recognised.'

'Do you think your soul is lost, Séverine? Do you think that if you died today, with no confession, you'd go to Hell? Because that's a lie.'

'Adding blasphemy to your sins?'

He took the verbal strike. 'You have the most complete soul I've ever known.'

'Remember what I said about Warstone

praise?' She looked away. 'I'll go to the abbey today.'

'I'll go with—'

'No, I'll get what I left there, then you'll be gone. If what you're looking for is not there, I won't help you find anything else. You may have helped me tell my boys the horrific tale of their father and his family, but you're all part of that. And just as I don't want them involved, I don't want you involved. I don't want to see you ever again.' She rose. 'Now, excuse me.'

He moved to one side and watched her walk past him with her head held high. He kept the door open so he could watch her turn the corner and go out of his sight.

He felt everything. Her pride, her acknowledgement that he had told her about his brother's death. He had felt Clovis's small arms around his waist. He loved them all.

And he knew he'd protect them like his brother had wanted to.

Chapter Twenty

'What are you doing here?' Séverine said.

'You're not walking to the abbey on your own,' Imbert said.

Had Balthus told them? 'It's a short walk. I simply need to see if they kept those books and things I left there.'

Sarah pointed to the pouch at her waist. 'To retrieve them? I thought they knew they were only to protect them.'

She'd only brought a few coins. She'd given much over the years to both this abbey and the one near her parents' home, but it had been some years before, and it was best to be prepared.

'If they're there, you might have more than you can carry,' Sarah said. 'Perhaps I can help there.'

'I'm here to keep Imbert company,' Henry said.

It was more than that. 'Did Balthus tell you all this?'

'Balthus?' Henry scratched his chin. 'I think he's with the boys and Lionel.'

She almost asked about Lionel, but a conversation wasn't what she wanted at all today. It was supposed to be a quick walk to the abbey and back. Not her and a thousand other people. She needed to think.

Scowling at all of them, she hurried her pace. None of them got the hint, though, and followed alongside her.

'Lionel is the son of Paul, the old watch guard. Did you know he died?' Henry said. 'I remember him well. Couldn't hold his ale. I'll have to test this Lionel out soon.'

'You won't get a boy sick!' Séverine said.

'Lionel's a man,' Imbert said. 'Inherited his father's sword. He's quite skilled from what I can see. Balthus is testing him.'

As if Forgotten Keep were some great manor house that needed trained watch guards. Why was Balthus bothering? He would be getting his parchment and leaving. As for her... She'd only wondered whether his parents knew of this keep, not that she'd be staying here.

Except she *was* thinking about staying here. But she needed to study all the consequences of that and couldn't do so in peace because she had a stablemaster, his wife, and a butcher for company!

'And the boys?' she said.

'They have sticks,' Imbert said. 'You'll be pleased to know they've already impressed Lionel with their skill.'

She swung on him. 'What skill?'

'You don't think that over all these years they hadn't picked up a few ways of fighting?'

Sarah patted her arm. 'It was inevitable.'

During all the years of rejecting their heritage, maybe she had been fighting a battle that couldn't be won. Or maybe Balthus was right, and she'd unconsciously given them an upbringing that was in between.

Henry burped. 'They're happy. That's all I can say.'

Happy. She could envision it. Balthus, the boys, Lionel all training and playing. Bonding more while she walked away from them.

They knew their true father was dead, but Balthus was there, and he was family. Wonder had filled Pepin's eyes, and Clovis had hugged Balthus as if he knew he wouldn't be rejected.

They were proud that Balthus was family. Regardless of how they'd started, how they'd run from him twice, and she'd trapped him in the pit. They were comfortable around him. Did they see what she did? A man who tried?

No. She didn't want to think about this now.

'What are you doing here?' she said. 'I thought you left?'

'I did, to come here and ensure all was as it should be for your family,' Henry said. 'Or as much as I could. You arrived sooner than expected.'

That explained how their arrival hadn't been all that much of a surprise and bedding and linens had been replaced and made ready for them all.

'I miss Denise, though. Think I'll ride back and see if I can't talk her into staying here.'

Denise was the widow that Henry seemed to like, but... 'You're not staying here.'

'You don't have a butcher, or a cook for that matter,' Henry said. 'Not that I'm skilled with that, but I know a way around roasting that I think you'll like.'

She hadn't mentioned staying to anyone. She'd asked Balthus about his parents. They were still to be hidden, and she didn't need more people from Warstone Fortress. Could she even trust this man?

Being responsible for more people wasn't what she wanted. She hadn't survived this long without help. All of Ian's former servants had assisted her along the way. Her own family had hidden her in the escape tunnel just a few weeks ago.

But this felt different. Personal in a way that nothing ever had. Perhaps because before she had been running and leaving people and items behind with her only thought to keep running. Now she was tired, wanting to stay, and Pepin and Clovis had too many questions and too many needs to just keep on the road and play hide-and-seek.

These people who walked beside her to an abbey she'd been surprised, but delighted was nearby.

'What makes you believe I would want you?' Séverine said. 'I hit you on the head!'

Henry laughed. Imbert and Sarah looked at each other with a knowing look she didn't understand.

'That you did, and it was a good one, too.'

Séverine walked faster. What was she to do? She had gone from a life of study and quiet contemplation to one of cruelty.

Ian was dead. No matter how many times she said it to herself, it wasn't true for her. He had been too all-encompassing to be struck down by a mere dagger. But then Balthus had said it was so, and it hadn't been an accident. What had he meant by that?

There was a hollowness in her heart at the thought of Ian gone. His parents' fervent belief in him had forced her to see him from their point of view. How were they coping with their son's death? Would they now demand Clovis and Pepin?

If she were a grandparent, she'd raze the world to find her grandchildren, but Ian's parents? She didn't know.

Ian was dead, and with heaviness in her heart she knew she mourned him. Not the man who'd wrenched her from that hall so long ago, but the one who with much tenderness had taken her to his bed, lain with her and fallen asleep at her side. Who'd mumbled and muttered and tossed and turned. Who, with wild eyes, had realised what he had done and had left the next morning. She hadn't seen him for months after that first night.

His mad mutterings and endearments hadn't turned her away from Ian, rather it was him abandoning her to his parents that was unforgivable. And he hadn't done it just once. Constant messengers, late-night meetings, disappearances, and after Pepin was born, he'd watched her with eyes she hadn't trusted.

There had still been the tender words when he'd slept, but she'd begun to not trust those anymore, either. Then he'd bundled them all up in the middle of the night and they'd left for a keep he'd called forgotten.

Had she loved him? No, she had never been given the chance. But she'd cared, and he was the father of her children. She'd run from him, but she hadn't believed it to be indefinitely. She'd only wanted to give her children a chance to know the world like she did.

For six years she'd run, hidden, survived. The moment she'd captured Balthus she'd feared she'd be plunged back into Warstone life; she'd even contemplated healing him to sway him to her side. Because there were always sides! One was either with the Warstones or their enemies. They pitted themselves against the world.

But Balthus…a favoured Warstone…had revealed a path she hadn't known existed, one she'd never dared hope for, for her or her children. That of breaking their malevolent reach.

Which came at a cost: that of finding a legend, which would require games and intrigue. Of travelling and running and fighting. Another life she didn't want for her children.

Fortunately, it appeared she didn't have to.

She'd get the documents, they would or would not be what Balthus needed, and he'd be gone.

There was a chance, too, that the Warstone parents didn't know about this keep. With the boys tired of hide-and-seek, with Imbert and Sarah getting older, and now somehow she'd acquired Balthus's butcher, maybe she had a choice about whether to stay or run again. Perhaps in a few years Balthus could contact her and let her know if their scheme had worked.

The abbey was up ahead. It was smaller than she remembered.

'Can you stay here?' She turned to Henry, who somehow took a few more steps before he stopped along with her.

From Sarah's perplexed expression, they must have been talking while she'd been deep in her thoughts.

'It isn't close enough,' Imbert said.

'For what?'

Henry ducked his chin. 'You know why we're really here.'

Balthus had requested them for her protection. As if he had a right to request or protect.

'He wanted to come,' Imbert said, 'but didn't think you'd agree.'

'If there is danger on this walk and at the abbey, what good do you think any of us would be? Even now Warstones and their mercenaries could be taking the boys.'

'Séverine.' Sarah laid a hand on her arm. 'That's not what I meant. I know there is inadequate protection for you or them with what we have. We care. That's all.'

She rubbed her forehead. 'I know. Let's see what the abbey still has.'

Sarah opened her mouth, closed it again.

'What is it?'

She waved and ordered the men to the side and pulled Séverine with her.

'He's not bad for a Warstone,' Sarah said.

She didn't need to guess who she was talking about. 'No, he's worse. Did you know he knew of Ian's death and didn't tell me? All these weeks I worried that we'd be caught because we stayed too long, and I had nothing to fear from my husband.'

Sarah shook her head. 'I do grieve for that boy who never stood a chance, but he was never your true threat.'

Ian had felt like one, since he'd chosen her at the betrothal announcement, but Sarah was right. If it hadn't been for the parents, being married to Ian wouldn't have been a love match, but it wouldn't have been the frightening experience it was.

'Did Balthus tell you why he needs these books from the abbey?' Sarah asked. 'I'm assuming you're retrieving them at his request. Otherwise I'm surprised we're here at all.'

'A parchment,' Séverine corrected. 'I think I know which one, too. It isn't very large, but it is intricately beautiful. And if I told a few people about it, it'd get him killed.'

'So he trusts you, then?'

'Pardon?'

'He trusts you with his life?'

Did he?

She wouldn't have any questions if he was simply cruel. None of this would be hard at all if Balthus hadn't said...the kind of things he had to her. If he hadn't kissed her, held her. Why have contradictions like his brother? Kind, protective and then...

Didn't she confuse things just as much? Didn't she want those touches and those words of his? Was torturing him for answers all she'd wanted when she shoved him in the pit?

'The Warstones have harmed you, but has he?' Sarah said.

'You know what he's done.'

Sarah nodded. 'He's also helped. It took some time, but eventually Imbert understood why he had to tear down the walls in that village, and as many times as you compromised your safety, he never harmed you.'

'That's because he was playing games.'

'Weren't you?' Sarah said. 'You told us yourself that you healed him to sway him to our cause.'

She didn't want to hear this. Wasn't it enough to know her husband was dead? That there was possibly an end to the Warstone nightmare she'd been living? To contemplate Balthus being good, wasn't that simply inviting more conflict into her life?

'I thought you were better than this,' Sarah said. 'I thought you of all people would understand about second chances and lives.'

'I just want to get to the abbey and be done.'

No matter how long they walked, there were no answers for her here.

Chapter Twenty-One

When he was beaten by Lionel again, the boys put down their sticks and just sat. When sweat poured from him and Pepin stacked pebbles in the dirt, Balthus finally called a stop to the training.

'How did you learn?' He locked his legs so as not to fall in front of Séverine's boys.

'From my father,' Lionel panted.

'No Warstone watch guard knows those manoeuvres,' Balthus said, moderately comforted that Lionel looked as exhausted as him.

'No, because you only hire them when they're young.'

'My father was the only one who travelled with them that day and stayed. He got old.'

'And then?' Balthus said.

'He learned how to fight a different way.

To strengthen his arms for fluidity as well as strength.'

'So you could do that flip,' he said.

Lionel gave a smirk. 'To disarm you.'

When Lionel had first done it, Balthus's instinct had been to grab his sword with his other hand for balance. It was a habit that must be broken, and that would take more practice.

'I think you'd better show me again.' Balthus straightened, widened his stance for balance.

'Not today.' Lionel looked alarmed.

He was tempted, but the boys had lost interest. Balthus shook his head and Lionel stepped back, staggered and crumpled to the ground. 'I haven't any legs left. If you had swung one more time…'

At least he still had some skill left to fell an opponent. 'You're good at holding your own. That's often all you need, but now that I know, we'll see about it tomorrow, then.'

Lionel huffed. 'Day after, I beg you.'

Laughing, Balthus turned to ask the boys questions, and saw them. Séverine was tall, but Henry dwarfed her. Sarah and Imbert were involved in some heated argument.

His eyes took in the bags Henry carried

but rested only on the woman he loved. She'd walked to the abbey and back and she was safe. Home.

Not home, though this odd place felt comfortable enough. Only the bottom of the keep was from some ancient structure. The rest was new, with fireplaces, garderobes and anything else that could be found in the grander structures being built.

It was small, secure, not well protected, but then it would definitely not blend in with the landscape. But to call it Forgotten Keep when it was this near an abbey...? It was too large for that and that needed an explanation.

On shaking legs, he walked towards them.

'Is there a lake around here?' Henry said. 'Someone needs to use it.'

'If I had any arms left, I'd shove you in,' Balthus said. Henry burst out laughing. Balthus did, too.

It felt good, better because Séverine was watching him instead of walking away. He'd take that odd expression on her face over her avoiding him.

'Are those they?' he asked.

She nodded. 'We need to talk.'

'Let me get cleaned up, and I'll meet you—'

'In my rooms.'

* * *

With hastily dried hair and a change of clothes, Balthus took the stairs to the spacious rooms at the top. Again, he marvelled at the design of this keep. The floors were finely sanded, every stone well mortared. It would be cool in the summer and warm in the winter.

Facing the closed door, he knocked before he entered. Here was sumptuousness he hadn't seen for many weeks and hadn't expected. How had this room survived the six years of her escape? How much coin had Ian left her?

'Are you wondering why I have so many pillows?' Séverine set down the book she was reading.

'I had noticed them,' he said.

She looked weary, beautiful, but tired. He almost suggested she sit, but he was in her home now and if he followed her wishes, he wouldn't be for much longer.

'It was a crumbled heap when we first arrived, but Ian had ordered much in advance, and I couldn't take everything with me when I ran.' She turned away and grabbed a scroll.

Balthus rested his hand in the small of his back, felt the door behind him and waited. If Séverine wanted to talk a bit longer and keep him in her presence, he'd stand here.

'I wanted nothing to do with your family, had no intention of attending that betrothal announcement. I never got along with my sisters very well; couldn't understand their obsession with gowns and men. My life was meant for the abbey. I was never happier than when I was alone, but I was taken from that life, and it changed me into a person I didn't like. I became suspicious; unkind to others when Warstone eyes were on me and I had to be so careful. But I love my sons so I ran. When you found me, you brought it all back, and then you reminded me what it was like to be lied to.

'What were you thinking when you didn't tell me about Ian? I can only think you didn't trust me, yet I knew your parents, and had lived in your home. I was married to Ian. After coming from my family, you didn't think I could detect the difference between a family that trusts and one that doesn't? Why could you not trust me, even a little?'

'I feared you'd run at first, but after that?' he said. 'No, I didn't trust you. You say you were broken again, but that implies that there was something there to begin with. Trust was never in my family. All those years you were with my family, do you think you were one of them? Did my mother ever sit down with you and share a drink?'

'We spent many hours together with needlepoint in the solar, we visited and chatted.'

'But no drink,' he said. 'She wouldn't have shared a drink with you, even if she'd ordered it herself. In her own home, she only ever drinks out of my father's goblet and only after he drinks first.'

'That can't be true.'

'My mother didn't trust her own husband, let alone an outsider who married into the family. As for her children, we were half of our father. Hence we had to prove our loyalty to her by holding our hand over a flame. My father wasn't innocent or naive in any of this... his cruelty was simply more direct.'

'But you were her children; I was a spouse of her child.'

'No one is spared. I was the youngest. What do you think that did to me?' he said. 'Do you think I escaped it all because I was the last born? No, I was honed from all the errors my parents had made before, then I had the benefit of siblings who added their own ways of educating me. So, trust? It's a word, but one I've learned to wield...until you.'

'But you still lied to me.'

'If I had thought matters through, I would not have—'

'Lain with me?' Séverine tossed the scroll back on the bed.

Why was she talking about any of this? What would change from their previous conversations? The parchments were here, all he had to do was sweep through them and find what he was looking for.

Except… Would that change things between them? It felt like Balthus was thrumming with some emotion not yet disclosed. And for her? He was right, his mother had never drunk in front of her. She wasn't truly a Warstone, regardless of her marriage or the children. She wasn't trusted, and after six years Balthus shouldn't have trusted her. She could have been anyone at that point.

'Wanting you is the most truth I've ever shown anyone,' he said.

'How am I to believe that?'

'You weren't like this when I first saw you. We hurt your ability to trust, didn't we? My family, Ian and I.'

'You're simply reciting facts, Balthus. Yes, my trust was damaged. Why do you think I ran? What I don't know is why you followed me, why you didn't tell me immediately.'

'You would have run if I'd told you at first. If Ian was dead, and I was stuck in a pit, you would have run.'

That was true, but that only helped his cause a bit. He tapped his left foot as if he was feeling a bit restless or was holding himself back. From the way his grey eyes were pleading with her, she knew what his direction would be. The room was large, but not that big, and he was blocking the door.

'Afterwards?' she said. 'After your fever broke, or when I entered the stables? You acted like I mattered. You told me about the legend. I didn't appreciate what that meant or how much trust you placed in me, but I understand that now, and yet you still lied to me about the most important fact!'

'I'm…trying!' he said. 'Some deeds and words I say and do are just impulses I fight against but can't always succeed. For years I relied on the Warstone training simply so I didn't die. But I hate that what I do hurts you.'

He stepped forward, and she gave him a warning look, and he suddenly stopped.

'I'm a coward. That's the reason I didn't tell you. I…kept my dead brother between us in the hope that if I couldn't stay away, you would. I've wanted you for so long, Séverine, it seems more than a lifetime. The memory of you standing in front of that tapestry has fulfilled my soul more than water ever did my body. I had no chance against you once I stood next to you, once I truly understood you as a mother.'

'But why keep me away, then?'

He held up his truncated arm. 'This is one of the reasons.'

'Your arm?'

'I'm not whole. I'm not…like one of your beautiful tapestries.'

She studied his tortured grey eyes. Despite her feelings towards him, he was beautiful, but in that raw unfinished way she found far more intriguing than any completed tapestry. He'd said he was trying to be good, and despite everything…she believed him, responded to him.

Was she being fair to him? Was Sarah right that she wasn't looking at everything?

She had in the beginning. She'd kept noticing the differences in him, but then…the parchment and Ian. But were those just…messages? Balthus was no messenger, he was a Warstone after all. Maybe, just maybe she needed to look at him like a man again.

Maybe he wanted to be seen like a man

since he showed her his arm, thought himself not beautiful because of it. But that wasn't all.

'What's the other reason?'

'I'm a Warstone!' he said. 'You ran from us before, and I don't know what you had to endure. I could guess, but—'

'Do you know Ian threw a fruit tray at me? Apparently, your mother isn't the only one who hates fruit.'

She tried to keep her tone humorous, but he turned his head, his eyes snaring hers before his lids dropped.

'I'm...sorry,' he said.

Séverine waited for him to continue, afraid he might. It wasn't a good memory. Ian had thrown the tray at her. She'd ducked, but the mess behind her, the noise...

Shaking, embarrassed, she had picked it up, and he'd been very tender afterwards. That was the only violence he'd ever shown her. Never had he hit her, never had he truly harmed her, but it had taken her years to understand the rigidness of his needs.

'What else?' she demanded.

The corner of his mouth curved. A smile, as if she pleased him. 'Everything I say to you is going to be disjointed.'

'Why? Because you can't tell the truth and are still trying to hide?'

He nodded solemnly. 'Some of that perhaps. Even now I'm struggling to tell you the truth.'

'That's a start,' she said. 'Does it hurt?'

'Everything I do since you came back into my life pains me. Tell the truth, my feelings, showing my vulnerability, my weaknesses. Undoing a lifetime of doing the opposite. Undoing a lifetime of being taught and then punished that I *must* do the opposite. Standing here before you, carving out whatever this is in my chest, it hurts. *You* hurt me.'

She snorted.

He spun in a circle. 'I'm getting this all wrong, but there's too much to tell. Do I start with Ian or me?'

She saw it then. The pain. Some of it reflected her own, but there was more for him. Somehow she knew there was more agony. 'What's easier?'

He huffed out a breath. She'd surprised him. 'Ian, though if I told you everything, you wouldn't believe it.'

'I've been gone for six years, but he's haunted everything I've done. I want to know everything.'

'I thought Ian married you because you were

the youngest and maybe the most impression-able, but I think it was because you didn't need him for anything. You didn't need Warstone money or power. He'd have to earn you.'

How would he?

'You were at the most lavish event I've ever attended, and all you did was stare at a tapes-try as if you hadn't a care in the world about any of us. Then you escaped and eluded him for years.'

'Because he didn't care about me or his chil-dren!'

It was the sorrow in his eyes that doused her anger and frustration. 'He cared, and… he did return to this keep. Once. I didn't want to tell you.'

Because the truth was horrible. 'To kill me? To kill our boys?'

The look on Balthus's face told her the truth. That spike of fear and horror that had dimmed over time surged again. She covered her mouth to hold back her cry.

Balthus stretched out his arm as if to stop her thoughts. 'He might not have done it, Séverine. He might have just come to see you, but I do know he was frustrated you were out of his reach because after that…he came after me.'

How? To kill him? It seemed he mourned Ian's death. 'I cannot believe he is gone.'

'I've known a few months more than you.'

'I ran from him for six years. He terrified me. I haven't seen him in all that time and yet... Why did he pick me? I know I keep asking, but...'

'I can only guess, as I have done a thousand times since then. Your sisters are beautiful but polished and hardened. The announcement was coveted by many and the Warstones were meant to be the sun. You, however, were staring at the far wall in the hall, turned away from everyone.'

'That tapestry,' she said. 'I wasn't malleable or naive.'

He gave a small smile. 'Maybe he just wanted to be near something pure in a way we never were.'

'He got my fear. That's all I felt when I turned, and... I don't think I tried to change for him.'

'He wouldn't have encouraged anything else. Your fear kept you wary and probably safe.'

'I'm piecing together the man, but even if he told me everything, I couldn't love him. I think I understand what you mean about my sisters. Ian was hardened like them, but because of the boys I miss him.'

'There's always more.'

Her expression dimmed. 'What is it?'

'I miss him, too, though Ian tried to kill me.' He gave an uneven smile. 'See, I told you it wasn't easy.'

Balthus exhaled. 'He came after me. I went to Reynold. But Ian and I still had a confrontation. Ian's death occurred at the same time I lost my hand. When I came to, I didn't know what hurt worse. But I know it hurts now just telling you this.'

This part of their lives was terrible, and yet he'd said it was easier than telling about him.

'I'm…glad you told me. I knew one part of him. If you tell me the other…or at least more, I can then face my children one day when they ask and tell them why I forced them away from their father.'

'Don't…don't go there.'

Something he'd said pricked her heart and she felt the bitterness and fear pouring from her. 'Why not? I had no other thoughts than those. He talked in his sleep, and I came to care for him because of those mutterings, but when he was awake, he terrified me. How can I explain the contradictions to the boys?'

'When they do want to know, they'll be ready. That time doesn't have to be now. I'm a man, Séverine, and have waited to understand about family and love all my life. Trust me when I say they'll wait for the story. They'll wait because they know it's worth it.'

Was it simply because he was a Warstone, and therefore something for her sisters but not for her? She thought of the life she'd wanted at the abbey, but she loved her sons more. She wished for quiet, for study, to read books and question philosophers again, but she'd never give up her children.

'You gave me little reaction when I told you he loved you.'

'Don't.'

'You need to know.'

'He never said it to me, and he was dying when he said it to you.'

'But it's our actions, isn't it? You always said you trust my silences. You can't trust what a Warstone says, but you can our actions.'

'He threw a tray at me. He left me to your mother who—'

'Some of that was his madness, but also…' He looked down at his feet, the left one tapping a little, before he looked up. 'I didn't believe he loved you at first, either. The more time I spent with you, I almost convinced myself that he couldn't have loved you or the boys because if he had, how could he have stayed away? But then… Did you ever wonder why this keep was here or why he called it "Forgotten"? It couldn't truly be forgotten when an abbey was so close. I think the foundations were here and he had it built for you because it was near an abbey. Something he knew you cared for.'

Could it be true? Could Ian have been a better man that she'd thought? Could Balthus?

'My brother loved you,' Balthus said, as if he'd heard her inner thoughts. 'I understand it now because I'm doing the same thing as Ian.'

'Lying to me?'

'Trying to keep you away from me, and that's why I lied. Maybe at first, I was scared to trust, but when that went away, I was scared of my feelings for you. I'd had them so long, and then you were suddenly there. It was too much.'

'Is this the difficult part?'

'And easy.' His eyes were stormy grey.

'Why me, Balthus?'

He took the steps necessary to stand in front of her. 'I love you. I've always loved you since that first day. Over the years I called it obsession or fascination, but I know it was something more because I couldn't… I couldn't stop thinking of you.'

'You noticed me.'

'I couldn't look away from you.'

'Because of my hair, because I was the fourth sister,' she said. Her tone still held some bitterness, but even though she questioned and accused, she heard in her own voice, felt in her own breath, the need for his words.

'Because you were lost in that tapestry,' he said. 'Do you remember it?'

'It was a hunting scene.'

His brows drew in, his eyes a little in awe as if he couldn't believe she remembered. What would he say if she told him it reminded her of him?

'When you saw something about it you liked,' he said, 'you hovered your hand over it as if you were tracing the artistry or thread. And you smiled, you *smiled*, and I swear the gold in that thread dimmed in the brilliance of your joy.'

Joy. It was one of the words he'd used when he'd been feverish. When he'd slept. He'd meant…her.

'How?'

'That day you were all I could watch. I couldn't keep my eyes off you. You moved and

I swear my body moved with you. Even when Ian took your hand and walked you across that hall to stand by his side at the dais, even when he took you away completely and you disappeared. You have been, and will always be, all I can see.

'So I lied. I lied for reasons I didn't understand until I did. I wanted you by my side. So what if I lied to do it? Was is a lie just to steal a touch, a few words, to see your eyes soften as you looked at your boys? How terrible is that in all the acts of depravity I've had to do?

'I could even justify it. If I was gone, who would protect you? The irony is not lost on me that I was the darkness you needed protection from.'

'You love me.'

There was something in Balthus's grey eyes. Something warm, tender, wanting, and Séverine couldn't look away. Not when he placed his hand on her cheek, not when he brushed his callused thumb against her chin, the roughened tip just scraping the bottom of her lip.

'I could never forget your smile. Even when I tried, when you were my brother's wife, when you gave one son and then another to him, when he protected you from our parents. When he was trying to be good to you in the madness of his mind, I tried to not feel that warmth in my heart. Because there were days, weeks it hurt, it *seared* because you could never be mine.

'You were the only one who showed me happiness, the only memory in my long life that gave me any warmth. How could I not love you?'

'I'm sunshine, aren't I?' She grabbed his hand in both of hers, pressed it between them just above his bound arm.

His brows drew in, and she loved the bewildered expression on his face. That vulnerability. How could he be a Warstone when he showed his emotions so? Or was it just her he showed them to?

'When you were fevered you kept muttering these words about joy and sunshine, I didn't know what they meant, but then you said them again.'

'I was asleep under the tree when I was supposed to be protecting you,' he said.

'You turned towards me and called me sunshine, and I knew with all my heart that that was what I wanted to be.'

'What are you saying?' he said, his eyes half wary, half hopeful. Underneath their entwined fingers she felt his heartbeat increase.

'That you trust me…that you…have feelings for me? Or did I ruin it all by not telling you, not explaining enough?'

'Earlier you talked of wrongs, and how you couldn't do anything right…but that would imply there was a right.'

When he looked as if he would talk, she released her hand and patted his chest. 'I know you won't believe this, but for once it's not all about you and your family.'

He looked as if he couldn't believe his good fortune.

'If you could see your expression right now.' She snorted. 'I think I'll memorise this.'

'What am I doing?'

'You look…worried. Hopeful.'

'I'm both. I'm more,' he said eagerly. 'There's more I can tell you, if that will help. If that would make a difference? I would do anything to—'

'Balthus, let me talk.' When he stilled, she continued, 'I did believe Ian was alive when I kissed you, touched you. I believed he was alive all those times when we talked and you helped with the boys. There hasn't been one moment with you when I haven't been unfaithful to my husband.'

'But he's gone.'

'I didn't know that when I did those actions. You don't understand yet, do you? You say you're a coward, that you have this family. You say you have all these flaws and that's why you keep fighting against this, but you forget… I'm flawed, too. I've made mistakes. I knew my husband was struggling, but he also scared me. I didn't appreciate that he dropped me off at the keep to protect me until you told me, but I should have seen the truth of that. I should have known there was a part of him deliberately not finding me. Maybe I didn't deserve to be found.'

'Never,' he said with such vehemence she wanted to believe him.

'I'm not perfect. I took a man's children away from him. There was still good in him. And though he may have harmed me, I could never see him harming them. My reasoning was that I didn't want them to turn out like him. That was possible. But now he's dead, and I'll be haunted by the fact that I wounded him by running. And to make it worse, there was only one man I wanted, and he wasn't my husband.'

'You're saying you're flawed…like me.'

'I'm also saying I don't think there are rights and wrongs. Not when it comes to love. It just is.' She breathed in. 'I'm saying the same thing you said to me.'

'Which is?' he said shamelessly. He knew. The light in his grey eyes, the wicked smile. The man knew what she wanted to tell him.

'I love you, too.'

He nodded as if she'd given a correct answer. 'What is my expression telling you now?'

'You. I think you're showing me you. That feeling in your chest as if something is squeezing it tightly and you can't breathe, that's love. I feel it, too. I liked your smile that day, Balthus. I liked you looking at me. I liked it that you reminded me of the tapestry I was looking at.'

'The hunting scene?'

'It had gold and a lot of red. It was brutal and trapped in a moment, but still very much alive. When I turned to you, I saw the same thing. You have always been alive to me. I don't know if that makes sense.'

'To me it does, and you could not have said more encouraging words.' He captured her hand within his again, kissed her palm, once, twice. 'Séverine?'

'Yes?'

'I think I like this expression you're showing me,' he rumbled.

She wiggled her hand free and brushed her cheek. 'The one where my face is all red and tears are welling up my eyes?'

He gave a slow nod. 'It's now my favourite.'

'You had one before? Oh, yes, at the betrothal celebration.'

He trailed his finger along her lips as if he remembered her smile. 'No, that got usurped by your expression when you peered into the pit.'

That wasn't a good memory. 'My fear and anger at you was your favourite?'

'No, your worry and anger *for me*. The time in the woodcutter's hut, you were worried for Clovis and Pepin. But that time you peered into the pit, your feelings were for me.'

Her heart turned over. This man. How could she not love him?

'And so this is it?' she said.

Balthus had never thought he would be so fortunate. Never dreamed a wish he'd made when he was young could actually come true. Séverine, telling him she loved him. He didn't want to talk anymore. He only wanted her in his arms for as long as the boys would let them.

But she had demanded he tell her everything, and he would do his best. He wanted no secrets between them. And there were other consequences that needed to be pointed out.

For him, they didn't matter. He'd do anything, be anyone, to ensure they had a life together.

'There's more, but none of it good.'

'Then let's not talk of it.' She looked up at him, her eyes tracking from his hair, which was still wet, to his fresh clothes. When her gaze dipped to his mouth, Balthus didn't want to talk, either.

'Do you want to see your family again? Or mend things with your sisters?'

'I do want to go and see my parents, but my sisters are long gone. Perhaps it is time to write to them.'

'And tell them I signed papers to lose Warstone Fortress?' he said, forcing the words between them. 'I gave away Clovis and Pepin's ancestral home. It's not finalised yet, but I gave the man my word and the legal documents have already been sent to King Philip's advisers.'

'I hated that place and all it represented. I wouldn't want my children there.' She ran her hand along the bound arm across his chest. 'Who wrapped your linen?' she said.

'Henry. It's so tight, my arm may fall off.'

'It won't be for much longer. No more bleeding?'

'No new tears or swelling. It's good, Séverine.' Inadequate words for what he truly wanted to convey. The deep gratitude. How humbling that she'd taken the risk. His life wasn't useless agony anymore.

Her green eyes rested on his, took in a curl that had fallen across his cheek and dropped to his lips before darting back. There was a colour to her cheeks now that called to him.

'Now that we're fine…'

'That smile,' he said. 'That smile, Séverine, just isn't…fair.'

Her grin turned knowing.

He growled, 'Let me get the words out first.'

She raised a brow. 'Like…'

'I think we can live here. I want you and the boys. Oddly, I wouldn't mind Henry in my life, and I still need to persuade Imbert to like me.'

'I should let you know Henry wants to stay here with Denise.'

That butcher. 'Did he ask you?'

She laughed. 'No.'

'I don't think we have servants,' he whispered, as if it was a secret.

'Most assuredly not.'

His life of order, dominance, wealth and

power didn't exist in this little keep named Forgotten. He couldn't be happier.

'What of the rest, Balthus? You want to talk. Just because we hide ourselves here, it doesn't mean the world won't find us.'

The world of demanding monarchs, politics, legends. His promise to his brother to help, but he never wanted to be parted from Séverine, Clovis and Pepin.

He gazed at the bed where she had placed the satchels. 'Should we look at what you brought?'

It didn't take them long. There were a few books, some scrolls. 'This is it.' He sat down.

She looked over his shoulder. Her hair was cascading down his arm with the familiar scent of thyme and her. That was far more poignant and vital than any treasure.

'How do you know? It's beautiful, but it doesn't talk about anything.'

'The drawings at the corners.'

She pulled it out of his hands and shifted it around, seeing it from other angles.

'Wait.' She took out one of the books, flipped the pages. 'See here? There's a pattern.'

He didn't see it.

She set it down. 'I still don't know what it

means, I'd have to study it a bit more, maybe make comparisons to other pages.'

'How did you know about the book?'

'The parchment is a similar size and the handwriting is the same. But in the rest of the book the handwriting is different. It was as if a story was being told, the scribe was tired for one page and someone else did it, and then he went back to the original. That's why this book always fascinated me.'

Her eyes were alight as she turned the pages slowly as if she'd never looked at them, though it was clear she had studied the pages before.

'You're excited.'

She looked up, her hand in the book. 'I've always studied books or tapestries. I find it interesting to see who the artist was and what they meant.'

'You and your tapestries.'

She laid a hand on his cheek and he leaned into it. He'd never get used to her touch.

'My tapestries are beautiful, but they are cruel to the people who make them. Crippled hands, endless hours lost, eyesight weakened, blood shed.

'And you say I'm like them?'

'You're not that pretty, but I could stare at you for hours.'

He clasped her hand. 'Don't.'

'I think you're blushing. Think I'll find flaws?' she teased.

He yanked her onto his lap. She squealed and protected the book. 'No, if you study me that intensely, I'll think you're plotting against me.'

'I'm always plotting against you. Perhaps I'll order a dozen spare buckets to be made in case I need to throw them.'

He laughed. 'Then I have no worries.'

She went back to slowly turning the pages. He found none of it interesting except deciding then and there that he could stare at her for hours, as well.

What were the boys doing now? Eating if they were around Henry. That sounded fine to him. His bones were tired, but now that he was settled with Séverine the fact he hadn't eaten for hours was felt.

'Are you hungry?' he said.

She paused, looked up at him in surprise. 'I am. The boys brought me some bread, but I don't remember if I ate it. Now that these are in front of me, I just want a few more moments.' She pulled back. 'You're staring at me. Are you now plotting against me?'

'I think I am,' he said. 'How much do you hate Warstone games?'

She stiffened in his arms and he quickly kissed her. When he pulled back, her voice was almost breathless. 'You know how I feel about them.'

He loved the softer look in her eyes. Wanted to kiss her again, but knew he'd then crush all the documents as he spread her out on the bed. 'I was to bring this all back to Reynold for his protection and study.'

'Oh,' she said, looking at the book in her lap.

He rubbed up and down her arm. 'You don't want to give them up.'

'Now that you say there are some clues to be found with the scribes, I thought I'd...' Séverine pulled herself up. 'Oh, you are plotting against me.'

His arm tightened around her waist, and she took in the feeling of safety, of warmth, of love.

'Is that so terrible?' he whispered. His breath and words skimmed her ear.

He was offering her a chance to study the beautiful books and scrolls, to investigate and find the scribes with all their meanings. It wasn't terrible, it was what she'd wanted and so much more. She'd have a family, laughter, conflict and beauty.

'Do you think there could be more scrolls or books?' she said. 'These were what Ian left, but that doesn't mean this is all of them.'

She felt him smile against her neck as he trailed kisses along her collarbone. 'No, it doesn't. The process could take years.'

'It doesn't mean we have to travel or fight battles?'

'It means I'd have to spend coin to build walls, to hire watch guards and protect you.'

She already felt protected. 'Can I have a room where I can study, with absolute quiet and as many pillows as I want?'

'As long as I can throw them and you on the floor as much as I want.' He skimmed his teeth along the curve of her neck and bit.

She shivered. 'I thought you were hungry.'

'I am,' he said, soothing the spot he'd bitten with soft kisses and darts of his tongue.

'Shouldn't we be worried about what King Edward or Philip—or your parents—will do with the boys?' she gasped. 'There'll be orders, perhaps even decrees.'

He kissed her again, but now his hand was untying her gown's laces and his fingertips were skimming the edges of her breast.

'Balthus?' she said. Her voice was breathless.

Seizing her waist, he whipped her around and grinned. 'Trust my silences, remember?'

Oh, he would be the most impulsive man she'd ever known. 'Trust your silences. How am I to—?'

He kissed her. Soundly. Thoroughly. With no more thought of plots and schemes, she dropped the book from her lap to the floor, kicked the scrolls off the bed and kissed him right back.

* * * * *

MILLS & BOON

Coming next month

A PROPOSAL TO RISK THEIR FRIENDSHIP
Louise Allen

He could let go and Melissa would lift her head and those warm, soft lips would no longer be clinging to his … and this kiss would end. And he did not want that.

Nor, it seemed, did Melissa. It was an inexperienced kiss, he could tell. Her mouth remained closed, but she made a little purring sound deep in her throat and every primitive male instinct demanded that he turn that purr into a moan.

Henry sat up. Where he got the willpower from he had no idea, but there they were suddenly, somewhat breathless and, in his case, most inconveniently aroused.

'That was very quick thinking,' he said when his brain allowed speech.

'I hope it was convincing,' Melissa said. 'I have absolutely no practical experience of that kind of thing.'

'Of course not. I think you may be certain that they suspected nothing,' he said.

'It was the only thing I could think of to stop them seeing your face,' she went on, looking round. She located her hat and blew dust from it. 'I think there is no permanent damage, thank goodness.'

Not to the hat, at any rate. What was the matter with him? He had been kissed by lovers of great experience. One innocent pressing her lips to his as part of a charade could hardly weigh against those encounters. Melissa was a friend, not a lover. An innocent, not a woman of the world.

A friend. We have something special—do not ruin this.

'Have they gone, do you think?' Melissa asked.

Henry looked out. 'They are walking away. No point in trying to catch them up.'

'No, I suppose not.' She put her hat back on and tied the ribbons in a rather lopsided bow.

Without thinking, Henry went across and retied it. How had he not noticed her scent before? 'Rosemary?' He realised he had said it out loud.

Melisa looked perplexed, then laughed. 'Oh, my hair rinse. That tickles.'

'What? Oh, sorry.' His fingers were still on the bow, touching the smooth skin under her chin. He removed his hand as casually as he could. 'It is safe to follow now, I think.'

A lot safer than staying here. Melissa is a friend, he reminded himself as he followed her out of the summer-house. *She trusts you, as a friend, not to be reacting like this to her, not to be thinking about her scent, the feel of her. Her mouth.*

Continue reading
A PROPOSAL TO RISK THEIR FRIENDSHIP
Louise Allen

Available next month
www.millsandboon.co.uk

COMING SOON!

We really hope you enjoyed reading this book.
If you're looking for more romance, be sure to
head to the shops when new books are
available on

Thursday 27th May

LET'S TALK
Romance

For exclusive extracts, competitions
and special offers, find us online:

facebook.com/millsandboon

@MillsandBoon

@MillsandBoonUK

Get in touch on 01413 063232

For all the latest titles coming soon, visit
millsandboon.co.uk/nextmonth